'*Buon giorno, I trust you slept well.*'

The Prince turned from the fire, invariably lit in the chill depths of this medieval fortress even in the heat of July, his expression as formal as were his words.

'Thank you, yes. In spite. . .' She stopped herself on her waspish retort.

'Of being kidnapped? Was I so very Gothick about it? I'm sorry.'

He neither looked nor sounded the least bit sorry. He was, she was certain of it, amused at everything he had done. Consequently, Cecilia decided she had every right to behave as badly as she chose.

'No need to be sorry at all, sir,' she murmured sweetly. 'Of course, I am abducted every day. I like nothing better than to be told I may not go where I wish to go. I cannot think of anything you could have done to please me more!'

'I'll think of something!' he retorted softly.

Louisa Gray was born in 1959 and attended what was, for someone as incompetent at games as she is, a disconcertingly sporty boarding school in Wales. She read Italian at university but left after a year, a decision she has never regretted—on the grounds that more than one tutor loudly debated the wisdom of trying to educate her at all. Her interest in history was everything to do with several generations of glamorous—even wicked—rebels for ancestors, of all of whom the family are stubbornly, if misguidedly, proud. She has an incurable weakness for Chopin, violets and her very patient Italian fiancé who generously admitted it was fun to be made the hero of her first Masquerade story. She now lives in the heart of Regency Bath and is completely under the thumb of her yellow labrador, Cressy.

This is her first Masquerade Historical.

THE MANSINI SECRET

Louisa Gray

First published in Great Britain 1991
by Mills & Boon Limited

© Louisa Gray 1991

Australian copyright 1991
Philippine copyright 1992
This edition 1992

ISBN 0 263 77584 4

Masquerade is a trademark published by
Mills & Boon Limited, Eton House,
18–24 Paradise Road, Richmond, Surrey, TW9 1SR.

Set in 10 on 11 pt Linotron Plantin
04-9202-83507
Typeset in Great Britain by Centracet, Cambridge
Made and printed in Great Britain

AUTHOR'S NOTE

THIS story is set in 1817 in the Italy of the last remaining city states—sovereign territories of ancient origin, some no larger than cities, some the size of small countries—the absolute control of these states now snatched from the hands of the great ruling families and in the clutches of one or other of the occupying imperial forces, Bourbon Spain and Austria holding almost equal power throughout the disunited Italian territories. Napoleon's incursions on to the scene a decade earlier confused the issue still further; the somewhat emasculated Vatican also had the fingers of both hands—and more—in this chaotic political pie. For the original ruling families such as the Sforza, the Estensi, the Visconti, it was a time of decay . . . unless they could play the system and harness the irrepressible urge of the Italian people to rebel against whoever was in charge at the time, often, it seems, just for the hell of it. I have made my hero just such a former sovereign prince, a man playing the game with a great deal more panache, if personal danger, than most of his kind actually ever did.

Aquila Romana is an invented territory, planted—because it's my favourite place—between Tuscany and Umbria, and has nothing whatever to do with the actual town of Aquila in the Abruzzi further south.

Having thought up the names of my characters I have discovered—rather, have had discovered for me—that one or two have been influenced somewhat by the Italian World Cup soccer team of 1990. This is a complete—if admiring—coincidence. Because of it, this book is for Francesco d'E., who made me watch all their matches . . . either in thanks for the fun it engendered, or revenge!

CHAPTER ONE

July, 1817

CECILIA saw the man running across the square and knew he was not going to make it. He was pouring blood, his once white shirt soaked with it, and he was stumbling erratically as if hardly aware what he was doing; in the still, burning midday air the sound of his agonised breathing rose to her even where she stood, horrified, on the hotel balcony. And there was nothing she could do. Or was there?

Cecilia had lived among the Italians long enough to tell herself, even as she raced down the treacherous marble stairs and out beneath the portico across the scorching stones of the square, not to get involved, a lesson she had learnt well but now ruthlessly threw aside; the sun was so hot that the blood had dried already against the cobbles and perhaps that was why—if she thought at all—Cecilia ran on as if in a dream, shouting out automatically in her native English for everyone else to get out of her way. So imperious was her tone that the gathering crowd stopped short in their tracks and hung back; they had not the least need at all to understand her actual words—her manner was quite enough. The man had collapsed on to the edge of the fountain by the time she reached him; as she flung herself down beside him, feeling for his heart, her loosened hair spread out across the soft spring water, its vivid gold mingling with eddies of blood as the basin of the fountain clouded to red and she knew that he was dying.

Instinct told her what to do, what he really needed.

She read without thinking the anger raging across his contorted, whitened features.

'Tell me!' she whispered urgently. '*Tell me*! I'll do whatever you want!'

She must have spoken in Italian after all—at least he understood her. Strangely his eyes cleared even as his frown deepened and he struggled with what he knew to be his last few breaths for the words he needed. They were beautiful eyes, Cecilia thought irrationally, a beautiful, pure, childlike blue, so radiantly alive. He was, she saw it then, such a beautiful young man. And he was smiling at her.

She knew the smile to mean the thank-you he could not waste his breath on saying aloud. Then, ragged, faint, she heard it.

'Mansini. I know the Mansini secret! You must tell. *Tell*! Mansini secret. The Duke!'

She thought that he said it once more, just the last two words, 'the Duke'. But even as she thought so his head fell back into the water and he was dead.

Cecilia was still in a daze as she rose to her feet, only vaguely aware of the avid silence at last broken by the hush and scurry of murmurs through the crowd. She looked about her. But for a few women of the market, a servant or two, there was no one there any longer. No one who counted, nobody to whom she could turn. A good thing, then, she thought, that it had been a long time since she had ever had to turn to anyone. So thinking, the Lady Cecilia Sherringham, youngest daughter of the late Duke of Downside, pushed her soaking hair back from her forehead and made her way down from the fountain steps towards the doors of the hotel in which she was staying. The now sparse onlookers parted round her, gaping, almost afraid of her, as she walked so gracefully towards the icy slabs of shade at the edge of the square. Even as she reached it a darker shadow detached itself from those around it and a man rode forward, his horse stepping delicately as if trained to silence. She knew him at once for a man of absolute authority.

Cecilia spoke quickly, even before he had raised his head from his courteous if chilling bow.

'My name is Cecilia Sherringham; I am English. That man by the fountain has been murdered. He spoke his last words to me.'

'And?'

Never in all her life could she have expected such a response. No concern, no interest, not even suspicion. Simply abrupt, as brusque as inherent good manners would allow.

Just one word and Cecilia was stung right out of her stupor.

'*And*,' she flung back her head and threw at him her most dangerous of glances, 'I intend to see that justice is done him, sir, even if you do not!'

Even in the shadow she saw him smile at that. It was a sardonic, almost laughing smile.

'I would be obliged,' she finished, almost disconcerted for the first time in her memorably disconcerting existence, 'if you would take me at once to whoever is in charge of this town.' How was it she invested the words 'this town' with all the contempt she was feeling for its uncaring citizens? 'Take me at once to His Highness the Duke!'

If his smile had been unnerving, how much more frightening was his complete expressionless silence. But Cecilia—if only just—stood her ground, her eyes not wavering from his half-obscured face. She was still watching him, minutely, as a cat would watch a viper, when with one swift, lazy movement he jumped down from the great chestnut, threw its reins carelessly aside, and leaned almost languidly against the great beast's uncomplaining neck. Even so, she almost *felt* that there

was nothing the least bit careless about that movement,
or ever would be about anything he did.

Then he spoke.

'No need to take you anywhere, then, *madonna*. I am
the Duke of Aquila Romana. And this town——' he
spat her words back at her so sweetly '—is mine!'

Back inside the hotel, with the dead man's body taken
away by the friars of the Monastery of San Francesco for
inspection by the authorities and his family, Cecilia,
sunk weakly on to the nearest ice-blue silken settle, had
time to wonder at her audacity, a thing she had never
wondered at before. Years of moving rootlessly about a
war-torn and dangerous Europe with her impoverished
if not quite degenerate parent had hardened Cecilia
against feeling even the smallest fear, if it had taught her
at least to recognise danger. Or so she had believed. In
all that time, with all the people she had ever met, no
one had impressed her quite so dramatically as had the
silent, frozen Duke of Aquila Romana. And to think that
she had come here only by accident, as a stopping place
on her long, sad journey hcme to England. She did not
want to go to England. . .

'My dear *madame*!' The proprietress of this elegant if
wilfully expensive establishment, a woman who, like so
many of her kind, liked to call herself a Countess,
bobbed and dipped like a frantic pheasant in front of
Cecilia, peering at her, eyes burning with an excitement
that could only offend, so ghoulish was her fascination
with the dead man's blood. Cecilia's gown was stiff and
black with it. 'My dear *madame*! You must change your
gown, you must! How terrible!'

Cecilia had always been careful in her manners, but
she forgot them now. She felt suddenly so utterly
disgusted—that and helpless, sent in here to wait until
the Duke saw fit to come and question her. He was
taking his time about it, and Cecilia had never been a

patient person. With a half-gesture of her hand she dismissed the gloating 'Countess', asking only that she be brought a glass of fresh lemon water. She was tired, but not too tired to be angry, and the 'Countess', sensing as much, was quick to see the advisability of leaving the room.

When she had gone Cecilia thought about that hurried exit; thought about how easy she had always found it to just insist, perhaps with no more than a look, and whatever she wanted would be done upon the instant. Even by people who had not the least idea who she was, nor any reason for fawning to the offspring of an English nobleman. It was this easy control over others—something she had, occasionally, a few qualms about—that had deserted her now, with the Duke of Aquila Romana, and she was almost afraid of how she would behave without it. He had already stung her into an open display of temper. It should not matter in the least what he thought of her, of course—except that somehow she felt the dead man's self-appointed champion owed him at least that she perform her task with dignity.

Cecilia looked down at the spoiled gown of ivory muslin and lace, torn badly once too often and mended so lovingly by darling Piggy. It was thinking of her old nurse that told her what it was she was feeling now; for the first time ever Lady Cecilia Sherringham was vulnerable, and she knew it.

She heard his footsteps even before he spoke.

'May I come in, *madonna*?' The Duke's request was perfunctory, no more than a commentary on what he was already doing. He was striding across the softly waxed French oak of the salon floor as if he owned the place. Which, she supposed suddenly, he almost certainly did. Absurdly, as she forced herself to rise to her feet to greet him with due correctness, the first thing she noticed was that he was carrying her glass of lemon water.

'Please sit, *madame*.' It should have sounded considerate; instead it sounded nothing less than the curtest of orders.

Suddenly shaken—by the murder and the sun and the strangeness of it all, she told herself—Cecilia sat. In front of her stood the Duke of Aquila Romana, Prince Federigo d'Aquilano himself, handing her lemonade as if he were perfectly used to playing lackey to strange females, bored, indifferent; interested, it seemed, only that she pulled herself together before he began what she knew would be his interminable questions.

The lemon water was excellent and badly needed. Cecilia took her time, sipping slowly, accepting that she really craved its comfort. Images of things she had not even realised she had seen had a way of swimming before her eyes as she closed them against the sun. Images of pure horror.

She was tired, of course, and shocked. The Prince d'Aquilano saw as much and, impatient though he was to hear what she could tell him, he knew better than to speak until she did.

At last, her head cleared a little by the icy sting of the lemon, Cecilia set aside the glass on a small inlaid Persian table at her side and looked up at him. Looked up and saw him as if for the very first time.

Sardonic, yes, to every last line of his dark, handsome face, but something more she had been unable to see in the shadows—he looked tired. Tired and a great deal older than she had supposed. He had jumped down from that horse with all the insouciance, the physical arrogance of a youth of less than twenty, and yet she saw now that he was possibly double that age. She could not have explained to herself how grateful she was for this knowledge; without those lines to his face, those marks of responsibility and care, she could never have believed as she did now that he was the very person to share what she had heard. As he was now, his face devoid of all expression, he looked more than capable in his hawk-hard repose. His eyes, as dark as they were flint-cold, unexpectedly did still more to reassure her. This was not a man she could like but she could—and it was all she needed—trust him to do everything he must for the dead man.

Suddenly, almost as if he had read her thoughts, the Duke smiled. A slow, surprising smile that heated into the depths of his chestnut eyes and reminded her why she had first thought he was so young. Even the slight beginnings of silver in the thick mahogany hair were belied by that unexpectedly beautiful, boyish smile.

'So you have made up your mind that I will do, have you, *madonna*? That you are going to trust me?'

Had she said that he was disconcerting? He was astonishing! Forthright in a way she had always thought she preferred, he almost unnerved her now. He saw too much with those quick predator's eyes of his.

Even so, she managed a smile in return, knowing that any weakness in her voice was only to be expected in her unenviable circumstances.

'Yes. Yes, I have.'

'I see you know Italy well, *madonna*!'

She understood. And this time she relaxed completely into her laughter before she could help herself.

'Meaning that one never knows quite where to turn in an emergency?'

'Meaning exactly that.'

Cecilia lifted her hand to her hair, suddenly irritated by a still-loosened frond. Really she should have called for Piggy to make her more presentable before this difficult inquisition. As if made aware by her dishevel-ment of her need for added dignity, she said quickly, 'Oh, I do beg your pardon, Prince! Please sit. How uncivil of me!'

'Not at all, *madonna*. You have more to concern you than your manners, I think.'

Again Cecilia heard the smile behind his low, lazy voice and was surprised at it. It sounded, as it had not done before, encouraging, if not quite kindly meant. Certainly she found herself more comfortable at last, becoming more herself. God knew, she must need to be!

'That's true, sir. Please ask me anything you wish. I should dislike to take up too much of your valuable time.'

Quite to her puzzlement the Prince d'Aquilano turned suddenly away at that. Why it was she thought from the set of his powerful shoulders that he was really laughing at her, or trying not to, she could not fathom.

She must have been mistaken. His voice was cool and even.

'It is your time that is valuable, *madonna*. I believe that you are returning home to England?'

'Yes.'

How heavy that one word sounded. Certainly her companion heard it. Sitting—rather casually, thought Cecilia, not quite surprised—on the edge of a nearby table, His Highness gazed down at a speck of dust on his otherwise immaculate boot and said abruptly, 'And you have no wish to go?'

Never had she admitted it before, barely even to herself, let alone out loud——

'No!' It was almost a passionate reply, though what was behind such urgency, she barely knew.

He heard this too. But his voice remained as steady as if he had heard nothing.

'You have been in Italy a long time?' It was only half a question, and she knew as much at once. And then she understood.

'I see.' She did.

And the Prince smiled again. 'That I know everything about everybody who passes through my territory? Of course I do. I have to.'

Cecilia was not sure the thought was a comfortable one.

'I know,' he went on, plainly amused at her discomfort, 'that you are the youngest daughter of the tenth Duke of Downside, that he died thirteen months since at Siena, that there is no heir, that there is no money. . .'

Brutally put, but true all the same. Even so, Cecilia felt a slow flush of anger rise to stain her cheeks. She remained silent as a sign of her displeasure.

For her pains the Prince d'Aquilano laughed out loud at her, deeply amused. 'Oh, really, *madonna*! To be so delicate. . .*you*! Now! After. . .how is it you say. . .ringing peals over my head in my own town square for being so remiss as to let a man die in my fountain?'

At his accusation, her second flush was unmistakably one of pride. Eyes glittering with it, Cecilia, feeling a whole lot better, looked him boldly in the eye.

'I did, didn't I?' Her tone was all of satisfaction.

'Yes. I quite enjoyed it.'

And suddenly, as if her whole first impression of this man had dissolved in the power of his personality, Cecilia herself began to laugh. When she could speak at all she accused, inelegantly, 'You would!'

That she was talking to the sovereign Prince of this state—a man whose prisons were, for all she knew, crammed to the rafters with people who forgot their manners in his presence—had never struck her for a moment. But if her recklessness had struck the Prince it did so favourably, for he seemed to relax himself, as if relieved by her laughing informality.

'Why are you going home, Lady Cecilia? You would not do in England—you speak your mind too freely. No, you shouldn't go at all.'

'Because——' was it true? '—I have nowhere else to go.'

Once again the Prince was intent only on his Hessians. Even so, his abstracted attention was as unsettling as anyone else's closest scrutiny.

'Have you anywhere to go in England?'

'My sisters. . . I have two, both married.'

'And both with a parcel of brats and little fortune, grateful for the advent of their baby sister as drudge?'

How true that was! Her sisters' letters had been frantic. Papa had barely been buried in his beloved Tuscan gardens when Persephone had hurried in first to cut out Eliza for their younger sister's services. So useful, had wittered Persephone—Cecilia could teach little Frederick and little August to speak Italian. Persephone was a cat, Eliza had fired off desperately, a horrid cat who had criticised her own darling George for his bulbous nose and jug-handled ears—which George she had meant, her husband or her baby, it had been far beyond the recipient of these outpourings to decipher; Cecilia must not go to Persephone, for such would be treason and Eliza would never speak to her again! As if, thought Cecilia wryly, God should ever grant me such good fortune as to be cast off by either of the penny-pinching creatures! Moreover, they had never once written to Papa in all the years of exile. They had only surfaced on his death in the hope that there might, however unlikely, given His Late Grace of Downside's proclivities, be some few and unexpected pickings.

Cecilia was not to know that her every opinion of this grasping pair was written all over her ever-expressive features. Certainly a man as perceptive as the Prince d'Aquilano could not have failed to see them. Even before she could answer he put in, with the bluntness she had come to expect, 'You can't live like that. Nobody could, but you least of all. I think you belong here. You should stay.'

She knew she should. It was here, among these casually melodramatic people, that Cecilia had first felt at home. She felt safe in a place where each and every emotion was pinned firmly to the sleeve and paraded for all to see. Enmity was as open as love, and that was reassuring. She wanted to stay. But with no money it was a dream beyond possessing. It was a loss that really hurt.

Because it hurt, she spoke almost too abruptly, to change the subject.

'However, sir, discussion of my affairs does not help you catch a murderer.' The instant she had said it she was sorry; how could she ever have been so gratuitously snubbing?

If he was snubbed, His Highness did not show it. But then, he never would. For he had a quality that was paradoxically also very Italian, a coldness and restraint of manner such as she had never known elsewhere and which was in such dramatic contrast to the openness of the general nature.

'No,' was all he said. Then, 'Tell me what happened. Everything you saw.'

That was easy enough. At first. . .

'I was restless; my nurse had made such a fuss about my sleeping for the afternoon that she made it quite impossible. . .anyway, I was far too hot. I went out on to the balcony just to look at the square—it is so beautiful. I was too hot there also, and dazzled. I saw very little. I suppose I was dreaming, you know how one does. . .'

'I know.'

'Well, then I heard footsteps, running, even before I saw the man. They came from that alley to the left, beyond the cathedral. It was so dark there. He simply erupted into the sunlight—it was a nightmare thing! Everything drained of colour by the sun, everybody else black and white, and then him. . .and all that blood. He looked so young. . .'

'He was.'

There was nothing in the Prince's tone to give his feelings away. Yet Cecilia sensed something behind the words. What it was—sadness, regret, anger—she could not tell. But it made her say, 'You knew him, sir?'

He looked at her then, the sun-gilded planes of his face harsher even than she had thought, animal-hard, threatening.

'I knew him.'

'Who was he?' Suddenly she needed to give the man—boy—a name. After all, she had held him in her arms while he'd died.

'His name was Giulio Mansini. Giulio the Poet. He was seventeen.'

Cecilia had sprung to her feet even before she realised it, driven by a rush of shock and anger and horror that had nothing to do with anything but the fact that the boy had been a full nine years her junior. Little more than a child. The Prince d'Aquilano read her shock far differently. He was at her side, taking her elbow in his hand to steady her before she realised he had moved; even as she felt the strength of his fingers and the reassurance of him, of any human touch, Cecilia was aware of the excitement coursing through him. . .an excitement that was a tangible heat and that had nothing whatever to do with her at all. He had almost forgotten she was there.

She was sure of this urgency when he spoke. A soft, gentle query, and yet it burned into her with its carefully controlled intensity.

'Mansini! When I said Mansini it meant something to you. Please tell me.'

Courteous, kindly. And yet, she knew it now, powerfully dangerous. And suddenly Cecilia was no longer sure of him.

What had Giulio the Poet said? What had he meant? Had he meant her to tell the Duke? Or had he meant something else? Did he mean to tell someone, anyone, *about* the Duke, that the Duke was behind his vicious murder? Her head was spinning; she even felt a little faint. Dizzy enough to sway suddenly, half towards him, and then, instinctively, to snatch herself away. Several yards away. She was shaking but she could not have said why.

What had Giulio meant that she should do?

As warily as a forest animal, cornered and distrustful, she watched the Duke of Aquila Romana as he watched her. And now all she could see was the threat she had first seen in him, and regretted too late the fact that she had ever dismissed that impression and come to trust him. Her every last nerve told her that Giulio had meant beware of this man.

'Please tell me?' His voice was as it had ever been, calm and infinitely reasonable, persuasive, irresistible.

Like a hypnotised bird, she found that she was saying, 'He said he knew the Mansini secret.'

Against her will her eyes were caught then and held by his and the searching, penetrating need to know that burned in them. He held her like that in silence for a full two minutes, then he smiled and said, softly, 'You didn't understand him, of course?'

As if her very life depended on it, Cecilia whispered urgently, 'No. . .how could I know? I know nothing!'

Another silence, and then the Prince d'Aquilano nodded.

'That is good,' was all he said.

Without understanding why she ever did it, Cecilia hurried then from the room, desperate for the sanctuary of her own chambers, the chance to think. Had she betrayed the dying Giulio or begun to avenge him? How was she to leave this town tonight—as she knew she must—when without the permission of this man she could go nowhere in his territory? He had not given any such permission to leave and she knew he had not fully questioned her. But she would leave. At once. Any other option simply did not feel safe. Cecilia flung herself down on the faded green silk of her counterpane and thought hotly, How to get away? From a man like that— *how*?

CHAPTER TWO

'PIGGY! Piggy, darling, please wake up!'

Cecilia bent over the bed which now held her old nurse and shook the woman into wakefulness. At least she tried to. But years of becoming inured to all manner of dangers had taken their toll of Miss Margery Pigg, and Miss Pigg, smiling, slept on.

At any other time Cecilia would have found this amusing. Now she was almost in tears at the frustration of it. They had to leave, and leave now. She had spent all evening packing their few belongings and she was ready to go. Getting out of the city might prove a real problem, for the Austrian garrison in charge would almost certainly have been warned by the Prince that she must not leave it. It all depended on just how much power he really had.

He spoke like an absolute ruler, and it was all too easy to believe that this whole territory bent to his will and each last whim. And yet she knew the city to be officially in Austrian hands, that there was an Austrian governor, that the power of the Princes of Aquila Romana, like all others of their kind, had faded from the total domination of the past. But if the governor was weak, and the Prince was strong. . .and this one was, beyond any doubt of it. . .then it mattered not in the least that the Emperor of Austria thought himself lord of these lands. It all depended on how the Austrian garrison felt about this Italian who knew that by all the rights of inheritance the city and all its territories were his. She might have to play on the loyalty of the Austrians to law and order and empire and their dislike for this princely thorn in their side, but that was something she knew that she could do. After all, she was not a Sherringham for nothing. And if all else failed and she was trapped here after tonight she could within a week or two get His Majesty of England to intervene on her behalf.

Why was it, then, that she was sitting shivering here on this bed while her old nurse dreamed on? Other than the fact that she knew that if the Prince d'Aquilano meant to keep her here—and she was certain that he did—a mere King of England would mean less than nothing to that autocratic gentleman?

'*Piggy!*' But it was absolutely no use. There was only one thing for it, and Cecilia had been putting it off as long as she could.

Miss Margery Pigg awoke to the unexpected and unwelcome rush of the contents of a water jug about her muffled ears. Blinking, muttering, she sat bolt upright, with her sodden lace cap askew. Then she said distinctly, 'Really, Cecilia! What a shockingly thoughtless child you are!' Even before Cecilia could catch her and prop her up she had sunk again into the deepest, if dampest, of slumbers.

It was inevitable really that Cecilia should burst out laughing. She was laughing so much that she was crying with it. That last was a sound that had woken Miss Margery Pigg as her duty all her charge's childhood years. In an instant she was out of bed, her arms around her shaking favourite and murmuring, 'Now, now, Silly; now, now. There, there, my angel, never mind!' So how could it be other than that Cecilia should collapse completely in a rocking, aching heap of real, if affectionate, hysterics in her old nurse's bemused and startled arms? It was a full five minutes before she had any control of herself at all. When at last she could speak she wasted no words.

'Piggy. We have to leave. I saw a murder!'

'Oh?' Miss Pigg was not even interested—why should she be? She had heard infinitely more disconcerting things in the Sherringham employ, and expected before she finally retired her position to hear much worse.

Cecilia could not help herself hugging her nurse at that. How many other elderly English countrywomen could travel the world as Piggy had done, sleeping even through the chaos that was Waterloo? Sleeping most of the time—indeed, Cecilia's mongrel Gulliver weighting down her rheumatic knees. Even the disastrous discomfort of the only carriage the Duke of Downside had been able to afford had made little headway in the matter of keeping Miss Pigg in the world of even the semi-conscious for long.

'I've packed already. Only, Piggy, we can't light candles or anything. There's a good moon, so that will have to serve.'

'Can't we pay our bills again, my love?' It was the only thing that really concerned Miss Pigg or ever had done.

'Of course we can!' Cecilia retorted as if this were a state of affairs that was normal. 'After all, there is no Papa to gamble the money away any more. I have left payment for the Countess in my room—a letter too. We must wake Jemmy at once and hurry.'

'What about horses? Those old hacks will never pull us far.'

'They might get us to Florence, or back to Siena. All I need is for them to take us out of the Aquila Romana. They'll manage that.'

'Well, I must say,' put in Miss Pigg, wringing out her nightcap rather sadly, 'I cannot see why you should wish to leave—apart from the murder, of course, which, I own, must have been a mite objectionable; I think this such a pretty place, and was so looking forward to exploring the cathedral.'

'Well, I'm sorry too, for it *is* a beautiful city. Only we can't remain. But you like Siena just as well.'

'Are we not travelling the wrong way if we go back

into Tuscany, my love? I had thought we were bound for Rome and the coast at Ostia—to go home.'

'Well, we are. But we need other horses and we can't possibly make it *south* out of Aquila Romana before he finds we are gone. . .'

'He? *Ah*!' Plainly to Miss Pigg this one word explained everything.

Cecilia was exasperated. 'No, Piggy. Not *he*—at least, not like that.'

'Not another desperate suitor, in fact?'

'Not this time.'

'May I know who precisely?' asked Margery Pigg with uncharacteristic sternness.

'The Duke of Aquila Romana, Prince Federigo.' Even as she spoke his name Cecilia found that she had shuddered.

'But I had thought,' protested Piggy, 'that he was a very handsome man.'

And, since only the absurd ever made the least sense to Piggy, Cecilia replied, 'He is, darling Piggy! And that is why we are leaving after all.'

Even as Miss Pigg was saying, 'I see,' as if she really did see something, Cecilia was running from the room with a whispered,

'Now do dress, Piggy. And *do* hurry up!'

Twenty minutes later, a disgruntled Jeremiah Pigg— nephew of that ilk—hauled unwillingly from his bed, and her own horse saddled, Cecilia was riding alongside the crumbling Downside carriage as it creaked its way out into the moonlit medieval square of Aquila Romana, past the fountain still stained with the poet's blood, beneath the brooding towers of the great twelfth-century castle and towards the western gatehouse to the road beyond. Above the gatehouse, limp in the humid summer night, slumped the flag of the Emperor of Austria; perversely, catching the only breath of breeze, the standard of the Prince d'Aquilano himself fluttered free and proud against the icy light of the starlit sky. Black on white silk soared the Roman eagle that had given the house of Aquila Romana its name, and, savagely speared in its talons, the writhing body of a spitting viper. Suppressing a shudder of recognition— dear God, but did his coat of arms suit the man who had made her so afraid of him!—Cecilia raised her whip to clip briskly at the bell placed for the convenience of travellers and to spare the occupying soldiers the discomfort of being woken to the sound of the door being battered in. She was just about to rap on the sweet-sounding bronze again when the door opened and a man, his uniform askew, stumbled out into the light of the gatehouse lanterns. One look at Cecilia's startled distaste and he was to attention and gibbering his apologies over and over again as if his life depended on them, in three different languages at once.

Cecilia cut across him.

'Yes, well, never mind, I do see that you are sorry and ashamed of yourself and all that; now would you kindly open the gates and let us pass?'

She had not even heard the approach of another horseman. But she heard his laugh.

'Oh, I'm sure he will, *madonna*. He'd be quite delighted to do anything you please. Only on this occasion—I am sorry to say it—he is doomed to disoblige you!'

At the sound of that drawling voice the soldier turned sick to the stomach and showed it. His salute fell a great deal short of what would have pleased his commanding officer, let alone the governor, who was going to have his hide if ever he heard of this débâcle.

'Sorry, Your Highness; sorry, ma'am!' Sorry all round. Then the soldier gave up saying anything at all and simply waited.

Cecilia, recovering at last from her shock, rounded then on the Prince d'Aquilano.

'You cannot keep me here, sir!'

'I think you know that I can.' Cecilia had no need at all to see his face to know that he was laughing still.

She was just about to reply when a bonneted head popped itself out of the carriage window and peered through teetering spectacles at the newcomer.

'Hmm!' remarked Piggy after a suitably long pause for close inspection. 'Very handsome! Are we staying here after all, my angel?'

It was shock, of course; quite in the teeth of her very real frustration Lady Cecilia Sherringham began to laugh. Her bridle was in the Prince's hand and her horse turned back towards the lowering bulk of the *castello* before she could even recover herself to stop him.

'Oh, yes, *madame*,' His Highness addressed the hugely impressed Miss Pigg, 'of course you are going to stay.' To Cecilia he added, in a voice so quiet as to be menacing for all it was full of amusement, 'You did not seriously believe that I would let you go?'

Cecilia found that she could see his eyes clearly in the moonlight, darkening beneath his permanently sardonic brow, hot and alive with something she was certain was more than laughter. Something that meant that when she spoke—rather, tried to speak—her voice would not come out at all.

He smiled then. 'You see,' he added, far too innocently, 'you belong in Italy—so much is obvious; how was I ever going to let you go back to scheming sisters and to slavery?'

Cecilia just managed to say something then. It was not respectable and a lady should not have uttered it.

'You bastard!'

Miss Margery Pigg's, 'Now, *really*, Cecilia!' was drowned out in the most infectious, the most open of laughter from His Highness.

'And you, my child, are the most shocking little hoyden I ever encountered. I like it!'

In stunned silence Cecilia allowed herself to be led ahead of the struggling carriage, across the heavy wood of the medieval drawbridge and into the shadows of the central courtyard. It was a forbidding place, but nowhere near as forbidding as the man now raising his arms to lift her down from her horse. Cecilia, shaking too much with temper at him to speak again, landed quite deliberately on the most vulnerable part of his feet.

'As I said,' he sounded, if anything, even more approving than before, 'appalling little hoyden! You will deal very comfortably with my daughters.'

Defeated utterly by his infuriating refusal to be anything but amused at her, Cecilia allowed herself to be taken by the elbow and steered into the depths of the ancient fortress of the Aquilano Princes. That the doors clanged shut with the iron thunder of doom was, she told herself grimly, very much what was to be expected in the circumstances. She had always enjoyed Gothick novels—but she had never wanted a prominent role in one.

'*Udolpho*,' she muttered, half to herself.

'Oh, that is too ridiculous—it's not even a very good book, besides the villain's being so oafishly menacing as to be tiresome to the point of vulgarity!' he countered. Then added, 'That dog, by the way. . . I gather it *is* a dog, it seems to be growling at me. . .would you mind telling him—it?—I have not in fact abducted you and to behave in a more becoming fashion?'

Cecilia's head was spinning with the absurdity of it all. She had no longer the least clue what was going on. Consequently she said the first thing that came into her head.

'He is not an it, he's Gulliver. And if you come within a yard of me again I shall make certain that he bites you!'

From a staircase lost in the grimmest of shadows she heard them—two loud and childish squeals of delighted laughter.

'How brave!' yelled one voice.

'*Really* brave!' yelled the other.

And down the stairs into the firelit hall raced two perfectly matched little girls of about eight years old, swamped in oversized nightgowns.

'Nobody speaks to Papa like that!' they announced together.

'I like Gulliver.' One was already cuddling the startled mongrel to her chest.

'Gulliver?' puzzled the other.

'Because he's been everywhere on his travels,' Cecilia explained, 'like the character in the book.' What she was really thinking was, This isn't real at all, of course, and I am dreaming it. It is so completely idiotic.

'Would Gulliver——' neither could pronounce him properly '—*really* bite Papa?' asked the one with the hapless dog in stranglehold.

Yes, please, thought Cecilia, succumbing to the general madness of the Italian moonlight. *Please*. Or bite *me*! Then at least I shall know that I am awake at last, and not here at all, but safely back in my bed at home in Tuscany. . .

'Oh, he won't bite anyone, my loves,' put in Miss Pigg in her Somersetshire-accented Italian, 'least of all a gentleman as charming as your father.'

Cecilia was not too surprised to hear the Prince d'Aquilano burst out laughing. But there was a completely different sound to his laughter now, something indulgent, something soft, even tender, and she found that she was looking at him again. Two seconds ago she could happily have murdered the man; now here he was, pounced under a heap of dog and small, giggling children, laughing at it all and hugging whichever was the nearest to him of the squirming mass of bodies. Gulliver, not caring to be cuddled, complained loudly, and the Prince, his thickly waving hair dishevelled in a manner that suited his youthfulness more than ever, smiled up at Cecilia's bewildered scrutiny.

'These,' he said proudly, 'are Iphigenia and Atalanta.'

'Only we had an English nurse once. . .before we frightened her away. . .*she* called us Figi and Talia.'

'She did?'

'Yes. So you can too. I'm Figi.'

'And I'm Talia.'

'Who are *you*, by the way?'

'Are you the one who's going to marry our Papa?'

Cecilia would have fled then, if she could, just as she would have run for her life—or sanity—in a real dream. Only there was nowhere to run. Nor any way she could turn from his blatantly mocking smile.

The Duke drew out her punishment with a long silence, while Figi and Talia speculated with horrendous glee. Then, just as Cecilia felt the blush of real embarrassment steaming into her cheeks, he smiled, and gave the most offensive of bows. Then deflated the twins with a soft, 'No, repellent creatures. This is Lady Cecilia Sherringham, who saw that grisly murder you have been so revoltingly inquisitive about. She is going to stay here for a while.'

He sounded no different from any old friend announcing a long-expected visitor. But to Cecilia that lazy voice was the turning of the gaoler's key.

'If I may——' she poured all the ice she could muster into her voice then '—I should be more than grateful if I might rest now, sir, for I am very tired. As, indeed, is Piggy.'

The Prince d'Aquilano swept the room with his lazy eyes for a moment, swept them most offensively of all over Cecilia, and she felt herself burning up again with helpless irritation; then he said, 'Oh, I think not. I imagine you will find that Miss Pigg is asleep already.' As, indeed, she was, before the cavernous hell-mouth of the castle fire, that traitor Gulliver snoring on her sensible travelling boots.

'Oh, Piggy!' Cecilia lost control of herself completely. 'Come, Gulliver! At once!'

Anywhere would do, so long as it was not here. Cecilia, for the first time in her life, picked up her skirts and fled. That she was carefully rounded up by a graceful and impeccable manservant was less a matter of luck than it spoke volumes for the iron management of this extraordinary household.

'This way, *madonna*; please follow me.'

It was when Cecilia saw the rooms that she knew they had been made ready for her long before the Prince had captured her in the moonlight. The fire was burning well, water heating in brass kettles above the grate, and soaps, scent and combs were already laid out for her on a truly exquisite French satinwood dressing-table. The scent was her favourite jasmine. She remembered then how the Prince had held her for a moment that afternoon, while she had still felt safe with him, before he had made her tell him the poet's final words. She had been wearing jasmine then, and he had noticed it.

Of all the things that had unnerved her thus far it was this that worried Cecilia the most.

She woke to the brilliance of hot sunlight penetrating the chapel coolness of her chamber through the ancient slatted wooden shutters, and to the wriggle of Gulliver on feet now numbed by his huge and painful presence.

'Get off!' She pushed him urgently, suddenly afraid for the immaculately embroidered silk counterpane under which she lay. Gulliver leapt down, his claws catching at a perfectly executed briar rose. Cecilia sat up and stared at the tear in horror; she was still inspecting a lily and a violet for more destruction when the door opened and a maid came in, carrying a brass jug of scalding water, followed by a second, bearing a cup of sweet French chocolate.

The first maid dipped a curtsy. Perhaps it was because she was still tired that Cecilia sensed something insolent in the demeanour of it. Certainly when she thought about it she could not imagine what it was. But it put her on her guard; reminded her too that her position here was quite the most peculiar and the servants must be fascinated by it.

'Thank you. . .?' It was plain from her tone that she was asking the girl's name.

'Arietta, *madonna*; I am the little Princesses' nurse.' And, so saying, she tossed aside her mane of perfectly blue-black hair from her even more perfect features. Cecilia was sure, then, that for some reason or other this girl did not want her here. But she had not been brought up to worry about the opinions of servants, so dismissed the matter from her mind, accepting the chocolate from the younger, plainer girl with real gratitude.

But it was her bath that made it possible for her to face the day with something like her usual command— hot, cleansing, soothing, and scented with pure jasmine oil. As she sat before the silver-mounted Venetian glass and let Piggy begin the long work of teasing her hair into its elegant Grecian curls, Cecilia watched herself in the mirror and began to think.

Twenty-six years of age. She was old, in terms of the marriage market, so old that no one could possibly place the least unseemly construction on her being here at the *castello*. She was undoubtedly—if, it had to be said, from choice—irretrievably on the shelf by this time, the shelf on to which her father's impecuniousness had precipitated her and where she had remained because the only offers she had ever received for her hand were from gentlemen who, though rich and well-bred enough to please him, had been even older and more degenerate than her father. The Duke of Downside had been bad-tempered about her refusing them all but she had shouted back at him in a comfortably Mediterranean fashion and he had let the matter drop. Papa had not perhaps—she smiled at it—enjoyed being reminded just whose fault it was that all her suitors were such disreputable ones. Whatever, none of that was the point now; the point was that she was here, unmarried, and beyond the hope of marriage—something she had not had time thus far to regret or otherwise—and as such surely safe from idle gossip, for all she was here in the Prince's house, alone save only for the somnolent Miss Pigg.

Safe, anyway. Cecilia studied herself critically: she had never been beautiful, at least not for the fashion of the day, which was turning away from her imperious, classical looks to softer and more childlike features. Her face was, her father had complained, almost too intimidatingly sculptured, delicate yet strong, her mouth stubborn for all it was soft, and her eyes, despite their size and luminosity and the shading of preposterously long black lashes, could be ice-hard in their unexpectedly deep and vivid blue. But only when she was cross, she soothed herself. She had always thought that otherwise her eyes were her prettiest feature. Along with her hair, a thick, heavy Saxon gold that had been all she had inherited from her beautiful mother. At least, too, she was small; she only wished that did not mean that she was—if only just—a bit too thin.

No—pale, tired, unladylike, as he had accused her of being, she was safe from the Prince d'Aquilano's attentions. That she knew by instinct he was a man from whom women were generally far from safe might hurt her pride a little—for he had barely noticed she was a woman at all—but it was safer to be offended than pursued. Much safer. Cecilia shivered at the thought of his dark and uncompromising features. It was an unexpectedly pleasurable sensation.

'Keep still, Silly! You have dislodged all the pins!' It

was a familiar wail from Piggy, always in danger of swallowing half the pins tucked precariously in the corner of her mouth. She never seemed to talk as much as when to do so put her in immediate danger of choking.

Silly. Suddenly Cecilia froze.

'Piggy! But don't you dare use that name for me in front of hi. . .the children!' she amended hastily.

'Afraid he will tease you for it, my love?' Damn Piggy for always going straight to the point! 'Now let me look at you. Yes, that will do, very well indeed. I particularly like the innocence of that butter muslin and the yellow ribbons. . .'

'Innocence?'

'Well, you must own, my love, that it wasn't really the thing to call His Highness a. . .well, what you did call him. No, really, Cecilia, I insist it was very bad of you. The more ashamed of yourself you appear this morning, the better. . .'

'But I'm not the least ashamed of what I called him! He *is* a——'

'You don't know anything of the kind, child, and I feel certain that his parents *must* have been properly married or he wouldn't be the Duke, now, would he?'

Literal, absurd, wise old Piggy! Cecilia was still laughing when she left the room to follow Arietta down to the dining hall. Behind her Piggy muttered, fairly, 'But he is an arrant swine!'

It was only when Cecilia realised she was to be alone with him that she began to wonder why it was she had known for certain that the Prince d'Aquilano was not married. He had been once, of course, but she had always felt certain that he was not married now. It would have been so much better, she thought helplessly, had there been Princess d'Aquilano to turn to.

'*Buon giorno*, I trust you slept well.' The Prince turned from the fire, invariably lit in the chill depths of this medieval fortress even in the heat of July, his expression as formal as were his words. So much for my looking innocent and sorry, Cecilia mocked herself—he hasn't even noticed me at all!

'Thank you, yes. In spite. . .' She stopped herself on her waspish retort; she had half promised Piggy to be good.

'Of being kidnapped? Was I so very Gothick about it? I'm sorry.'

He neither looked nor sounded the least bit sorry. He was, she was certain of it, amused at everything he had done. Consequently Cecilia decided she had every right to behave as badly as she chose. Only when he gave her real cause, of course. . .

'No need to be sorry at all, sir,' she murmured sweetly; then could not help herself. 'Of course, I am abducted every day. I like nothing better than to be told I may not go where I wish to go. I cannot think of anything you could have done to please me more!'

She would have much preferred that he be cross at her impertinences than smile in such a lazy and maddening fashion. When he smiled like that she noticed all over again how handsome he was, and how unusually unceremonious for a man who was—she had to face it—little short of the King of all he surveyed. It would not do to remember that he was capable of being charming.

'I'll think of something!' he retorted softly. Then, abruptly, his whole demeanour changed and she saw at last the very thing she had just thought was absent in him. She saw his deliberate opening up of the great gulf between them; the man who was royal in all but name was pulling on the mantle of his authority to distance her. She knew what was to come. More questions.

'Please be seated, *madonna*.' Had she doubted that this was now an official interrogation, that doubt now fled. So it made it somehow all the more absurd that he then waited in patient silence for his servants to serve

her with the hot bread, peaches and glass of lemonade
that was all she had wanted for her breakfast. Disconcerting, too, that he allowed her to eat for a while, eyes
never leaving her, though she felt this rather than saw it,
for she could not look at him. She was almost certain he
was doing it on purpose to unsettle her.

Well, she wouldn't be unsettled! Not this time. This
time it was not the middle of the night; no more had she
just seconds ago been cradling a dying man in her arms.
If he meant to harass each answer from her she would
fight him. He had to know—for her pride's sake, though
she refused resolutely to admit to such pettiness—that
he was not going to be able to control her, for all his
exalted rank and, if she faced it, his absolute advantage.
Nobody was treating her as a prisoner, but then no more
would they; it was the Italian way to be so much more
subtle than that. Even so, she was one. It was only the
why she was that eluded her.

When she had finished one of her peaches and a
manservant had poured her out a second glass of lemonade the Prince dismissed everyone else from the room
with nothing more than the almost imperceptible lift to
his brows.

'Now, then, *madonna*. We must talk about the death
of Giulio Mansini——' he saw the look of resentment
flash into her eyes at his official manner and added,
dampeningly '—so that you are saved the trouble of
repeating it all before the Austrian governor. Yes,
madonna, he does exist—no need to look so surprised! I
believe, in fact, that I am meant to be under his
jurisdiction. That is of not the least consequence, of
course; however, he does like to know what is going on,
and it seems harsh to deprive him of his little pleasures.'

Had the contempt in his voice been more pronounced
Cecilia would have suspected bitterness, resentment, that
he was indeed fettered by his Austrian masters. But the
disdain was light, almost amused, even tolerant, and all

the more astonishing because of it. Cecilia found she had
paused with her glass halfway to her lips, staring at him
in near disbelief. Not even her impossibly arrogant and
selfish father had ever behaved with half such assurance
as this.

'Very well,' she managed, because she had little
choice. She knew what was coming next. Did she
remember who was in the square, or who followed Giulio
into it. . .?

She was wrong. He was turning away from her as he
spoke, so he did not see her expression of utter
incredulity.

'How long had you known Giulio Mansini, *madonna*?'

Cecilia could not believe she had heard him correctly.

'Known Giulio Mansini?' she parroted stupidly, and
was surprised at the anger in his eyes when he at last
turned back to her. Anger and a great deal more. She
could not look away from him.

'That is what I said.' His words were granite-hard.

Condemning enough to bring her to her feet in a heat
of rage. How dared he suggest such a thing? What
nonsense was this?

'I did not know the man at all. I never saw him before
yesterday afternoon!'

She knew even as she spoke that he did not believe
her. It was the way he did not believe her, with the
sardonic, almost casual smile of one who had been
expecting her to lie to him that angered her the most.
Until he said, 'For someone who had not met him,
madonna, you were very. . .tender with him.' And she
exploded.

'And so should anyone have been! And *would* have
been anywhere but in this benighted country!'

'Meaning?'

'Meaning, Your Highness, that anywhere but in a
place that lives, *feeds* on suspicion and intrigue people
would have rushed at once to his aid. As I did!'

'A lone girl, in a strange city, with all those other people able to do more to help him, and nearer to him when it happened? You cannot really expect me to believe——'

'I don't in the least care what you believe, for you are being so ridiculous that it is shaming to see it! I saw a man in trouble and I went to him——'

'And held him in your arms—just as a lover would?'

Cecilia had long ceased trying to unravel the separate strands of his thoughts, let alone wonder how he could have come to think them in the first place. She could only react to each new thing as he said it. And react she did, erupting into such a flood of temper that she was aware just for a moment of the greatest sense of release, almost of power; she was far too angry to be afraid of him any more.

'That, sir, is unforgivable! The words of a fool! And you know it!'

'I know nothing of the sort.' For all its velvet blandness, something stirred beneath the surface of his quiet voice. Something that stirred in Cecilia too, but she could not say what it was. Other than that she had to challenge him, fight him. She needed to.

'In fact,' he continued, his voice devoid of all expression, 'I know little about you at all. Other than that for two years past your home has been but sixty miles from here, and Giulio Mansini was for much of that time in Tuscany also.'

'Oh, but this is monstrous! And so utterly absurd that it is laughable!'

'Is it? I see nothing ridiculous in it at all. He was a handsome boy. You would hardly have been the first——'

'The first *what*?' Cecilia's fingers bit so deeply into the peach she was holding that it was crushed in a stream of scented juices. His smile as he saw it was hateful. Hateful

and smug! Cecilia came within a hair's breadth of
throwing the peach right at him.

'I wouldn't!' he warned, reading her mind to the last
intention. 'I meant you would hardly have been the first
to—er—*respond* to the poet's charms.'

Had he had a wife Cecilia might have understood him
in that moment. She knew, incredible though it was,
that she was hearing jealousy in those acid, icy tones.
But she was too angry to heed it.

'Succumb was the word you were looking for, Prince,
as if I should ever *succumb* to any man. . .least of all just
a pretty child of a boy!'

'Giulio was no child!'

'He was seventeen! Good God, surely you cannot
suppose. . .? I am six-and-twenty years old, and you are
quite beyond your place to speak to——!'

'Six-and-twenty?' For the first time ever Cecilia heard
a note of indecision, hesitation, in his voice. At any other
time it would have flattered her; now she laughed right
in his face.

'Yes, Prince, six-and-twenty. Rather beyond being the
object of a young boy's attentions. Or any grown man's
either!'

The way he looked at her then was impossible to face,
impossible to handle even in the heat of her rage; his
eyes had always a quality that could sear to the very
depths of their victim, burning out the truth. But this
was more than that. Smouldering like fire, and yet it was
much, much more than just the power of his overwhelming personality working to undermine her now. Too
much more.

'You think that?' There was speculation, nothing
more, in his even voice. But Cecilia found that it shocked
her to the core to hear it. It sounded, her bewildered
brain was warning her, like the response to some kind of
challenge. A challenge he had accepted—that she had
never issued. Never would issue. . .

'My age is not the issue, sir.' She forced out the chilling words in the teeth of nerves shaken to snapping-point. 'The only point is that, beautiful as an angel though he was. . .and he *was*. . .' she flung at him defiantly '. . .I never knew your poet. No more would I have had the unkindness to let him attach himself to me if I had done. I never met him!'

'So why. . .?'

'I told you why. I went to him because he *needed* someone. The only person willing to go to him was me. If you cannot understand that, sir, you can understand nothing at all!'

Cecilia had had enough of this. Even as she finished the sentence, she was turning to leave the room, and to the Devil with his absolute power in his petty city state! He had no control over her and he was going to know it.

As she reached the doors she thought she heard him call out, 'Just a moment, Lady Cecilia—wait!'

Certainly the youth who now came into the room heard him. Cecilia found herself facing almost a perfect copy of the man standing so silently now behind her. He was even wearing the same sardonic smile.

'Oh, I would not wait, *madonna*. For he won't ever understand. Will you, Father?'

Even as he spat out the final word with a bitterness that spoke of real hatred, Cecilia stood rooted to the spot, shocked by her mistake. He was not so like the Prince, after all; he only had the colouring and the manner. He did not have the eyes. These eyes were blue. The eyes of Giulio the Poet. And they were smiling at her in a way that wanted her to know it.

Behind her a voice spoke, soft with the flickering menace of a striking adder.

'Ah, Massimo. Allow me to present you to the Lady Cecilia Sherringham.'

Cecilia found herself looking in disbelief from one to the other, her head nodding an automatic response to the younger man's exquisitely executed bow; father and son. Impossible! Impossible that two men could ever hate each other as much as this. Impossible most of all that she should be trapped here between them as if all that scalding venom were centred on herself. Intolerable.

'Prince Massimo,' she murmured, stunned.

'Massimo d'Aquilano-Mansini,' he replied with the utmost elegance. With the utmost irony.

Mansini, again. What in God's name, thought Cecilia then, is going on in this place?

CHAPTER THREE

WHAT was going on was the most elegant, the most courteous minuet of loathing that Cecilia had ever been privileged to witness. Father and son smiled, but the smiles threw such contempt at each other that she could almost feel it physically poisoning the atmosphere. Cecilia, forced by good manners into staying in a room she would have given anything to leave, could only watch and fight as best she could any threat of their manipulating her into being some new pawn in their bitter game. A violent game. The air reeked of physical threat only just reined in.

'Please don't run away, *madonna*.' There was almost a purring quality to Prince Massimo's beautiful voice. Cecilia had no choice but to take her chair by the fireplace, closer to the man whom seconds ago she had come near to hating so much herself. The tension in the Duke as she approached was palpable, but, for all it felt directed at herself, his eyes remained unwaveringly on his son.

How beautiful the Duke must have been as a boy, she thought idly, still trying to come to terms with the fact he had this son at all; beautiful now, for all his harshness and the strain evident about his eyes and in the lines of his face. But as a boy—as Massimo still was—he must have been the closest that man could ever get to being a god.

Massimo was nineteen perhaps, maybe twenty, no more, and Cecilia had to mentally revise her assessment of his father's age. He would be forty for certain. He did not look it. Paler of skin, and with his carefully wind-swept hair and decided air of cosmopolitan fashion,

Massimo was as beautiful as anything she had seen in the works of Michelangelo or Bernini; even so—it struck at once and it was an impression never to leave her—for all the sweetness of his smile, the soft openness of his sleepy blue eyes, he was much more closed a man, more secretive even than his father. Simply, the one she would trust—if she really had to—the other she could not. Even as he smiled winningly at her, Cecilia knew that she would never like Massimo d'Aquilano-Mansini. Because she knew it and felt guilty because she had no grounds for such a prejudice, she responded with her most dazzling smile.

As she did so she saw the brows of the Duke lower into a deep frown, his eyes darken and his mouth set into an even harder line. All he said was, 'I would be obliged to you, Massimo, if you would allow me to continue asking Lady Cecilia what she saw yesterday afternoon. You know, of course,' his tone was silken, 'that your cousin Giulio is dead?'

For a long moment the silence was so heavy in the room that Cecilia felt she could have reached out and moulded it between her fingers. The Duke had meant something by that. But what he could have meant was beyond her.

Then Massimo murmured, 'I know.'

'I'm glad I did not have to shock you with the news,' returned his father innocently. 'Now what I must do is get to the truth of the matter as soon as possible. . .'

Again there was something more in that innocuous statement than the meaning of the words. Prince Massimo reacted with the same wary silence.

Then, 'Of course.' And, to Cecilia's surprise, he was bowing to her again. 'Forgive me, *madonna*, I must allow myself to be cast from the room. You and my father have clearly so much to discuss. . .'

Polite, banal words, stinging with some message that went far above Cecilia's reeling head. Before she could reply he was gone again, leaving behind him an atmosphere so savage that she could not for the life of her think what to say to bring the Duke round from his brooding silence.

Eventually, after what must have been a minute at least, he seemed to remember where he was.

'My apologies, *madonna*. You must think us all sadly wanting in manners. It is just that——'

'Of course. I hadn't realised until now that Giulio was related to you.'

'Related to me, *madonna*? No. Related to my son.' He succeeded in saying the word 'son' as if he had taken arsenic.

'Oh, to your wife, then?'

'My wife.'

So flatly did he say that word that Cecilia knew it was more than her life was worth to ask the questions now bubbling to her lips. Desperately she wanted to know what all this was about, but all too plainly she wasn't going to find out.

So she said, the way one did when a silence was impossible, something undeniably stupid.

'I had not thought you to be old enough for a son of Prince Massimo's age.'

She paid for it. His tone was all mocking pleasure.

'No? I count myself flattered, *madame*!'

Cecilia felt snubbed; although she knew she had asked for it, she had not said anything offensive, after all, and he had no reason to be quite so nasty about it.

The Duke seemed to sense something of her hurt—and it was hurt—for he came closer to her then, almost as if he might take her hand. Whatever he had been meaning to do, he did not do it.

But he did say, 'Forgive me again, *madonna*. If you can.' He smiled at her then and she would have had to be a great deal more hurt or angry to resist the self-mocking wistfulness of his manner. 'I seem to have done nothing but what requires penance and absolution. No wonder you made that comparison with *Udolpho*.'

'Well,' Cecilia could not resist—she did not even really try, 'it *is* all a little like a novel by Mrs Radcliffe, you must own. Dark castles, dead of night. . . I know you must have a dozen dungeons. . .'

'And a father and son at each other's throat like savages!'

Cecilia shuddered. Because it was true. Yet they had been so frighteningly courteous about it.

'Perhaps that is because you are too young and he resents your authority as a result.'

She could easily have said because Massimo was too old. But that was not the way it had occurred to her, and she was only saying what she meant.

He smiled at it; it would have taken a much angrier man to resist such honesty, least of all the unconscious compliment implicit in it.

'I am eight-and-thirty, *madonna*. And yes, perhaps I am too young. Perhaps. . .well, many things. . .'

For a moment Cecilia felt the stirrings of real regret. She knew by instinct that he had come very close in that moment to confiding in her. Knew something else, too: that he rarely did confide in anyone at all. It was the burden of Princes, after all, to have no one to whom they could safely turn. Even less could a man in his unenviable position trust and know he was safe to do so. She felt in that moment real sympathy for him. And wondered next what he had ever confided to his wife. That was all such men had, after all—the hope that somewhere there was a woman who would care for them more than for politics, who would be loyal, and listen. She must have made some movement, a half-gesture. That, or he had sensed the train of her thoughts as he had done all too often before. He did reach out a hand to her then, and Cecilia took it without the least sense of alarm or even thought for what he meant to do with her own hand.

What he did do was hold it for a moment, looking down at where it lay, white and fragile in his own strong, sun-gold fingers. Almost absently his thumb brushed her upturned palm. But only once. Just as he smiled only once, in a way that set her heart beating out of step—and had her looking properly at him just at the moment he looked at her, and holding his eyes not because she could not help it this time so much as because it was what she wanted very much to do.

Then he said, his voice sounding unexpectedly strained, almost as if he was having trouble speaking, 'Let us be friends, *madonna*. We've behaved despicably, both of us, you know we have! Let's not do it any more.'

Cecilia spoke before she even thought about it. Her voice, too, was not much more than a whisper.

'Yes,' she answered, and really meant it. He would make a very dependable friend. Just as he made a terrifying enemy. 'Yes, I'd like to be friends.'

It was only when he raised her hand to his lips that she realised, somewhere inside and to her dawning horror, that she might like them to be a great deal more indeed.

Beyond the formidable fortress that was the Castello d'Aquilano lay the most unexpected, the most magical of gardens. For all their intended formality, the plants had long since taken control for themselves and run riot, a mass of roses, irises, violets, jasmine, carnations—even, here and there, where the gardeners had decided that they looked quite pretty after all, a cluster of wild poppies. It was here along the cypress walks that the Duke now led Cecilia, her hand tucked lightly into the crook of his arm, talking with her as easily now as if she had been any ordinary guest. It felt like that to her. Easy, comfortable, where before everything had been so puzzling, so disturbing. But then perhaps that was because they were at last out into the morning sunshine, free of the pressing shadows of the *castello* towers, strolling between the gentle swaying of the vines, the rustle of fountains and the golden flash of carp in the Chinese lily ponds.

'I married when I was seventeen.' The Duke led Cecilia to a bench of stone carved with the arrogant eagles of his coat of arms. 'Hardly welcoming, are they?' He smiled at their incredible ugliness, but he went back, as she wanted him to, to the subject he had started on. 'Elettra, my wife, was the only child of the last Count Mansini. . .last legitimate child in the whole family. The heir. My parents and hers had always been at odds with one another, though I never understood the reason, when the families had always been on such close terms before, but when the Austrians came they decided to bury their differences. It was only sense then to consolidate our power and wealth into one family and fight the Austrian invaders from the stronger position. The fact that Elettra and I had hated each other all our lives was of little consequence. Such things never are.'

He had spoken the words so easily, as if hatred for one's wife were normal—so much so that Cecilia almost thought he believed it was and she felt a shock far beyond any she had known so far. He was not bitter at it, simply bored, indifferent. In that one dismissive phrase she knew again why it was she had always refused to be married, how soul-destroying it would be, unless she respected her husband, trusted and liked him. . .if she was fortunate, really loved him.

'Elettra was older than me, three-and-twenty.' He laughed then, remembering his disbelief at hearing Cecilia's age and her insistence that she was positively faded. 'Almost,' he teased, 'as crabbed with age as you are!'

Cecilia laughed at it. 'Absurd creature!'

'It's your own fault, for being such an absurd child. And don't say you are not a child—you are to me. In your terms I must be irredeemably ancient.'

'Crumbling to dust. . .'

'Well, there you are, then. I shall call you a child if I want to.'

'You were telling me about your wife.'

For a moment, when he replied, 'I was, wasn't I?' the Duke sounded almost startled at himself. As, had she but known it, he was. He had never talked to anyone like this before, and in all honesty could not say why he was doing so now. Other than that, he found he wanted to.

'We fought like cat and dog if we were in the same room for so much as a minute. From which you will conclude that Massimo is not my son.'

He said it so much as lazily as what had gone before that Cecilia at first was not sure she had heard him. Then she was, and she felt herself jump at it. Felt too the Duke of Aquila Romana take her hand again, this time in both his own.

'Don't be missish now, Cecilia. I like you much better when I can't shock you at all.'

'Very well!' It was the way he had said 'Cecilia', so easily, without thought that he should not, that made her throat go dry; she had never heard her name sound half so pretty before.

'Good. If you were ever to turn into a copy-book English lady it would be a shocking waste!'

'I'll do my best to be completely unacceptable, sir.' How she managed her old dryness of tone she never knew—her head was reeling at the things she had just heard.

'I know you will.'

'Iphigenia and Atalanta. . .?' Somehow she had to break the silence.

'Did Elettra and I stop fighting long enough to conceive the twins? No. Their mother was. . .she was a. . .friend.'

'Was? I'm sorry.'

'I loved her, but I was already married. She died when the twins were born.'

'But surely, could you not have annulled your marriage, in the circumstances, and married the woman you really cared for?'

Had she gone too far? Certainly the question was grossly indelicate and Cecilia knew it. Inevitably he smiled at it.

'I wanted to. Dear God, I *did* want to! But I couldn't. Politics. Even here in Italy, where I thought we had more sense, politics will always take precedence over love.'

'It seems so sad. . .' Cecilia was speaking mainly to herself. She was remembering how he had seemed with the twins, so happy and so free of all care. He should have been married to their mother. To the Devil with politics and war! Even as she thought it, the very idea of his being happily married at all made her a little sick, but she failed to understand it.

'It was Hell on earth. Hell for Parisina.'

'Parisina was her name?' Again Cecilia was speaking to herself.

So was he. 'Parisina. Parisina Mansini. Giulio's elder half-sister.'

'Oh. . . I see.' And, almost, Cecilia thought she did.

How complicated it was, these two families so often inter-linked, like the threads of an ancient plait now impossible to untangle.

'Giulio and Parisina were my wife's bastard cousins. Their father was Cardinal Ippolito Mansini.'

'That rather explains it!'

'Doesn't it? He lived very happily with his mistress— she had fled her royal Spanish husband to be with him; they built a villa just outside the city here. His children had the most perfect childhood—as I hope Parisina's children do. *My* children.'

His only children, Cecilia thought of it now. His heir

in law was not his heir by blood. What it must mean to a man like this that his titles and inheritance pass into the hands of the son of the wife he so hated, Cecilia could not begin to conceive, except that he would hardly be able to bear it. And Massimo would know that. It explained so much of what was wrong between them.

'You might have married again, after your wife died?' she said, following her thoughts to their logical conclusion.

'I never met anyone I wanted to marry—not even to save all this.'

'Not after Parisina. . .?'

'No.'

Cecilia felt that stabbing pain deep inside her again, and this time she knew what it meant. It was jealousy. Envy, anyway, of a woman who had been loved so deeply, as she would never be herself; what else she might be jealous of, she did not understand enough to question.

She changed the subject abruptly.

'Who was Massimo's father? Did you know?'

Oddly, it was as she asked it—such a grossly impertinent question that she was appalled at herself—that she noticed he was still holding her hand. Even as she noticed it, so did he. For a moment it looked as if he would retain his hold on it, but, even as she thought he was going to, he smiled, almost sadly, and let her go. Cecilia felt strangely bereft.

'I knew. The first thing Elettra did when we were married. . .and I mean the *very* first thing she did. . .was tell me she was already with child. The child of the Austrian governor of the time. . .and I had married her solely to gain the power to oust him from this city!'

'Dear God!' Even to Cecilia, with no personal loyalty to this city and this land, it was a terrible thought that it must one day pass absolutely into the hands of the son of one of the hated imperial overlords.

'Baron Lorenz von Baden. That is what all this will be one day—the inheritance of the Bastard von Baden!'

For a moment Cecilia felt compunction, a real sense that, whatever else he might prove to be, Prince Massimo was innocent of his birth.

'Oh, Federigo, is that fair?' In her turn she found she had used his name without thinking, even without really realising she had heard it before.

'No, it is not.' She had never met a man more honest than he was, even with himself. 'I tried to be fair. I would have succeeded perhaps. Only that would not have suited Elettra. Only this—this farce, this hatred—would have been enough to satisfy her. By the time he was five years old she had made sure that he could never love me.'

He was not perhaps the easiest man to love, perhaps least of all for a lonely little boy; even so, Cecilia believed him. A belief perhaps unfair to Massimo and based solely in her instant and unreasonable dislike of the boy.

'And I had thought my own family to be a sad one,' she sighed.

'Isn't it? If not in such a Gothick manner?' It was a relief that he was able to laugh at her again now; she had not known how to begin to lift the atmosphere of regret that had descended upon her.

'I do not like my sisters, if that is what you mean. They were cruel beyond forgiving to Papa when he lost all of his fortune. . .'

'Every last scrap?' Still the Duke was teasing her, making her own ignominious story easier to tell him.

'To the last crumb! Papa really was completely penniless, and Eliza and Persephone would never forgive him for it. No more would their *odious* husbands. How even my sisters contrived to find two such unappealing gentlemen I cannot for the life of me conceive! In fact, I can barely imagine it possible for there to be *one* gentleman quite so beastly.'

'You can't go back to that.'

'Where else can I go?' Cecilia had not meant to sound even a fraction so desperate.

'I've been thinking about that. . .' As the Duke spoke she felt him drawing a little away from her along the bench. Certainly, despite the sunlight, she felt colder.

'Oh?'

He was looking away from her, out across the sun-parched lawns towards the high cascades and the vast lake beyond. His gaze seemed so fixed on the horizon that it was almost as if he were looking for something in particular, though she knew that he was not.

'I thought you might like to stay here.' He might have been talking about nothing more important than tomorrow's weather.

Cecilia had known just before he said it that this was what he was going to say. Even so, when he did so she felt considerably shaken.

'Here?'

'You are parroting me again. It sounds so *silly*.'

He used the English word then and Cecilia leapt instantly to her feet in a blush of horror.

'Where did you hear that? Who told you? Oh, but I will murder *darling* Piggy!'

'You would be committing the greatest injustice if you did!' Federigo shaded his eyes against the sun and looked up at her. 'Figi and Talia were spying into your room this morning. They ran at once to ask me what it meant, and why in particular I wasn't meant to hear it!'

'Oh, but. . .!' Cecilia felt her cheeks burning with embarrassment. Of all things for the twins to have overheard and repeated, that was the most humiliating of all.

'It's not so bad.' He smiled—no, it was almost, she was astounded at it, a grin. 'I shan't use it unless you are being particularly foolish. One can use any jest too often.'

'It isn't in the least a joke, and I think I hate you!'

'Good. That means you are going to stay!'

The strange thing was, Cecilia knew that it did.

'Only. . .*why* am I staying?'

'Oh, I think to teach Figi and Talia a little English, don't you?'

'But——'

'Nonsense, it's the perfect—um—cover.'

'Cover!' Cecilia was alarmed again, but couldn't begin to see why. 'Cover for what?'

'For the fact you love Italy and you want to stay but it would have been most improper to ask me!'

She knew then what it was that had frightened her. She was frightened that he could so easily guess the truth, even though it had only this moment become clear to her. No, not just Italy, she thought; I could so very easily, unless I am really careful, begin to love you!

'Of course!' Never would Cecilia have believed she could have sounded so matter-of-fact, least of all with her nerves churning as riotously as they were at this shocking revelation.

'That's settled, then—you'll stay?'

'Yes.'

Only when he got to his feet and took her hand in his arm and led her to find the twins to give them the news did she suddenly realise what she had done. She had willingly locked the door of her own prison on herself and thrown away the key. She half wondered, as she cast a glance up at him and saw that he was smiling gently to himself, if that were not the reason he was smiling—that he knew it.

'We know plenty of English already,' said Atalanta, finishing magnanimously, 'but you can stay anyway if you like.'

'We think we are going to like you,' explained the Princess Iphigenia kindly.

'We like Gulliver.'

And plainly as anything the overgrown and monstrous-looking mongrel liked them. He was scrabbling at the edge of the lake, his multicoloured hairs as full of mud and water as the twins' muslins were plentifully spattered with both evil-smelling substances.

'How disgusting of you,' Cecilia commented.

Hurt for him, the twins dived at Gulliver to hug his injured feelings better.

'Lord, but where did you find such an unprepossessing animal?' asked their father, trying to keep the laughter from his question.

'Waterloo.'

Cecilia knew that would win an excited reaction. It did. The twins she had expected to squeal, but it was good to see their languid parent well and truly startled just this once.

'Waterloo!'

'On the battlefield. Or, rather, running off it, singed and absolutely terrified. A friend of ours found him, Viscount Savernake—but he has a dog already, even larger than this one, so he gave Gulliver to me.'

'Who called him Gulliver?'

'I did. Perry—Lord Savernake, that is—had called him Griswold, and it really *wasn't* kind of him.'

'I can see that *you* might think so,' the Duke put in delicately. But the twins as well as Cecilia were against him.

'Gulliver's a much nicer name.' The twins looked sternly at him.

'Even though you cannot say it!'

Watching as he teased the children, Cecilia found herself thinking how different he was simply because of their bubbling presence. And wondering how like Parisina Mansini they were. Certainly they were the most beautiful children she had ever seen, hair a mass of unruly mahogany curls, eyes of warm chestnut-brown.

Their father's eyes. The thought made her blush. And to her horror she found that he was watching her.

'This sun is getting too hot for you—come back into the house. *All* of you.'

It was kind of him to pretend he had not noticed her confusion.

'Gulliver too?' The twins prepared for battle.

'No.'

But, sovereign Prince though he was, there was no absolute authority here.

'Yes, or we don't come! He'll be lonely.'

'Oh, good God. . .!'

Cecilia, just a little, needed her revenge for his having seen that blush, however nice he had been about it. Tucking her arm confidingly through his, she murmured, 'Oh, but he *will* be, you know.'

It was already very important to her to know that she could make him laugh like this, with a complete relaxation of all that wary tension.

'Oh, very well, I can't fight all of you! But under duress. I——'

'No, you don't—you think he's adorable!' Cecilia smiled innocently past him.

'The only thing I think at this moment,' retorted the Duke of Aquila Romana succinctly, 'is that you are the most shocking little minx that was ever born!'

For someone on the very edge of falling really in love for the first time in her life, it was a very reassuring, even inspiring, comment.

As the little troupe reached the shelter of the vines below the terrace a figure came hurrying towards them. Dressed in the stiffly braided uniform of a commander of the Austrian garrison, the man was carrying his silvered helmet beneath his arm; one enfeebled finger was doing its best to loosen his choking ceremonial collar.

'Ah, Governor!' Whatever he felt about the man's wardship of his lands, the Prince d'Aquilano was impeccably polite to him.

'Ah, Prince!' And the Governor laughed out loud, gesturing weakly to his pocket. Atalanta got there first.

'Here you are.' She took out his handkerchief and stood on tiptoe, where he bent to let her mop his sweating brow.

'He has two children of his own and he misses them dreadfully,' confided Iphigenia, taking Cecilia's other elbow. 'The Countess insisted they stay behind at Salzburg.'

'And very wise she was,' laughed the Governor, overhearing her remark. 'They would have completely baked themselves in this appalling climate!'

'Help the Count with his collar, Atalanta.' Her father was smiling quite easily at the ministrations of this twin. 'Then he will be able to bow without strangling himself. Allow me to present you to Lady Cecilia Sherringham, Count. Lady Cecilia, this is the Count von Regensberg.'

Even as the Count bowed with unmistakably Austrian precision, the twins were swinging from his arms and playing with his helmet.

'Only he lets us call him Uncle Axel, don't you? So you don't feel so very lonely.'

'Is everyone lonely around here?' asked the Prince vaguely. Quite naturally the Count looked puzzled.

Cecilia took pity on him. He looked the kind of man she had always liked—intelligent, good-natured, easy of manner, if at this particular moment his startling blondness was very much stewed beetroot in the blistering Italian sun. He was young, too, for so important a position, perhaps no more than six years older than she was.

'The Prince is referring to my dog, Count. The twins would insist on bringing him into the house. I really think that he must stay outside, however; your uniform is far too elegant to spoil.'

'My dear ma'am,' the Count accepted her outstretched hand with grace, 'he may *eat* the thing for all I care! You cannot begin to conceive how uncomfortable this is. Twice as uncomfortable for me as for my troops—at least they do not have to wear this merciless helmet.'

Since at this point the helmet was being worn by Iphigenia, right down past her chin to the neck of her dishevelled muslin, Cecilia laughed easily. It seemed to be the way the Prince d'Aquilano wanted things to be. Certainly his manners could have countenanced nothing less. How Federigo really felt at this moment she could not say, for she had withdrawn her arm from his to offer her hand to the Count von Regensberg. Even so, she was certain she would have felt the tension in him, if it had been there. She always had so far.

'Please look where you are walking, Figi. Come along. . .yes, Gulliver too.' Federigo's tone was martyred. 'Some wine, I think, Count, and then perhaps you can tell me why you have come this morning.'

It was when he spoke, and Cecilia felt the swift glancing of the Governor's eyes from herself to the Prince and back, that she knew why he was here. To talk to her about Giulio. Knew, too, what it was that Federigo had done for her. She was under his protection, a fact he had just made explicitly clear—certainly the Count von Regensberg understood it. There would be no unpalatable questions for her from that quarter—unless prompted by the Duke of Aquila Romana himself.

As indeed there were not. Atalanta, Iphigenia and Gulliver were sent about their undoubtedly messy business, hauled from the room by a far from pleased Arietta, whose skirts had been until this moment dazzlingly clean. The Count laughed as they left, his tone almost wistful.

'You daughters are right, Prince; I do miss my own children terribly.'

'You might always——' here Federigo paused as he passed the Count a glass of icy white wine from the *castello* vineyards '—of course, go home.'

It was when he smiled, and the Governor met that smile with one just as sardonic of his own, that Cecilia saw at last true the position between them. Of personal enmity there was nothing at all, but loyalty to their own cause was absolute, the Count to Austrian domination, the Prince to his stolen birthright. In the sheer sophistication of their dealings they were frightening. Certainly Cecilia had never admired Prince Federigo more than in this moment.

The Count knew not to extend the jest. Other than to say, 'Not unless I may take every last bottle of this excellent vintage with me.'

The two smiled again, and Cecilia thought what a great pity it was that two such men, with so much in common and such unforced mutual respect, could never really be friends.

'And now, Count, to the purpose of your visit.'

'Of course. It is most distressing for you, Lady Cecilia, but I fear I must ask you a few more questions.'

'Please, don't concern yourself on my account. What is it you wish to know?'

It was the Count's duty, after all, and she wanted to make it easy for him. That her sweet and genuine compliance raised a smile of ironic astonishment from the Prince d'Aquilano she chose, studiously, to ignore.

'Only whom you saw in the square, ma'am. Oh, I know you cannot name them, but describe them if you will.'

'I shall try. Only. . .'

'Yes?'

'Surely the murderer would not have been in the

square at all, but in the alley beyond the cathedral, from where Giulio Mansini came?'

'I would say yes, ma'am, under normal circumstances, but I cannot help feeling that he must needs have followed, to be certain Giulio did not speak before he died.'

'But in that case the murderer must of necessity have been the first person to reach him. . .'

Even as the words hurried out in all their innocence Cecilia felt the air grow a little colder.

'Not necessarily, ma'am.' The Count was treading very carefully. 'Suffice only that he be able to discover what was said.'

'You mean that whoever it was Giulio spoke to might be bribed to silence?'

'Yes.'

'But I should never. . .'

She heard then the soft chink of Federigo setting down his glass.

'Bribed, Count, or more permanently silenced.'

A shiver of such disquiet shook her body that Cecilia knew it was visible for all to see. The Count, she knew, had seen it for his fastidious face took on a look of real distaste and he flashed a quelling look at Federigo. A brave gesture in the teeth of a man like the Prince, and she was more than grateful for it.

'But—I have told His Highness what I know. So I am perfectly safe.'

'Of course you are.' The Count's smile did not quite reach his eyes.

Why did those otherwise comforting words upset her so badly? Make her feel suddenly so insecure?

'Tell us who you saw in the square, Cecilia.' It was Federigo, speaking as quietly as ever. And again she heard the menace in his voice. And she thought, Who is it you want me to say, I know you *do* want me to? What is my part in all this? Remembered, too, who was the first person to question her, to make sure he heard Giulio's last words before anyone else did. Only that was ridiculous, for Federigo was here with her now, letting her repeat them to the Governor.

Only. . .there was something at the back of her mind. The faint, residual memory of her initial response to the man with whom she knew she was almost in love. The instinct not to trust him. All too easy to trust when she was alone with him; all too easy, perhaps, to be manipulated?

Because she had to, because she could not bear the way her thoughts were travelling, Cecilia kept her eyes resolutely on the Count von Regensburg.

'I saw only peasants, sir; a few women of the market. An aged countryman with a very tattered goat.'

Yes, it was all coming back to her now. Much more vividly than she had realised she had seen it at all. The young girls in their fresh white cottons. Arietta—the maid had been one of them, hovering by the steps of the cathedral. She had been in the group around the fountain too. And someone had been going into the cathedral itself. She even had the notion that he had only just finished speaking to Arietta. The trouble was she had seen only the back of him, and he had been dressed as all gentlemen of standing in such a city were dressed, in the sober black coats and elegant biscuit pantaloons that were to be seen from Bond Street to St Petersburg. Even so, the man had been familiar.

Then she thought, It was Federigo. But it couldn't have been.

Massimo, then; his son, who wasn't his son at all?

She came round from her thoughts to find that the Count was leaning forward a little, certain from her expression that she remembered something.

Right up to the time that he said, 'Ah, I think you *do* remember something important!' she had been going to tell the truth.

When he said it she replied, 'No.' Never had she sounded more convincing, or needed to. 'No,' she repeated, 'I thought that I did, but it was nothing.'

Was she imagining it or did she hear the Duke of Aquila Romana give the faintest laughing sigh?

From out of nowhere clouds had gathered, tumbling towards the *castello's* battlements in the abrupt, sulphurous charge of rain and thunder that she had seen so often before in these wild hills. Soft as the landscape was in the sunshine, as amber-gold as if soaked in vintage brandy, like this, with the lightning forking savagely into the valley below, it was primeval, frightening. Exciting too. Or it would have been had Cecilia not been feeling so completely cornered.

When the Count rose to take his leave she made to escape after him, making her very genuine tiredness her excuse. Even as she curtsied politely to Federigo and was heading for the door he caught up with her. . .took her firmly by the shoulders and pulled her round.

There was no avoiding that penetrating, urgent stare. He was looking right into her and searching for something in particular. And he must not find it. Because she was unsure herself exactly what it was. Did she distrust his son, or Federigo himself? And why say distrust when she really meant suspect? And suspect of murder at that. It took all her strength to meet that gaze with one as steady as his own.

Even so, it was not steady enough.

'Why do I think you are lying, Cecilia *mia*?'

It was the fact that there was no mockery in that soft, almost whispered endearment that scared her the most. He sounded puzzled; more than that, confused by something he badly needed to understand.

'I'm not lying!' She knew her lips had shaped the words, but no sound came out.

His eyes, seemingly darker now than ever, swam

before her then as if sweeping in to engulf her, or was it that she had swayed a little towards him? She did not know. Whichever it was, his grip tightened like a vice on her upper arms and she gasped at it.

All he said was, 'I say that you are.'

Cecilia twisted a little to try to loosen his hold, for he was hurting her. She was too afraid of his forcing the truth out of her to be angry. She just wanted to get away from him.

'I am not lying!' she repeated. Surely he must believe her—even to herself she sounded desperate. But then she would, wouldn't she, if she knew something she should not know, and knew it about the man who was holding her so fiercely now?

It was the fact that every grain of spirit she had screamed that this was impossible and that she should trust him that made it so hard for her to fight him now.

He remained silent, his grip, if anything, tightening on the already bruised flesh of her arms.

'Please let go, you're hurting me!'

Much to her amazement, before she had even finished speaking he did let go, abruptly and with a look close to horror on his face. He sounded appalled.

'I'm sorry. I didn't mean to!' Then his whole mood changed, in a sickening swing from contrite to accusing. 'Or did you think,' and suddenly he was speaking so slowly, so assessingly, 'that I *did* mean to?'

This is mad! This is nonsense. I am being such a fool! But nothing Cecilia said to herself could make her speak now, beyond the most feeble of protests.

'No. I'd never think that!' How was he to know it was spoken from the heart? That she would not let herself believe such an ugly thing, because she could not bear to?

'You're lying again.' And where there had been real heat emanating from him, so much so that it had felt for a moment as if their bodies touched each other, there was suddenly only chilling withdrawal.

Even as he turned away from her and made to leave the room Cecilia thought, My God, he is hurt. It hurt him to have me distrust him! Why it should, she did not stop to think. Instinct dragged her across the room after him, and she caught at his arm, expecting even as she did so to have her fingers shaken off in cold, dismissive anger. She was wrong. Federigo stood absolutely still. Her fingers clutched stupidly at his sleeve as she struggled to find the right thing to say. After all, they were meant, were they not, to be friends?

Before the words would come he asked, his voice expressionless, 'Do you mean to trust me, Cecilia, or not?'

It was hearing her name that made her shiver then, made her fingers loosen, just fractionally, their grip on his arm.

'I see.' It was all he said. Then he brushed her hand away and he was gone.

Cecilia stood rooted to the spot, wondering how on earth it could have happened. Come back, you fool, she thought, you damned stupid fool! Can't you see that I'd trust you if I didn't think I love you? I'd know what to do?

She heard the words as if she had spoken them out loud. I love you.

How on earth had it happened, when she had known him only a day—when she had disliked him so intensely for most of it? But it was a pointless question, after all; all that really mattered was that it had happened, just as she had always known it would for her, instantly, and with no turning back. Whatever it was she had always been waiting for, she had seen it in this man, though she would never know how or why. She had found what she had always needed to find—somebody so much stronger than she was. And she had thrown it all away.

Then came the real rush of cold common sense. She had thrown nothing away, expect the beginnings of foolish hope. She could love him all she liked; nothing on earth was ever going to make him love her. Why should a man like Federigo—after Parisina Mansini—want Cecilia Sherringham, who was so very, very ordinary, after all?

CHAPTER FOUR

IT CAME as not the least surprise to Cecilia that she was unable to sleep when at last she reached her bed, earlier than she might normally have done and having more than convincingly pleaded a crippling headache. She had been fortunate that the Duke had been called away on urgent business at noon or she would have been obliged to develop her throbbing temples many hours sooner. As it was she had spent a quiet day—as quiet as any day could be that involved Gulliver and the twins—mercifully free of the leisure in which to think about what had happened to her, and she had successfully exhausted herself so that she would not think the night through either. But one did not make such decisions for oneself and certain things had to be faced. Cecilia did an uncomfortable amount of facing painful and humiliating truths as the night wore on and the thunder roamed in across the valley to hang, it seemed, with real malice above the *castello*; menacing and hostile, the rain lashed down, obliterating the moon.

First she was too hot, the air was thick with electricity, and Cecilia lied to herself that her restlessness was only the coming storm; then the storm came and she was obliged to close her windows against it, suddenly as cold and shivering as she had been stifled, and unable to avoid her troubles any more.

And what troubles they were; what a mockery of a choice lay before her. To remain here or to go home to England. Only England was not home; Italy had been all she had known for years, and all she cared for. Somewhere inside she knew that, if she had to leave, the greater part of her optimistic self would remain behind.

But she could not afford to stay alone. Papa had left her with barely the funds to pay for her journey and then only if she was very careful with the pitifully little she had. This morning Prince Federigo had offered her everything she had not dared to let herself so much as dream she might have—as much time as she cared to spend in this place. She could not impose on his generosity for very long but it meant a little more time before having to let her beloved Italy go forever. By this afternoon she had known she could not accept him, and all because she had shattered her dreams herself. She could not have more effectively fallen in love with the wrong man if she had tried.

Had she fallen in love with him?

It would be nice—she paced the floor with a cynical smile warming her frozen lips—to think that she had not, that this was an infatuation born of gratitude and glamour, of his undeniable strength and personal authority, that because she had known him but thirty-six hours she could not possibly be in 'ove at all. Cecilia knew better than that. She had been smitten before—what young girl had not?—and she even looked back on those wild and silly longings with fondness; they had been foolish but they had been the best of fun and ultimately harmless. This was not the same. Before she had so rashly seen only the god in the most ordinary young men, and when the infatuation had died she had astonished herself at how she could ever have imagined such dazzling qualities in what were, after all, but mortals, fascinating though they had been; this man she half suspected of involvement in murder—and if she did not he most certainly suspected her. One really could not be less blinded by another's charms than that. And yet she found, even as she thought these things, that she fought them harder than she had ever fought any agonising reality; she was fighting her instinct that Federigo had something to hide harder even than she had fought the news of her father's death. Federigo had been rude and arrogant, officious, domineering, utterly ridiculous in his accusations; but he had also been kind, and amusing, and gentle—generous too. Most of all she knew, somehow, that he understood. He had understood from the start how desperately she did not want to go to England.

But did she have to leave, even knowing that she did love him when he would never care for her? Because, despite his almost wilful determination to be obnoxious, she had not been able to help both liking and respecting him, and he had bound her to him with the one emotional chain it was impossible to break—curiosity. She knew he had spoken to no one as he had spoken to her this morning; he had wanted her to know about him, and more than anything in the world she wanted to discover the rest. She wanted to know because she had sensed in his spontaneous confidences something she believed he did not even know he felt: the need for understanding in return, the need to know that someone he could trust. She had felt that so strongly that she still felt it now, like a sudden heat, a prickling of energy along her skin. . .he had *needed* to talk to her. And was that not just the smallest step from needing Cecilia herself?

But this was madness! All her common sense and all her experience of people told her that men like Federigo had been too long in the realms of wariness and self-sufficiency ever to safely return; he might want to trust, but he had lost his ability to do so. With that loss, and the greater loss of Parisina, he had lost his ability to love.

Only was that certain? The thunder erupted as if filling the echoing courtyard with its writhing presence; through the slatted shutters she could see the lightning bleaching the sky to white-violet, then back to charcoal. Cecilia pulled back the shutters to watch the storm, glad that Federigo had given her a room facing out across the valley away from the town; like this, the lightning forking like adders' tongues between the cypresses and the mausoleum beyond the lake, illuminating the classical lines of the Palladian vault until it stood out carved in ivory against the English yews hedging around it, the Castello d'Aquilano was beautiful, the starkness of the central fortress hidden in the shadows behind her. Cecilia felt as she had used to feel as a child at Downside Castle, looking out across the Wiltshire plains from the battlements, huddling in a cloak from the shattering storm, excited as much by the sense of the age, the immortality of the great house, its impenetrable protection, as by the thrill of nature at bay and howling at the earth in abandoned rage and fury. It was this elemental violence against the impregnable security of these ancient stones that made her shiver now, alive to both, willing the storm to do its worst and the Castello d'Aquilano to defend her. As its master had done, she knew that he had; her interview with Governor von Regensberg would have been of quite another nature without Federigo there to guide its progress.

It was her excitement that asked the question again: had Federigo lost himself too far in pain and distrust to love again? It was excitement that made her answer herself: not if I can help it. And repeat, as she looked down almost laughing at the storm: not if I have anything to say to it!

It was in this strange exalted mood that she at last closed the shutters and made her way to the great curtained bed, its hangings ghostly in the reflected lightning, softened by the single candle-flame on the chest beside it until the embroidered roses and irises, the lilies and the violets, carnations and vine-leaves glowed with the deepest jewel colours, each so beautifully caught in silk and pearls that she felt almost that she ought to be able to smell them. She could smell the jasmine oil, fresh against her skin and hair. She would never sleep now, not like this. It was two in the morning by the tiny

French enamelled clock beside the candle. No, she would not sleep now.

Cecilia woke suddenly, out of what felt, the moment she sat up so abruptly, no real sleep at all; she felt strangely both utterly relaxed and frightened. Her body was warm from dreams she could not remember, yet she was shivering as if she had been left out in the rain.

Rain, that was it; she must not have fastened the window properly, for it had burst open with a crash against the casement that was fit to wake the dead—no wonder she had had such a powerful shock. Cecilia was out of bed and running to close it before she even realised that this was not the window she had stood at before; this was not the window she had opened.

Cecilia reeled against this second shock so literally that she had to catch at the casement so as not to stumble. The floor was slippery with water—the rain had plainly been coming in for quite a time. But she had not left this window open.

That was absurd! It came of reading far too many Gothick novels and then joking about them to Prince Federigo this morning. Cecilia slammed the window shut almost as if the noise would shake her to her senses. She decided that she must have left this window ajar, after all, or Piggy had. That was what she decided, and nothing was going to shake that decision. Any other conclusion was just far too disturbing to be entertained. She was just closing the heavy wooden shutters when her eye was caught by a movement in the faint wreathing of moonlight through the storm-clouds, a figure darting up the steps from the lower terrace of the gardens towards the *castello* terrace itself. But, even as she took in that it was a man, she knew that she must be mistaken. Nobody but the most helpless lunatic would venture out on such a night as this. Even so, she remained where she was for the next ten minutes, without really thinking about what she was waiting for, watching intently that one slab of moonlight cutting across the grass. But nothing moved, not even the distant cypresses in the breeze, and the storm was dying. Plainly she had made a mistake, and a not surprising mistake at that, she chided herself—after imagining windows mysteriously being opened it was only one small step to imagining intruders as well.

Who was to say it was an intruder at all? Really, she must still be half asleep! It would simply have been a servant hurrying for home, or one of the Prince's private garrison, disturbed by some unexpected noise into diverting the course of his usual patrol to investigate. With that she closed the shutters and scurried back to bed. There was nothing at all to have alarmed her in the first place.

So why was it that when she slipped beneath the now icy linen covers Cecilia huddled into the smallest ball, cold as much from the inside as out? Strange too that, just as she was falling asleep again she said to herself, What a strange thing—Federigo says Massimo is not his son, so how is it then that when I first saw Massimo I thought they were so very alike? They *are* alike. And on that final puzzling thought she fell asleep.

The air had cleared beautifully by the time the dawn rose above the valley with that gilded silver glow that Cecilia had never seen anywhere but here in Italy, bright with a chill of promised heat to come, scented with thyme and lemon and the peppery sharpness of cypress, and the softness of the roses in the English gardens just below her window. Cecilia always rose early, and had made a habit of riding out on Hereward before breakfast, washing and dressing herself as best she could in her formal riding dress of softest sapphire velvet, her rakish little Polish lancer's hat that had caused such a stir in Brussels before Waterloo on the pretty, if inexpert, arrangement of her golden curls. She saw no reason at all not to do the same this morning. After all, Hereward must have his exercise, and Federigo could not possibly want to discuss the twins' lessons with her until after she had breakfasted. It would inconvenience nobody, so she would go.

It was halfway to the stables that she realised, almost as if in her sleep, that she had made up her mind to stay. The excitement of the night was gone, but the confidence remained. And she had lived in Italy long enough to believe that she would rather risk the pain and unhappiness of rejection here than return to the stultifying drudgery of an empty future with her sisters in England. So thinking, and accepting it as a rational decision, she ran quickly round the terrace, down the steps and out across the cobbles to the stable block beyond. Ahead of her she recognised the homely, if gigantic, figure of Jemmy Pigg, up and dusted off—all he ever did in the way of washing—and already tending to Hereward, who was co-operating, as Hereward always co-operated with anything, willingly and with the sweetest of tempers, so long as he had his bucket of oats and his cabbages.

She smiled then, at the only horse she knew who ever ate cabbages and wine cakes, and called out to Jemmy, to be met by his usual splitting smile.

'I knew you'd not disappoint old Hereward, milady. So here he is, all ready for you.'

Hereward affirmed this statement by pausing over his breakfast just enough to remove his nose from the bucket and stare at her. Then he started eating again, snorting vulgarly into the depths and dreaming of more treats when he came home again.

'Wonderful place, this, milady.' Jemmy was plainly enraptured. 'Asked for cabbages, like Hereward 'as to have, and nobody turned a hair at it, just as if all horses are as strange as he is.'

Hereward objected to 'strange'. He blew a large mouthful of his oatmash into Jemmy's grinning face.

'He is a very lively animal, a good animal, beautiful.'

It was a strange voice that spoke then, deep and guttural, the voice of a Tuscan peasant. So deep was the voice that Cecilia turned, automatically looking far above her, for it was the voice of a veritable giant. She was never so startled in her life to find that she was gazing at only air. She looked down abruptly, at least five inches, and began—she could not help herself—to laugh.

The man was tiny, but never had she seen a man so tough. He had the muscled stockiness and the savage brow of a vagrant street-boy, the same air of casual distrust and competence; his nose was broken—probably more than once—and his face was a mass of scars that shone white against the burnt umber of his skin. His fighter's arms were filled with cabbages and he had, she saw it at once, the eyes of a Botticelli angel. They were eyes that could kill with a look and yet, happy as they were now, gentle, wide and curious, they were beautiful. He should have been an ugly man, but he was not. There was something most attractive about a nature so open as his. Had nothing else won Cecilia over his smile would have done so—it did do so. Slow, innocent, spreading at the edges into wicked, and his whole face lit up as he grinned again.

'Are all those for Hereward?' she asked the man—she really could not stop laughing. He had the physique of a hired murderer yet was come in the guise of St Francis. Hereward had recognised this at once, this extraordinary empathy with animals. . .completely ignoring the cabbages, as she had never seen him do before, he nudged them aside as if jealous of the attention they were getting and snuggled his nose deep into the little groom's shoulder.

The man laughed. 'Of course, *madonna*. If he likes them he may have all the cabbages he wants. Me, I think he must be mad!'

'Oh, he is mad. . . I expect Jemmy has told you about the beeswax candles?' It was plain at once to Cecilia that the two men had struck up a real friendship. But then they should have done; they were of a kind. The best kind, she thought suddenly, in the world.

'That Hereward—oh, what a name, how am I expected to call him Hereward?—that he stole the candles from a wedding table and ate them?'

'And was not sick at all.'

The man hugged Hereward closer and scratched behind one ecstatic ear. 'I said he was mad. . .you do not mind I say that, of course, not if I say he is also very handsome?'

'He's a bit scruffy at present. . .he lost a great deal of his mane when we had to rescue him from some railings.'

'It will grow back; he will be very elegant again. He's very strong for a lady to ride, *madonna*. . .'

Cecilia knew a compliment when she heard one; a typical Italian male compliment, admiring if just a little disbelieving.

'I manage,' she returned drily, and all three of them laughed.

Gulliver, who had been out and about since the very crack of dawn, came at this to join them.

'Ah, but that is a more ridiculous name even than Hereward,' the little groom protested.

'What is your name?' asked Cecilia, kneeling down to greet her loyal mongrel.

'Salvatore, *madonna*. But everyone calls me Toro.' And he spread his arms wide in a gesture of self-mockery and grinned even more angelically than before. And he was right—he suited his name exactly: he looked like a miniature—if powerfully dangerous—bull. The fact that he was so certain of his dangerousness as to make mock of it made Cecilia like him all the more.

'Have you worked for His Highness long, Toro?'

'Always.' Then, as if he thought his answer too abrupt, he added, 'My father, he worked for Prince Federigo's father. He died last year.'

'Your father did? I'm sorry.'

It had been an easy mistake to make. And Salvatore quickly corrected it.

'No, *madonna*, I meant Prince Francesco, His Highness's father.'

Why Cecilia was quite so shocked she could never afterwards really say, except that it was just one more thing about Federigo she had not yet known, one other recent sadness in his life. She knew just from the way Toro had spoken of it that it had hurt Federigo very badly.

'I had not realised. . .'

Toro understood. More than Cecilia would have liked, so fortunately a great deal more than she could guess. He was not surprised. Not surprised at all!

'His Highness does not speak of it, *madonna*, not to anyone.' Toro felt compelled to add this part simply because he had the strangest feeling that perhaps His Highness might want to, if it were that this beautiful girl were there to listen to him. Toro and Federigo were more than master and servant; they had been friends since birth, one but ten hours older than the other— Toro—and because of it feeling as protective as a much older brother. Not that *he'd* ever needed protecting, that one! But then the old Prince had thought the same. . .

'Forgive me.' Cecilia recognised forbidden territory when she strayed into it, for all the little groom's warning had been so delicately delivered.

Toro was horrified. He had not meant her to take it in that way at all. That was perhaps why he said, before he thought perhaps he ought not, 'Oh, no, *madonna*, it is not that. . .it is just that His late Highness's death was so sudden, he was killed. . .'

He had committed himself too far, and he knew it the moment he saw Cecilia's ice-blue eyes flash with the recognition of what he really meant. She was going to make him say it—and Federigo was going to have his hide for this!

'Killed, Toro?' Never had he heard such a commanding tone from a girl so fragile and so young. Her voice was as soft and gentle as ever, but the urge to obey it became irresistible.

'*Assassinato!*'

Cecilia had known that was what he had meant; even so, that one stark word appalled her. Absurdly she felt a deep stab of guilt for mocking Federigo's manner as Gothick. His whole life had held the quality of the most overwrought kind of novel. What she had meant as a defensive jest had been nothing less than true. Assassinated. By whom? Why?

All these questions were clear in her face as Toro shifted his embarrassed attention to Hereward, aware before she was of the shadow falling across the cobbles. How he did it, Toro would never know, but you could trust that man to be everywhere, and to hear everything when it really mattered that he shouldn't!

Even before Cecilia could form her questions, fighting herself all the time for the impropriety of questioning the servants at all, the Prince d'Aquilano was saying, almost idly, 'We do not know who, *madonna*, so we cannot know why.' Then, almost on a laugh, a sound so brittle that she knew that beneath his light manner he was very angry, he added, 'It is too good a morning to be speaking of murder, *madonna*. If you are going to ride out may I come with you?'

Cecilia looked at him then, thinking very much the same as his servant was thinking. How is it that he always catches me out in the most embarrassing situations? He was dressed casually in old buckskin breeches and an even older coat of blue English superfine, the garb of a country gentleman about his country pleasures. How is it, she thought again, that such clothes only serve to show him even more clearly for what he really is, the

Prince and statesman? The answer was simply in the man himself: he was what he was through to the very marrow.

And how was it that he had guessed what she was thinking now?

She knew that he had because of his smile. There was something about it that was not quite mocking, not quite appreciative, perhaps a little of both. Moreover those sleepy dark eyes had taken in every last detail of her faded riding habit, and—Cecilia flinched at the knowledge—every last detail of the thin body beneath it. It should not have made her angry, for she knew that neither his servant nor hers had seen it, and yet angry she was—very. Perhaps because that look came too close to what was really in her own mind, too close for anything but embarrassment. She had been so sure last night that perhaps it might be safe to love him after all— that perhaps she could make him love her in return; but such dreams always looked foolish in the cold light of day and faced with the very human object of their fantasy. Federigo the dream was a far cry from Federigo the man. Her confidence fled in a rush of girlish nervousness such as she had never known before, and because she despised herself for it she took it out on him.

'Of course, sir, I should be delighted.' Her tone was brightly quelling.

She had asked for him to laugh at her. Certainly the amusement was there in his voice when he remarked blandly, 'Civil, but not very encouraging!' Then added, and she felt the barb hit home, 'Never mind, we can pretend that I am only doing my duty and keeping you under observation. The Count von Regensberg would be most displeased were you to abscond.'

Cecilia had quite simply never met anyone like him. Nobody else would have spoken to her like that, least of all in front of two innocently smiling servants. It was going to be the talk of the entire *castello* before they had returnd from their ride. She had been cross before; now she was absolutely livid.

'Well, come along, then,' she rapped it out as she might to a niece or nephew who had never been her favourite, 'Hereward is eager for his exercise, after all.'

A silly speech, made even sillier by the fact that Hereward was quite patently not eager for anything at all, except perhaps having his ears rubbed again by Salvatore and getting his teeth into the first of those succulent cabbages.

'So I see,' murmured Federigo sweetly. Then compounded her humiliation by clicking his fingers at the dreaming horse and bringing Hereward alongside, all alert and alive and anxious to do his bidding.

You, thought Cecilia, eyeing Hereward in a manner that got through even his shield of amiable stupidity, are a traitor of the very worst kind and I shall never, but never, feed you so much as half a cabbage leaf again!

'Good boy!' Federigo patted his neck, but his eyes and tone were all for Cecilia. He was smiling so ingenuously that she could have hit him.

'Are you intending to walk, sir?' She glared at both, hoping to shake his superiority a little.

'Not at all. Er—am I, Toro? I don't see Malatesta about.'

He had known, of course, she fumed, that just hearing his name would bring the great chestnut trotting across the cobbles with a ridiculous whinny of besotted greeting. Hit Federigo? Only after she had kicked him first. On both shins. Hard. Very.

'And you accuse my animals of foolish names! I thought Malatesta to mean headache?'

Federigo was not to be ruffled. He stood quite at ease between the two huge animals as they eyed each other warily and Hereward shifted a little to protect his cabbages.

'It can do, *madonna*, and Toro here might tell you that

that is exactly what he is, from Toro's point of view. That half-moon scar on his left cheek was Malatesta's doing.'

'And the one on the left, but——'

'Precisely, Toro, but I'm not sure *la madonna* Cecilia needs to know about that!'

It was not in the least a reprimand. The smile that passed between them was that of old and valued friends.

'Maybe not,' Toro grinned with angelic sweetness that nevertheless conveyed a ribald humour, 'but I can show Madonna Cecilia the bite-marks on my arms!'

'Not if you want me to feel like eating my breakfast, I think!' Cecilia smiled vaguely in Toro's direction—she wanted all Federigo's attention on herself just at this moment—so he would know just how boiling angry she really was with him.

'Malatesta,' smiled Federigo, knowing exactly what she was about and approving it, 'can also mean bad in the head, bad blood, dangerous, belligerent. . .um, wild and obstinate. . .'

'Evil-tempered and cunning,' chimed in Toro, exchanging a grin with Jemmy Pigg.

'Yes, altogether an undesirable of the first water,' finished Federigo flatly as the chestnut took it into his head to rear up and cuff Hereward smartly on the haunch with the toe of his shoe.

Hereward, a kindly natured beast, and not a soul would say otherwise, was not a coward either. He bared cabbagey teeth, and Malatesta, surprised to see the worm turning, backed away.

Cecilia watched it all in silence for a long moment; then she began to smile.

'I had not,' she remarked limpidly, 'really believed it before when people would say how like their masters animals can be. . .'

She was forced then to stifle a cry of real outrage, because she was paid out for her impertinence by being swept from her feet and on to the startled Hereward's back before she realised what Federigo was planning. As she hung on to her hat and shifted carefully in the saddle for balance he kept the firmest hold on her boot. His smile was of a saintliness to rival Salvatore's.

'For that,' and there was real challenge in his voice now. . .it thrilled through the words like energy along a nerve and struck an answering chord deep in her own, 'you are going to have to pay a price, *madonna*.'

'Indeed?' It was meant to be haughty. It came out as the most feeble of whispers, and Cecilia clenched her fingers as if she really were about to hit him.

'You are always threatening me with violence, *madonna*.' He let go of her boot then, just when she needed him close to feel her real anger, and leapt up into Malatesta's saddle. Inevitably the chestnut reared and agitated, but Federigo—damn him!—had the bullying creature easily in hand. 'I think,' he went on, 'you are also in the vilest temper. . .'

It was Cecilia who forgot the servants then.

'Well, are you surprised? By God, but I never met so insufferable a man in all my life!'

'You don't altogether surprise me. Even so, that was very rude.' He was laughing with real pleasure at it.

How on earth to remain angry with a man who would not accept that anger, with a man who was always laughing at it? Especially when one could suddenly see the funny side oneself. But she would die rather than let him see it!

'I only answer rudeness with rudeness, Prince!'

'Oh, dear——' he looked genuinely disappointed in her '—and I had thought you could manage a better retort than that!'

She was so infuriated at herself for her urge to laugh that Hereward gave her tension away by shifting irritably along the cobbles and snorting loudly.

'Steady, Hereward!' Never had she had to speak to

him like this in her life. It was as if even he were
determined to show her in the worst possible light.

'Yes, steady, Hereward!' Federigo mimicked her tone
so accurately that Cecilia froze rigid in her saddle and
flung him a look of such venom that it almost silenced
him.

'You'll never hold him while you're in that temper.'
He meant to sound arrogantly mocking, she knew it;
even so, she took the bait.

'You think not, sir?'

'I said so, did I not? I think you should give him his
head.'

'I'd rather have yours, on a platter!'

'Race me instead!'

That was a challenge she could never refuse. Mainly—
Cecilia's eyes glittered then at something she knew and
he did not—because never once in her life had anyone
been known to beat her. She had seen a way of getting
her own back on him, with interest.

'If I win?' she demanded.

He did look startled then, but so briefly that she could
almost have been mistaken.

'I had rather been thinking in terms of if you lost.'

'A forfeit?'

'Something of that sort—why not?'

'Why not indeed, since you are going to be so soundly
beaten?'

Federigo laughed out loud then, and had either he or
Cecilia had eyes to notice it a wager was struck at that
moment between Jemmy and Toro, each betting enthusi-
astically on his own employer.

'Very well,' said Federigo kindly, 'I'm going to lose.
If I do, what is it you want?'

Cecilia knew the one thing that would make him
angrier than anything. The real challenge.

'*When* you lose, you permit me to leave the city!' She
heard the mockery in her own voice then, an almost

purring quality. She might not be completely confident of winning, but she was certainly sure he was going to have to really fight her for his victory.

For a moment she almost felt she had gone too far. It lasted not a second but his whole face seemed to close down, to shut her out, all laughter drained from it until it froze to the marble rigidity of real fury, real threat. She saw in the sudden hardness of his mouth that somehow this had stopped being a game. But even as she thought it the hardness melted as if it had never been, and he was smiling again. It was when he lifted his eyes to hers that she felt, like a blow to the stomach, that such laughter was even more of a danger than his anger.

'Very well,' he said evenly. Cecilia felt rather than heard him pause then, like a cat playing with a mouse; her nerves stirred uneasily but she faced him squarely. His voice was almost soft when he added, 'But when you lose, *madonna*, you stay here as long as I say.'

'I. . .'

'Those are the terms. I let you go. Or you stay for as long as it pleases *me*, not you.'

She wanted to stay, after all; she had only made her challenge because it would be such a pleasure to have him urge—if not quite beg—her to remain after she had won the race. She wanted to stay—so how was it that suddenly the very gentleness of his tone alarmed her?

What a ludicrously English word! She mocked it. Alarmed! When the truth was that it had really frightened her.

Cecilia knew only one response to fear. She lifted her head and looked directly into his eyes. They were quite expressionless.

'Very well. I agree the terms.'

'You want us to make sure you don't cheat?' put in Toro with the irreverence for which he was so popular throughout the *castello*.

'Elegantly put, my friend,' Federigo raised a dry

eyebrow at him, 'but I think we can trust to Her Ladyship's sense of honour, don't you? The English don't cheat, as a rule, or so they tell me.'

Jemmy Pigg was not having any of this. He forgot himself.

'Aye, but Italians do!' If Toro didn't like that remark they could sort it out between themselves later on. Toro was not the only one with meaty biceps.

Jemmy was rewarded with the Prince d'Aquilano's most dazzling smile.

'So I believe. But I shall do my best to behave like a gentleman. I shall even give Her Ladyship a few paces' start if you prefer.'

Cecilia exploded. 'The Devil you will!'

And before he could so much as raise his eyebrow at her she kicked Hereward into a gallop and was racing him out towards the open parkland even as Federigo was turning the protesting Malatesta.

It was a good race, through the early half-mist of light splintering between the olive trees, on towards the shores of the lake. But she had known from the moment Federigo had let Malatesta have his head that she could never win it, though she meant to make a battle of it if poor Hereward's stamina would let her.

Perhaps it was too many cabbages, perhaps it was surprise. Whatever the cause, Hereward was winded and she knew it even as she saw the great chestnut take the ground from her on the rise and begin the descent to the valley floor. Poor Hereward. But she had to push him.

'A hundred cabbages!' she urged him. 'Thousands!'

Hereward always responded to the words he liked best. So when at last he skidded to a halt in the damp grass at the water's edge she was only a neck behind Federigo and he knew it. He had won, but only just, and it had surprised him. Or something had. There was more to that unfamiliar glitter in his eyes than just the unholy pleasure of seeing her beaten, though the lord knew he was enjoying that enough.

'Poor Hereward!' he tormented. 'You don't deserve such heroism, *madonna.*'

Damn the man, he was not even breathless!

Cecilia struggled for her own voice but it would not come. It was all she could do not to slump forward to fight the urgent stitch in her side. She was sadly out of condition, no doubt about it. But then since Papa had died there had been nobody to ride with her like this. She had forgotten how long it had been. . .

'Don't be so proud—choke and splutter all you like,' Federigo added kindly.

Her voice found its strength then. 'It's you will choke, sir, and I shall do it with my own two hands!'

Yet it was his hands that were about her waist before she even realised he had jumped down from the steaming Malatesta. As if she were no heavier than swansdown, he lifted her to the ground and—this would teach her heart to thump with sudden fantastical hope and excitement!—pushed her head down and propped her hands against her shaking knees.

'Stupid girl!' he commented as he massaged her back as he might rub down a horse, and at last Cecilia felt the pain in her side diminishing and her breath, somewhat raggedly, beginning to return. That her hair was, thanks to his ministrations, all over the place but where she had planned it that morning, and her face flushed from being forced to turn her head upside-down in this undignified fashion, was but the smallest part of the humiliation she suffered. Never had she felt a fraction such a fool in all her life.

She made the strangest gasping sound.

In an instant Federigo was all concern. 'Cecilia?'

He knelt down to take her hands from her knees and hold them between his own. She had forgotten to wear her gloves, and her fingers were cold as ice. Urgently he chafed them between his own and said again, 'Cecilia? Are you. . .?'

Cecilia made the strange sound again and he saw her face at last. Try as she might to school her features, she knew the minute she looked into his eyes that she would fail. From the strangled gasps of before she gave way to quite hysterical laughter. She was crying with it. Never had she been made to look so ridiculous, and she was laughing at it as if it was truly funny.

He had every right to look puzzled. Any man would. Through her laughter Cecilia thought, *That* is why I love him, for Federigo d'Aquilano was not puzzled at all—he was laughing almost as hysterically as she was.

That was how she came to be in his arms, of course— she had not planned to be there. He had not planned to hold her. But somehow—they both felt it—they were shaking so much that they needed the other to stand up at all. Cecilia felt her own arms slide round his waist and she rested her head against his shoulder, for it almost hurt, she was so dizzy. She felt the blood pounding in her ears, she felt her pulse stumble and begin its race out of control. She felt the heat rise to her face, warm, paralysing. Even so, she could not stop the laughter.

Federigo held her closely, conscious of nothing but the fact that he was doing so, that he should not be— then that what did it matter what he should be doing or not doing at all? He too could not stop laughing. But what he felt most of all through the laughter was the most passionate sense of gratitude. Nobody, not since he was a child, had made him feel like this before, so innocently released, so free of who he was and all he must become. It was like being suspended in time with her, where nothing could touch him and he had no burdens, and he knew he needed this.

They neither of them were conscious of their thoughts at all, rather felt them and knew them by instinct. Cecilia had laughed herself to the point of tears and automatically he found his handkerchief and wiped them away for her. Strange that her lashes were so dark when her hair was so radiantly fair. . .

Quite without thinking why he did it, Federigo bent then and kissed her gently just between those feathered lashes and the gilded arch of her eyebrows. It silenced her completely.

Cecilia looked up and stepped back at once, horrified. Frightened, most of all, because she knew she could turn that simple, friendly kiss into something so much more. But it would not be love. She was aware then of the meaning of the almost liquid heat in her limbs, the weakness of them. Knew, with the instinct of one responding to something in him, that she could touch such feelings in Federigo, that perhaps she had already begun to. But it wouldn't be love. So she must not do it.

He was so plainly puzzled by her sudden withdrawal that she found herself saying the very first thing that came into her head, explaining stupidly, 'I have made the most shocking mess of your cravat.'

He dismissed this speech almost indifferently; one hand reached out and caught her wrist. Cecilia had ended his first ever moment of real freedom and he wanted to know why.

'It was a mess already.'

Cecilia carefully freed her wrist from his grasp, and he was aware in that moment of a deep and bitter anger. But it passed, because enough of the magic of his momentary escape remained. Cecilia saw the puzzlement in his eyes still, and knew that he wanted an answer—she could not give it, so she had to pretend she had not seen the question. Carefully she dabbed her eyes with the handkerchief and hurried on, 'I can't think why I laughed like that. It was just so. . .so *ignominious* to be tipped upside-down by a man I met only two days ago.'

Perhaps the moment had not quite fled after all. Her absurdity was preserving it a little longer. Federigo found that he was saying easily, 'Had you rather I called Miss Pigg to hang you up by your heels instead?'

'Not in the least.' Cecilia smiled up at him then, aware that the intensity of his mood was passing. 'You did it very nicely.'

'Thank you.'

'Would you like your handkerchief back, or had I best keep it now?'

In an instant, inexplicably, all that intensity returned, and yet he spoke so lightly.

'Oh, I think keep it, don't you, *madonna*? Since I have won our wager and you must stay now.'

So intense was whatever emotion lay behind those ordinary words that Cecilia could not even put up a show of grudging him his victory.

'Yes. . .' She said it almost silently.

'I think——' and when he took her wrist this time Cecilia did not fight him '—that we must talk, don't you?'

CHAPTER FIVE

IT WAS refreshingly cool here by the lake, and so restful
as Federigo led the way towards the canopy of the great
Lebanese cedar, where he took off his coat and spread it
on the ground for Cecilia to sit on. It was a gesture that
touched Cecilia; he had no thought at all for the fact
that, old though it was, his coat was so much grander
and more worthy of care than her much-mended velvet,
rubbed shiny now with age. Cecilia leaned back against
the trunk of the cedar and closed her eyes on the
unexpected threat of tears, and he sat beside her, no
more than an inch or two away, touching her with the
warmth from his skin if not his body, and she let herself
drift for a moment in the intimacy of it all. It was a
comfortable intimacy. Comfortable, and exciting, all at
the same time.

'Are you feeling better now?' His voice was not all
laughter.

She smiled and opened her eyes. 'Yes; the pain in my
side has gone.'

He smiled back. It was the easy smile of friendship,
all intensity gone. He seemed even more relaxed than
when she had seen him with the children. In his shirt-
sleeves he looked so much younger than before; the
white of it against his gilded skin softened the harshness
of his features, and the tiredness was gone. She noticed
for the first time what remarkable eyelashes he had, so
unusually thick and so long. Just like an Arab horse!
And she laughed silently to herself, knowing he would
never forgive her if she said so.

'What are you laughing at?'

How had he sensed it—or did she know? By the same

85

silent exchange of feelings through which she knew he was completely at peace in this moment.

'You, in the main.'

'I suppose it might be. Am I so very comical?'

Cecilia put her head on one side and thought with sudden seriousness, Yes, you can be. And I am glad you can, or you would be altogether far too perfect!

'A little.'

She saw him smile as his eyes drifted out across the lake. 'I'm glad,' he said quietly. And Cecilia knew to believe him.

The sun was above the far hills now, for it was perhaps seven o'clock, and the light was beginning to warm into morning, burning off the mist until the sun slanted down on the lake, guinea-bright and almost too dazzling to look at. Even if one shut one's eyes one could still see it. Cecilia watched the shading on the water and then raised her eyes to see the shadows of dawn slowly lift from the mausoleum on its little hill beyond them. It stood so beautiful against the semicircle of yew and the cypresses, remote, jewel-like, at rest.

'My father is buried there.' It seemed Federigo had followed her gaze. 'And I have arranged for Giulio Mansini to rest there too. They will bring him this evening. Will you come?'

'It is not tradition here in Italy for women to be present.'

'No more in England. But I think you want to be there, don't you?'

Cecilia did. She had been the last living person Giulio had said goodbye to; she wanted to be there to make sure she said goodbye to him. She never really could, of course; those dying eyes would be with her as long as she lived just as she would always retain the impact of his beautiful nature. She had felt it almost as if it were a natural part of death that every truth of him was laid bare. Guilio Mansini was a good man, and she was glad that he had friends to bear witness to it.

'I don't think I shall ever forget,' she murmured half to herself.

She felt his hand brush hers briefly, and he said, 'And I was so clumsy when I questioned you. I'm sorry. I suppose that I was angry.'

'And so was I. I *was*, Federigo; I've never been so angry in my life! Does it sound foolish to say I feel as if I had let him die?'

'Because you were too late to save him? Not foolish at all. That is how I felt about my father.'

She knew then that he was asking her to make him talk about it. She felt again what was almost pity for a man who did not really know how to confide.

'Was it the same. . .did he live a little while, as Giulio did?'

'He died exactly as Giulio died. In the exact same place, the *castello* square. My father died on the cathedral steps. I found him.'

It was Cecilia's hand that stole across the narrow divide then to tuck itself into his. It was an appalling story.

She felt his fingers close round hers and heard the almost dream-like quality of his voice. He was, perhaps for the first time, letting himself really remember that night.

'It was just over a year ago, and he had been to dine at the Governor's palace. He liked von Regensberg as well as I do. Better perhaps. . .he never seemed to feel, as I did, that the Austrians *must* be driven from Aquila Romana. But he was an old man; I think he had made up his mind a long time ago to leave the insurrection to me. Whatever his reasons, the city was a peaceful place in his time, he elected to walk home. He felt quite safe—nobody in their senses would have wanted to kill him if it would put me in his place. My father's reign was a lull

between two storms and everyone knew it; they knew
that once I was Duke the unspoken truce with the
Austrians would be ended, if not at once it *would* be
ended. I am trouble, my father was stability. . .he should
have been safe that night.' Even now, a year later, he
sounded almost disbelieving that his father had been
wrong.

'If Toro's father had still been alive perhaps things
would have been different—he would never have let
Papa be such a fool. He would have protected him. As it
was, his new servant was loyal but untested, and he was
killed instantly. Papa fought whoever attacked him, but
he had no chance of winning; he was shot three times
above the heart.'

'But you say that when you found him he was alive?
Could he not say who. . .?'

'No. He tried. I still don't know what brought me out
into the square that night—I had just felt restless all
evening and I made Toro come with me. I don't know
what I thought I was doing. . .'

He paused for a moment and looked away, down at
her hand lying in his own. The sunlight was just bright
enough for her to see why. There was the clear flash of a
tear trapped in his lashes. But she knew it for a tear of
anger, of bitter frustration. Cecilia could feel it stinging
through her as if they shared all the nerves of their
fingers. But again it was as if the magic of morning held,
and his pain was brief.

'We found my father just too late. He had lost too
much blood. He could barely talk. He said something,
but it was unintelligible. I. . .it's hard to think that my
father tried to tell something so important and I was too
stupid to understand!'

'Not stupid.' Cecilia remembered again the clarity of
Giulio's words, but he had been young and strong and
fighting death with every last drop of his being; even so,
clear as his words had been, they had been breathless

and she had had to lean close enough for his lips to brush against her skin to hear it. 'Not stupid at all. You had to try to save him, not waste your time trying to follow his words.'

It was meagre comfort, she thought, but it seemed to him to be enough.

'Perhaps. Toro and I got him home, meaning to give it out that he had died naturally in his bed, but a drunken Austrian soldier met us carrying him home and shouted the news to the whole town. I suppose from the moment that it happened the situation was too dangerous for me to take time to wonder what Papa had meant. I had to take control—instant, absolute control—over the actions of every Italian in this city in that moment or not at all. I could not risk riot and rebellion, and there so easily might have been, for my father was a good man; people loved him. They didn't love me.'

'Did they know you?'

'You want to make everything easy for me, Cecilia! No. Perhaps again you were right. Perhaps they did not know me. But what they knew they were afraid of.'

And they still are, she thought, certain of it. She had heard the quality of the silence in the square as he had appeared when Giulio was murdered. She knew just what to say.

'I think, you know, that it is better that they fear you than love you—for the present, Federigo. Love can come later, when the Austrians have gone. If you are ever to prise loose their grip you will need absolute support in this city. Fear will buy that much more surely than love.'

For a moment she thought he was going to burst out laughing. Certainly he dipped his head as if to shake away such an inappropriate response, and she saw that he was smiling. She felt a little of her old offence at it. . .perhaps to a politician such as he was her remark might sound naïve and childish. . .

He sensed something wrong and looked quickly at her—nothing must go wrong between them now. They had, imperceptibly, become real friends, and he would not risk that for anything ever again. But he could not quite stop the smile shining into his eyes.

'A child of Machiavelli? A true Tuscan!'

She knew she was being teased, but still said a little defensively, 'Well, it is how it was with Wellington, after all. None would claim *he* was loved. But he was very, very powerful.'

'I am to compare myself with the Iron Duke now, am I? Careful, Cecilia, you are in danger of flattering me again!'

And her defensiveness dispersed in laughter, and with it the shadow of his father's death, for now. He had talked of what he wished to talk about. Cecilia understood why he had spoken of it now. She was to be part of the *castello* household, if only for a while, and she needed to know what had happened in it, because most certainly what had gone before would shape its future.

'Austria will let go its stranglehold.' He followed her thoughts almost exactly. 'I shall make her. But the time is not right.' His voice clouded momentarily again. 'There have been one or two incidents; I need to find out how they started—small matters, but enough to put the Governor on his guard, and, were he not the man he is, extremely dangerous. In other cities, with other governors, men have been shot for lesser crimes than vulgar cartoons on the Governor's walls. There have been attacks on Austrian soldiers too, always explained away as drunken incidents, but I know I cannot afford to make my bid for power yet; someone is trying to force my hand.'

'To cause enough trouble to. . .'

'Have me removed from power. . .thrown in my own prison? That could happen. Again, were von Regensberg not the man he is, it would have happened already.'

'You have told von Regensberg your views?'

'He told me!'

'Then surely you are safe?'

Federigo laughed cynically at that. 'Axel told me he knows perfectly well somebody is stirring the cauldron and that I am pleading new-born innocence. But he knows just as well that tomorrow when there is trouble it will be I who ordered it. He knows that we are enemies.'

Cecilia moved then, on to her knees in a childish gesture of eagerness and frustration.

'But need you be? You are so alike. Surely something could be worked out between you? You have a good understanding of each other.'

'A compromise? Axel allow me free rein for the price of my accepting his precedence in public?'

'Why not?'

She knew the instant she said it why not, why it could never be.

'Because I am the Duke of Aquila Romana and he is the puppet of the Emperor. I *will* rule this city. But I will do it only over his dead body.'

'He said that too, didn't he?'

'Of course! Axel is no coward—he meant it. He would die rather than fail the Emperor, or return to Vienna with the shame of having been defeated by a petty Prince such as me.'

Petty Prince. She had called him that herself once, in her most private thoughts. How wrong she had been. There was nothing small about either his ambition or his courage, or his determination to liberate his people.

'I just wish. . .'

'Wish it did not have to be this way?' He smiled at her again, understanding, and absently pulled at one of her fallen curls. 'But it is, and it can be no other way until I take this city back. I—*we*, the Princes of Aquila

Romana—did not start this after all. The Emperors began it, and they must accept a bloody finish.'

Cecilia had nursed the wounded throughout the carnage that was Waterloo; she had not only seen men die in agony, she had helped to save their lives by sawing away putrid legs and arms herself. She knew what war was, and that the dangerous politics of Aquila Romana might bring the state to just such destruction as she had witnessed in Belgium. She might have to accept it, but he could not ask her to like it.

She said so. 'I know everything is as you say that it must be. But I hate it so!'

He took her chin in his hand then and looked at her hard.

'Would you believe me if I said that I do too?'

She could only nod.

She knew he was going to kiss her again. Oddly, it was the fact that he then kissed her forehead, in a gesture as much of respect as friendship, that allowed her to do something she could never otherwise have dared. Cecilia, quickly, with the softest butterfly brushing of his cheek, kissed him back.

The shadow which fell across them was not, as she had thought, the grazing horses after all.

A far from discreet cough and a warm, sardonic voice broke in.

'I'm sorry to disturb you, Federigo, but I think that you had better hear what I have to say.'

Cecilia looked up into the face of a complete stranger. A handsome face, with the ice-white skin, the amber eyes and the black curling hair of a Grecian god. But no ordinary god. There was spirit here that was quite remarkable, and the most powerful sense of a very private nature, almost of shyness, for all his gaze was direct, his smile challenging and his manner boyishly at ease. He was so beautiful that she almost felt he could not be real at all. Pan, the enigmatic god of the wilds, of pleasure, and feelings, but dimly understood; the god of instinct. He was not tall, and was as slim as he was powerfully strong. She knew by instincts of her own that this man never relaxed, never rested, and yet that this burning energy of his never tired him. He spoke to Federigo like the closest of friends, so she never really understood why it was that she felt uneasy in his presence, a real disquiet as those amber eyes blazed gold in the heightening sun.

Federigo shaded his eyes against the glare and looked up. The very fact that he remained lounging where he was showed the depth of the friendship between the two of them.

'*Benvenuto*, Sigi. Cecilia, this is Sigismondo Vialli. . .a friend.'

But Princes cannot have friends, she thought again, not and be completely sure they are to be trusted.

'Sigi, this is Lady Cecilia Sherringham.'

Cecilia held out her hand to greet the stranger. As he took her fingers briefly in his and bowed courteously over them she felt that ripple of real disquiet. It was difficult to know what to do about it, since she was sure more than she had ever been sure of anything that those amber eyes could see into her very soul. Even as she mocked herself for the over-imaginative trend of her thoughts she knew that she was right in the case of Sigismondo Vialli. This man's eyes saw every secret.

She was glad when Federigo got easily to his feet, cursing an unexpected grass stain.

'I've seen you look worse,' drawled Sigismondo Vialli with the same sardonic smile.

'In your company!' It was plainly an old jest between them. 'You said you had something to tell me, Sigi; what is it?'

'It is the Mansini palace. . .Giulio's apartments. The woman that keeps the place for him is dead. . .'

Cecilia had never admired Federigo's outer calmness

more than she did now as he merely raised an eyebrow and said, 'And?'

'Her body was discovered by the Governor's men, when they went to ensure there was nothing left undiscovered to give clue to what happened to Mansini.'

'Did they? What a waste of time when we had been already!'

Sigismondo Vialli smiled. So plainly that 'we' meant just Federigo and his friend. And possibly the groom Salvatore.

'They went there late last night. Yes, that is what I thought,' said Vialli, answering something Cecilia could not understand in Federigo's expression. 'They found the apartments burning and Signora Maldini with her throat cut in the kitchens.'

'And all this was last night, you say? And yet the Governor has not seen fit to inform me of it until now?'

The two men looked at each other then, and Cecilia began to understand. Federigo had not been told because the Austrian suspected he already knew. What she was not so sure about from the glances then exchanged between Federigo and Vialli was if it was covering Federigo's guilt in the death of Giulio Mansini that he was suspected—or of covering up for hers.

The magic of dawn was gone and the sky began to blaze. The mausoleum across the lake took on new shadows and looked just that—a mausoleum, menacing, a place one never wanted to go. And she thought, How far I have come from yesterday when I thought Federigo guilty myself.

Then she had the real revelation. Even if I *did* think it still, she thought with real shock, it wouldn't matter. Simply she belonged to Federigo, her loyalty belonged to him, nothing in the world would ever make it matter what he had done or had to do. So, although she was back with the reality of her suspicions—for, to tell the truth, she would believe this Vialli capable of anything, good or evil—Cecilia heard herself say, as easily as she might end any ordinary social encounter, 'I shall leave you gentlemen to discuss this matter, if one of you might help me with Hereward.'

There was good reason for her request. Hereward had nodded off and was likely to come to with a dangerous lurch if she tried to mount him unassisted.

As if they too were engaged in nothing more than a stroll in Hyde Park, the Prince Federigo and Sigismondo Vialli lent her their help, bowed courteously, and she was free to go.

Why she raced quite as fast as she did back towards the safety of the stables, she never would know. She turned only once to see Federigo turning Malatesta in the opposite direction. As he rode off towards the town she saw Toro racing to join him, warned by Vialli's groom that something was afoot and he would certainly be needed. Cecilia clattered to a halt in a stable-yard which was at peace, all but for herself and Jeremiah Pigg. It seemed too quiet now. She felt so much more than merely uneasy. She was frightened.

'Did you enjoy your ride, milady?' asked Jeremiah, who wanted to ask if he had won his bet with Toro but did not dare, for she was looking at him most oddly. Almost as if he were not there at all.

Cecilia shook off her thoughts when she realised he had spoken. 'Oh, I'm sorry, Jemmy, did you say something?'

'I did, milady.' So that was it—in love, was she? That would explain the vacant stare and the puzzled frown! He had guessed she would be, and was not at all sure he liked it. 'I wagered that fool Toro you would beat His Highness,' he finished flatly.

She smiled then, completely restored to her normal happy humour.

'Did you, Jem? I'm sorry. I hope it wasn't a great deal

of money. I lost.' Then she added with real spirit, 'But only by the shortest whisker!'

Something even more strange was going on here than just the mistress falling for some foreigner, mused Jemmy, and that was certain. The sooner he got in a word with Aunt Margery—if anyone could manage to wake dear Piggy up at all—the sooner he would like it. It was his and Aunt Margery's business to see that little Lady Cecilia was protected.

Cecilia hurried towards the shadows of the *castello*, for the first time looking up at the grim battlements and being grateful for the fearsome protection that they offered. All she could think about the fact that Aquila Romana was stirring, the viper's head was up and poised for striking, something dangerous was going on in this city and the man she loved could very well be behind it, whatever he had said to the contrary. That and—this is my home. He won me in a wager! So whatever comes now I shall stay here. I want to stay. Even if we are heading into war.

So thinking, she took the stairs at a run, startling a gasp of disbelief out of the ever-elegant and demure maid Arietta. Cecilia was frightened to the very core of her, but she was something else much more important. She was happy.

CHAPTER SIX

'WHAT a state you have got yourself into, milady,'
protested Piggy at the sight of her charge's hair. Then
laughed out loud because she had been saying the same
words, with but minor variations on the theme, for the
past six and twenty years. In many ways Lady Cecilia
had not grown up at all. That was why, sighed Piggy
sentimentally, gentlemen were always falling in love with
her. Piggy had wondered ever since she had come here
whether this latest gentleman might not be just as
susceptible as all the others; and if he did fall in love
with Cecilia whether her old nurse would like it.

The Prince was a strong man and Cecilia certainly
needed some sort of authority, if only because she had
never known it in her life. His late Grace of Downside
had been a hopeless parent and an even worse example
to his already headstrong daughter. Yes, a strong gentleman was a necessity. But this man was dangerous too—
his whole way of life was dangerous. Miss Margery Pigg
might live, it seemed to all the world, in a dream, always
three quarters—if not completely—asleep, but she saw
things more clearly than most, all the same. She had
known, for instance, long before Cecilia had told her last
evening, that they were to stay here in Aquila Romana.
She had even found that she rather liked the notion. It
was such a comfortable palace and the children were
little angels. . .even so. . .

Miss Pigg was about to embark on an even more
profound bout of thinking when these very angels poured
through the door, falling over one another and Gulliver,
and pursued by Arietta's forlorn wail, 'Come back, you
little monsters; come back here this very instant!'

97

No use at all, that Arietta, sneered Miss Pigg. All prim and pretty and no backbone! What use was that with small children, least of all with wilful little girls?

'*Silenzio!*' roared Piggy, wielding a threatening hairbrush. Atalanta and Iphigenia sat abruptly on the edge of Cecilia's bed and stared their incredulity. Even Gulliver stopped in his tracks and pondered the advisability of a quiet scratch, even if barking and cavorting like a puppy was more fun.

Gulliver scratched in a 'don't look at me, I didn't do anything' manner, and Atalanta—or was it Iphigenia?—at last found voice to break the silence.

'You're *ferocious!*' She was obviously much impressed.

'You are ferocious, *Miss Pigg*,' corrected Piggy, banging the hairbrush against the palm of her other hand.

'Ferocious, Miss Pigg,' they chorused cautiously. Then, irrepressible, 'Did she bully you too, *madonna*? Or just us?'

Cecilia turned round from her mirror and took in the scene before her. Piggy pretending to be an ogress, and the twins, neither of them the slightest convinced, but enjoying the show whatever. They were as scruffy as always, as flushed and as pretty; she knew to tell one from the other because Figi had soot on her nose and Talia was wearing a gummed plaster on her forehead.

'Not often,' she smiled, playing Piggy's game, 'but then I can't say I ever deserved it as much as you two do. What happened to you?'

'My kitten climbed a chimney.'

'Figi kicked me in the eye when I was helping her to rescue it.'

All this drama and it was not even breakfast yet.

'Are you going to tell us we're dishevelled?' They said half the sentence each. 'Because if you do you're a hyp. . .hypo. . .'

'Potomus?'

'I don't think that's quite right,' mused Figi seriously.

'Hypocrite,' supplied their victim, trying not to smile, for really they were being exceedingly naughty.

'That's it! Thank you very much,' added Talia politely. 'Thing is, you're dishevelled too. So is Papa—we saw him.'

For the first time ever Cecilia felt Piggy's eye come to rest on her in genuine anxious query, and blushed. How the twins had made it sound to Piggy, she could not guess, but she knew how it had sounded to her.

'I don't think our reputations are quite beyond repair,' she hurried out in a whisper to Piggy, knowing her nurse seemed to really need to hear her laugh at it; to the twins she said, 'Your papa and I had a race, I'm sorry to say.'

'Why sorry. . .unless he beat you?'

'Well, he did. . .'

'Of *course*.' Figi said it with passionate loyalty.

'But only just!' Cecilia had her pride.

To the twins this was the revelation they had been waiting for. Somebody had had a race with Papa and almost won! Since this could not possibly have been an accident, there could be only one explanation.

'Papa must like you *very* much if he almost let you win.'

'He did not let me! That is wickedly unjust! It was all quite fair and square, and if Hereward were not quite so fond of cabbages. . .'

'Cabbages?'

'Who's Hereward?'

'My horse. I raced your papa and Hereward was so brim-full of food that he was winded.'

'Oh. . .' It was a long-drawn-out sound and like an echo. The twins exchanged the most significant of glances.

'We don't believe you,' explained Figi for the uninitiated into the twins' private exchanges. 'But you have to say *something*, of course, we understand.'

Really, they were quite outrageous. Cecilia tried to sound as ferocious as Piggy, and failed.

'You two are quite the most shocking little minxes I ever encountered!'

Atalanta thought about it, then said, 'We can't be. Because Papa said *you* were the most shocking he had ever met, and he would not say so if we were, cos he knows us too.'

She recognised that she had got her statement somewhat garbled; Figi smiled patronisingly at her as if to suggest she might have managed it better. Talia took exception and pulled her hair.

That was going too far. Cecilia intervened before she had an actual mill on her hands.

'Be quiet and stop that this instant!' She spoke very quietly but she knew the effect. Figi and Talia stopped mid-punch as if they had been turned to stone.

'You, Figi, will go and clean that remaining soot off your face. You, Atalanta, will pull your skirts straight. You will both go at once to Arietta and see to it that you do not come down to breakfast before your hair is tidy.'

Even Gulliver stopped his scratching in awe.

Figi and Talia stood, heads hung, hands behind their backs, in a posture they had often mendaciously adopted to extricate themselves from any threat of retribution. This time there was nothing forced about their pose at all. Their very real meekness lasted until they were just beyond the door—where they broke into a run and shouted at each other in ear-piercing giggles.

'Isn't she wonderful?'

'Nobody else could make us be good like that!'

'I'm going to tell Papa he *has* to marry her. . .'

'Not before I do. . .'

'Bet I shall!'

'Won't!'

'Shall too. Ouch!'

'Ow, that hurt, I'll tell Arietta. . .'

'If you even *think* of telling I'll. . .'

A distant door thudded shut on the din and Cecilia had just one second to spare in sympathy for poor Arietta.

Then she looked at Piggy and saw the speculation in her eyes. And, knowing what was in her own mind, she blushed.

'I see,' said Piggy.

'I rather expected you would,' returned her mistress weakly.

It was a custom brought to the *castello* by a long-gone English heiress that the family eat all their meals together—even breakfast. So it was that when Cecilia descended at last to the great baronial dining hall the twins were already present. Prince Massimo was with them, keeping a form of mildly exasperated order.

He rose from his chair the moment he saw Cecilia, and well he might have done. He had been lounging quite openly in Federigo's place at the head of the table, and there was nothing the least innocent about his enjoyment of it. He did not even care that she guessed it. Cecilia felt her features freeze in a manner that had chilled even the Duke of Wellington to the core when he had forgotten himself somewhat at the Duchess of Richmond's ball on the eve of Waterloo; and all that poor gentleman had done was say she was far prettier than her mother. Prince Massimo, however, appeared to be impervious to the chill.

'How delightful you look, *madonna*. But then, I always think that there is nothing so good for the constitution as riding out first thing in the morning.'

Naturally the twins must have told him about the race. So why was it she flinched at his words, suspected them of a hidden and insinuating meaning? Her voice was barely above arctic when she replied.

'No, indeed.' She sounded exactly like her grand-mother, the ancient Dowager Duchess of Downside, whom everyone had long since designated 'that old dragon'. Even that was not enough to ward off Massimo d'Aquilano-Mansini's undoubtedly easy charm.

'I have taken the liberty of ordering freshly pressed grape juice for your breakfast. Father feels his guests will prefer it to this rather insipid lemonade.'

Did he mean her to notice that he could never say 'Papa' or anything but that acidly delivered 'Father'? Did he mean her to know that he was not Federigo's son?

'Thank you, I should love to try it. I used to drink little else when we were at Siena.'

'You were there for how long, *madonna*?' Prince Massimo helped her to her chair as he asked this question. He was behind her and she could not see his face, and yet she thought, I don't even like so innocuous a question as that. He is too close. He is too excited. What does he want from me?

What Prince Massimo wanted became no clearer to her as breakfast progressed, the twins so subdued as to be remarkable. To begin with Cecilia supposed that her telling them to behave had been the cause of this unnatural silence; then she knew. It was Massimo. The twins were drinking milk, sitting across the table from her; she could see them peering anxiously across their tall tumblers at the brother who was not their brother, and she saw that they were uncomfortable in his presence.

She knew why that was the moment she thought of it. There was not an ounce of joy in him, nor of understanding of such wild exuberance, such happy natures as these irrepressible children possessed, and he envied them. It was vivid in his blue eyes for all the world to see when he thought that world was not looking. But envious of what? She could not really believe it was their father's love. Simply, every time that Federigo was mentioned she felt a coldness in the air. And because it was she kept speaking of him Cecilia recognised that coldness for what it was. Massimo was jealous.

It was an impersonal jealousy, of course, such as she had seen between her sisters vying for their parents' attention when they had not really cared for either Mama or Papa at all. It was just that Massimo wanted all admiration for himself. He wanted all the attention. He wanted to be what Federigo was. He envied him with the envy of truly helpless hatred. Cecilia herself was nothing to him. Even so, she must prefer him to his father or pay the price. She could not favour him and she knew that he would make her pay for it. Yet all the time the only words exchanged were inconsequential. About England, about horses, the twins demanding to know about Waterloo.

It was when Massimo looked at her as she spoke of the battle, and he realised that she had been there, knew what she had seen, that Cecilia understood he was already her bitter enemy. In that look she saw him reassessing her, and how easy it would be to deal with her; he had thought her just a little English spinster, impoverished and helpless; now he knew what a tough and stubborn breed such wrongly pitied and slighted creatures could be.

'The worst injury was my Lord Leominster, that I saw for myself at least. It was such a terrible thing, for half his face was shot away and. . .'

These were the details the twins were hoping for, the grislier the better. Yet she recognised in them the beginnings of disgust and understanding that such devastation was not such a great adventure after all. Talia was even trying not to cry when Cecilia told of Sholto Leominster. Massimo, in contrast, saw Cecilia's still raw distress, and behind his glittering smile she knew that he was glad of it.

'Good God, such tales at breakfast! You must have

stomachs of iron in England, *madonna!*' She had not even heard Federigo returning. Not for the first time she noticed that he moved as silently as a cat.

'We don't mind!' But the exuberance had gone out of the twins, as she had meant it to. They would not ask such insensitive questions again; just a little—because they were kindly creatures—they were growing up.

Their father looked at Cecilia and back to the twins, and Cecilia found herself frowning at him, telling him with her eyes what she had been doing in teaching them so graphically not to exult in war. She saw his brow clear as he understood her, his smile. She heard too the cold shifting of Massimo's feet against the flagstones as his chair scraped back and he rose, his voice like icy water.

'It's not like you to allow breakfast to begin without you, Father.'

Did he never stop sneering and sniping? Cecilia saw Federigo's eyes cloud with weariness at it. He had had nearly half a lifetime of this.

'I had matters to attend to.'

'Oh?'

'Matters I shan't discuss in front of the children, Massimo, but if you come to my study I shall tell you after I have breakfasted.'

Cecilia saw that Prince Massimo would have liked to press for information now, but did not dare to. The fact he did not dare, and rarely did dare too open a challenge to Federigo's face, only served to fuel his jealous anger.

'Very well, sir.' It was almost as if Massimo, like his mother before him, could not be in the same room with Federigo for long. As if when he strode out, his meal unfinished, he had had to go, as if to remain would have been too much for his precarious temper. There was no doubt at all that Federigo relaxed, and even as he smiled at the twins they were squirming in their seats as if to make themselves more comfortable and at home. The atmosphere of cold was gone and all that remained was a very normal family at breakfast.

'I thought I told you not to feed Gulliver at table.' Federigo said it idly; in fact, Cecilia could barely believe that he had spotted this surreptitious transgression.

The culprit was not so surprised, but then to Atalanta her father was omniscient. 'I'm sorry, Papa.'

'Hmm.' He had heard that so often before.

'I am!'

'Well, you are certainly unprecendentedly tidy. Is this your work, Cecilia? I can't think of any other explanation.'

Cecilia was so startled to hear him say her name in front of the children that she dropped her bread in her lap and almost swore. He guessed it.

'That's more the girl I know! Even so, you have smartened them up considerably—how did you do it?'

'Rather by accident than design, I'm afraid.' She met his smile as best she could. 'I think Piggy's brandishing my hairbrush was the real incentive.'

'Very likely. Did she go on to use it?'

'Oh, no. Asking them to be good was all that was needed eventually.'

She knew herself to have been accepted into a long-running family game when she heard the twins deride this loudly.

'As if we'd do a thing we are told!'

'*I* never would!'

'Is that so?' Federigo smiled at them gently and Cecilia understood that the three of them had long ago written the rules as to how far the twins were allowed to go with their misbehaviour. That this was much further than most children had everything to do with the fact that their father badly needed their loving irreverence. The lord knows, she thought, there is such unremitting bowing and scraping among the servants and the citizens of Aquila Romana as to be intolerable to a man of Federigo's sardonic nature.

'Would you,' he added, 'go out into the garden now and play with Gulliver if I told you?'

'Can I finish my milk?'

'Do you *want* to?' Plainly Atalanta's question astonished him.

'Well, you always say I have to, but I hate it.'

'Then I'm a beast and a torturer and you don't have to——' his voice was almost lost in the ensuing hug, '——but only for today, as a reward for being presentable at breakfast.'

'Does that mean,' Figi half throttled him too, 'that if we're good as good every, every day we don't ever have to finish our milk again?'

Cecilia had to look away. How often did parents find themselves hoist with their own careless petard?

He dealt with it smoothly. 'That will very much depend on the *sort* of tidy you are. You will have to pass muster at inspection or it is two glasses each without fail.'

'Ugh!'

'You wouldn't!'

'If you are not out into the gardens before I count to ten I shall make it three glasses.'

Before he could draw breath to count, even had he been intending to, Figi, Talia and Gulliver were gone.

'You were very lucky to wriggle out of that particular corner,' mused Cecilia out aloud.

'I was, wasn't I?'

'Are you really pleased to see them clean and sober?'

He understood even before she had finished speaking.

'Do you know, I think that almost I'm not? They would almost not be my daughters if they were to behave themselves too often.' Cecilia was just turning back to her peaches when he added, oh, so innocently, 'After all, it seems to do no harm to let them grow up disobedient and wild. They would only turn out just like you.'

After breakfast Federigo had Massimo to attend to, and Sigismondo Vialli was expected with the private papers taken from Giulio's apartments. These would have to be read through, however distasteful the task. There were even a few collected from the Palazzo Mansini this morning that had inexplicably been overlooked before. They were charred but still just legible. Vialli would work on them with his secretary throughout the morning; Federigo had yet another visit to pay to the Governor before he could meet his friend and look into these new papers for himself. Cecilia therefore took herself off into the garden, where she occupied herself and the twins by strolling along the rose walks and between the clipped geometrical hedges of the formal gardens, pointing out each flower and shrub and herb and naming them in English. They learned a sad Irish song she had heard from a dying soldier in Brussels. When she told Figi how he had asked her to sing it with him over and over just as his mother had done when he was a child in Galloway Figi burst into a torrent of tears, waking Piggy from her doze, and, as Cecilia had done before her, rushed straight to the old nurse for comfort while Talia sat wet-eyed with Cecilia on the stone beach and said what a nice man he had sounded and it was so unfair. Gulliver snored and Arietta, freed from her duties and yet not the slightest bit grateful for it, drifted away into the gardens and was lost from sight.

Only two things disturbed the peace of the morning: Massimo storming from the *castello* an hour after he had gone to the study with Federigo, his face white with rage and so angry that he could not care who saw it; and a slight difference of opinion in the stables between Jemmy Pigg and Toro. Jemmy came away with a bloodied nose and Toro with a superlative black eye. Honours were even and they were again the best of cronies. Cecilia half dozed, telling the twins an old West Country folktale. When Sigismondo Vialli arrived and crossed the terrace she raised a languid hand to return his bow of greeting. It was a perfect morning.

Cecilia and the twins took their cold luncheon alone, nothing more than fruit and iced lemonade, and then she saw them to their room to settle them to sleep while the sun was at its highest, looking in on Piggy, who was already away to her favoured dream world, and sought her own.

It had been a strange day and it was only half over. Painful revelations, the birth of a real friendship; the acknowledgement that not even proof of Federigo's guilt in murder could alter that friendship now. Sigismondo Vialli. Federigo obviously trusted him. But ought he to? Did she? Was it just that no woman would quite trust a man as vivid and as fascinating as Vialli—not unless she was happy to gamble her sanity on his mutable affections? She suspected many had, and that they always would. Perhaps even those whose hearts he had broken were not completely sorry. One would never forget a man like that. He would, she saw it really, be worth any amount of pain. So was that her only reason for distrusting him, because he was not a safe man for any woman? Maybe he was, otherwise, the most honourable and loyal of friends. She knew even as he made her nervous that she had rarely liked anyone half so well.

But her thoughts turned inevitably back to Federigo and what he was doing now. A sad task, Giulio's papers, which must to a man as private as Federigo be an unpalatable one. He would hate the sense of prying even into the life of a man who was beyond concern for it. At dusk this evening, when the heat of day was gone, he would lead the cortège to the mausoleum to bury Giulio beside his half-sister. Beside the woman Federigo had loved.

It hurt so much to think of it—both of his loving anyone else, and of his agony at having lost her—that Cecilia refused to think about it any more. To force her mind into safer channels she picked up a box containing something that had always had the power to lift her moods. Letters to her father from his friend Lord Byron. Wild, fascinating, vivid, deeply witty, clever, they never ceased to entice her into the world the poet inhabited, as he meant these letters to. He knew that he was spinning wondrous dreams. He had always had a word for her too, and when her father had died His Lordship's was the letter that had meant the most to her; he had understood the most and cared the deepest. A good friend, a unique man. It did not surprise her to find that, as she at last began to feel sleepy in the savage heat of afternoon, and sank into heavy sleep, it was Byron's words that came with her and his images. It was a dazzling dream.

At first she thought the sound to be part of the dream, the sound of footsteps, ringing cold outside her door, the door opening, almost an iciness to the air as the footsteps entered and came towards her. Only they could not be part of this dream because it was beautiful and these footsteps were frightening. Abruptly Cecilia awoke to find Federigo towering over her. At first she was too dazed to think that he should not be here. She was confused with sleep and able only to raise her hand against the infiltrating sunlight to try to see his face. It was lost in shadow; even so, she saw the anger in it— almost, it seemed, betrayal. Whatever it was, it brought her to her feet before she was even fully awake. She swayed for balance, and as he had done before he caught her shoulders to catch her from falling. But not as before. These hands were painful in their fury.

Cecilia half shook herself, convinced now that this would only make sense if it were another dream.

Federigo was her friend. So why was he looking at her in this way? Almost as if he hated her.

'What. . .?'

It was enough that she tried to speak—it told him she was awake. Awake enough for what he had come to say.

'I want you to explain something to me, *madonna*.'

She had heard that flashing viper's tongue in his voice before, but never for her, never as cold and deadly as this. She had to be dreaming still.

'I don't——'

'Understand? That is for me to say, *madonna*! I am the one who does not understand. I thought you trusted me.'

'I do. . .'

'I thought I could trust you.'

This was madness! Cecilia tried to fight her befuddled head. 'You *can*!'

He let go of her so abruptly then that it was almost worse than had his fingers bitten deeper into her shoulders. It was like being cast aside in disgust. She felt adrift in confusion, with not the least idea what to do about it. This was not really happening.

'I can't, and you know why I can't!'

Somewhere deep inside, stirring independently of her predominant feeling of distress, Cecilia felt the beginnings of anger. It was her anger that fought back for her now.

'I know nothing of the sort!' Unfortunately she was so tired and so bewildered that what had meant to be the curt ring of warning sounded merely defensive and stained with guilt.

'You do know it!' He had turned away from her almost as if he could not bear the sight of her. 'You lied to me about the one thing that really mattered.'

'I haven't lied at all!'

If he had swung round, if he had shouted at her, even if he had struck her, she would have preferred it to the slow turning back that came now. In his hand he had a piece of paper, ochre at the edges with burning. She could smell the charring from here. Giulio Mansini's papers. What had they to do with her at all? Cecilia sat down then on the edge of her bed, almost slumped had she not had just the rag-ends of pride left to make it graceful. She could no longer stand in the face of this or he would see her shaking.

For a silence so long that it almost hurt she listened to the clumsy throbbing of her heart and felt her pulse beat erratically in her palms. She dug her thumb-nails into them as if to stop it. Her head was spinning, she was so exhausted. Federigo remained absolutely still, and she knew she would have to look at him soon. He was willing her to and she could not fight him. But she would look at him on her terms if it killed her. Cecilia took a hard, deep breath and held it. Only when she let it out on a calming sigh did she raise her eyes to his, direct and defiant; his own were absolutely empty.

'You haven't lied?' It was almost as if he was asking her to be able to convince him that she hadn't, wanted her to convince him. But he was the one who had to believe and he would not do it.

She could only tell the truth again. 'I've never lied to you, about anything.'

She saw his mouth twist in distaste at her words, at himself for wanting to believe them. She saw contempt and complete withdrawal.

'Then explain this.' It was all he said. And he tossed the paper into her lap and turned towards the door to leave the room.

All Cecilia's confusion fled in that instant. How dared he? Accuse her, then not even have the courtesy to wait for her reply.

'Damn you for a coward if you leave this room now!'

He walked two more steps as if he would be happy to be damned to get away from her. Then he stopped.

'Well?'

'Have the grace to let me see what it is I am meant to have done before you ask me that, sir!'

It was Cecilia who then turned away from him. The paper as she opened it almost came apart in her hands. Oddly, against the burning, the words stood out even more boldly. That they were written in a beautiful, flowing hand was the first thing she saw as she bent her head stiffly and began to read. The second was her name. As clear as anything, it was her name. And all around it were words of love and devotion, passionate, rushed, fierce, hopeful. Nobody had ever written to her like this and never would. This was no mere billet-doux, no pretty little trifle to amuse, no elegant, empty flirtation. This was raw, hurt, desperate love. It was written to her, about her, for her, and, clearer than all the rest of the letter, it was signed 'Giulio Mansini'.

Cecilia felt as she read it all the blood drain from her face. She should not read this. Of course, it was not for her, it was some other Cecilia. It was not an uncommon name in Italy. But, even as she tried to convince herself of it, she turned the paper over to where her full name was written across the fold. The Lady Cecilia Sherringham, and her old direction in Siena. Cecilia had let the letter fall from her numbed fingers even before she realised she had finished it. She bent automatically to retrieve it, but Federigo reached it first, and with a contempt that utterly disgusted her he kicked it out of reach.

Whatever he might feel, he had had no right to do that. No one had the right to treat such honest feelings with contempt. Only. . . Giulio Mansini could not have written it! She had never seen him until the moment he had died. It was impossible.

'There is more. . .journals, full of your name. And I am to believe you that you did not know him!'

'But. . .'

But she was as confused as he was, couldn't he see

that? She could not believe the evidence of her own eyes. She would have said it was so impossible that Giulio simply could not have written it, only any other explanation was equally incredible. There could be no other explanation.

'Perhaps. . .' her words were her thoughts flooding out before she was even aware of them '. . .perhaps he saw me. Perhaps that is it. You say he was a poet; perhaps he saw me and thought. . .well, I suppose a poet might think it intriguing to have been an English woman in exile; perhaps he had met my father in Siena and they talked of Lord Byron.'

It was the word Byron told her she could never convince Federigo now; even as she spoke it, he laughed at her, and it was a sound so cold that it burned her.

'He mentioned exactly that in his journal. Talking with your father about Lord Byron, hearing some of Byron's letters, admiring them, envying the facility of phrase. . .'

'But. . .' Cecilia stopped the thought where it was. Because what he had said proved that Giulio Mansini had met her father. Papa had treasured those letters; they had never been out of his sight until he had died, and since his death never out of hers. She kept them always beside her bed because they had brought such comfort to her in her loneliest moments. No one could know of them who had not known her father or herself. The mention of Byron could not be denied.

She amended, 'Plainly, then, he did meet Papa—everyone met Papa. He was one of the sights of Siena, God knows!' That much was true. Her father had held eccentric court at their small *palazzo* and, for all his foibles, for all his weaknesses, he had made a host of friends. But there had been some of them she had never been allowed to meet. 'I did not meet all his cronies. He did not consider it suitable if they were young men.' Meaning young men with no money and no useful prospects—the others Papa had welcomed with open arms; all up to the age of seventy, with or without their own teeth.

'That letter was not written by someone who never saw you!'

'I didn't say he could not have *seen* me!' Cecilia was hating this so much that she could have screamed at him to stop it. Not for her sake, but for Giulio Mansini's. This was private. If it was true she had never been meant to know it.

It was this rage for a dead man who had trusted her in his last moments that gave her strength. And the sudden memory of what she had never noticed at the time, for she had been too concerned to save him if she could: his smile. Giulio had wasted his last strength on smiling at her, and yet it had come easily. Those eyes had been so beautiful, so vivid, because—it was insane to say it—for that moment he had been happy. That smile had meant something very deep and meant it for her. Even as she at last knew it to be true, she found that she was saying, 'It isn't true, it can't be true!' She meant that it was impossible he could have felt like that for her. That anyone could. Least of all a man—boy—who had only seen her, never met her. She heard a phrase from the letter burst into her head: 'If I were older, if I were not only Giulio Mansini.' And in that moment she hated Federigo for showing her what she was never meant to see.

'You have no right. . .!'

She almost thought then that he meant to strike her. Instead he took her hard by the shoulders and almost spat the words back at her. The viper's tongue, striking with all its venom.

'No right?'

But he hadn't, none at all!

'That was private—you should not have read it!' She was defending Giulio, and yet she knew even as she

spoke that it sounded as if she were defending herself. . .that she was guilty.

Only guilty of what? Even had she known Giulio
Mansini, was not that her business and hers alone?
Cecilia caught his wrists hard to pull his hands away
from her. That her nails dug in and hurt him pleased
her—she had meant them to.

'Let go of me; I am not the one who was running away
from the truth! It is you who are the coward because you
will not listen. You are the one who is wrong. Too wrong
for me ever to forgive it! What you have done to
Giulio. . .!' She could not finish. What matter that he
could do nothing to a dead man? He had somehow
mocked his memory and she loathed him for it. She was
so angry that she began to cry.

Never in her life would she have expected what
happened next. The hands on her shoulders wavered,
then came in to her neck, soft, stroking, calming, and
with the backs of his fingers he brushed away her tears.
She saw in his face a pallor to match her own, the most
vivid shock. Even as he spoke, she knew. . .

'Don't; my God, Cecilia, don't do that! Don't you
know I understand? I understand better than anyone.
Why couldn't you trust me with this? I *do* understand!'

He believed her to be grieving for a dead love, just as
he was in this moment still grieving without comfort for
his.

'He was her brother—Parisina's.' He could hardly get
the words out. 'I knew he was in love. I asked him about
it. The whole town knew; we all tormented him about
it, but he wouldn't tell anyone who she was, who *you*
were. He never told. I'll never tell. . .!'

She could not let him offer his comfort to her so
openly when what she was feeling was only humiliation
and hurt. She caught at the hand that was at her cheek
and held it; she had to make him hear her.

'But he didn't love me, he couldn't have done; not

me!' Why couldn't he see that? That no man would ever love her like that—why should he? She would never deserve such a thing. It was what hurt her most about Giulio the Poet now, the fact that there was no escaping the knowledge that he had seen her and had loved her; all that generous ardour, and all wasted on someone as worthless as she was.

For a moment Federigo almost understood. But he could not really be expected to. He heard only that she could not believe that Giulio loved her.

'Why can't you believe?' He seemed almost stunned at the idea of it.

Cecilia tried to turn away; it hurt to see what he had allowed himself to show her.

'Because. . .because I am *me*.' Such a painful echo of Giulio's own helpless words.

She felt him reach for her then, pulling her round to him half by the shoulders, half by the waist.

'And why should that mean he could not love you?'

There was an intensity in his eyes that she could not bear to look on. Cecilia hung her head, feeling impotent and so very, very small. He seemed to be saying that she should believe it.

'I. . . I'm just not worth it. I'm not. . .' she flung it out helplessly as she felt him beginning to fight her denial '. . . I'm *not*! Not I!'

She could feel his eyes as if they were burning right through her deep into her thoughts to try to understand her. She could feel him shaking and his breathing was sharp and unsteady. Even so, when he spoke it was very carefully, almost without expression.

'If it were I to say that, there would be reason for it. I never understood why Parisina wanted me. But for *you*, who are so young and so beautiful, who could have any man in the world at your feet. . .!'

Cecilia was frightened of her feelings then. Because, as she opened her mouth to say 'I couldn't', she almost said, 'Yes—any man but you!' No, she almost said 'I love *you*!' One more second of this and he might force it from her.

Anyone might think he knew that he was trying to. Even as she thought it, his hand came under her chin and he lifted her face to look at him, and she could no longer fight it. She wanted to close her eyes against that intimate scrutiny of her tear-stained face, but she couldn't. She opened her mouth to say something, but he shook his head and she was silent.

'He *did* love you, Cecilia, because you are lovelier than perhaps you will ever know, and sweet and troublesome and so damned *silly*! I know exactly why he loved you. And I didn't *want* to read that letter. It's true it was private. I'm not angry any more because I know what it's like, when. . .' He could barely say it; he shook his head once as if to defy the choking of grief. 'When Parisina died I denied everything too. Everything. Even the twins for a while. . .'

Her gesture was instinctive; that was too horrible. That was pain beyond anything she would ever know. Her hand lifted to touch his face and he closed his eyes beneath the comfort of her fingertips. She saw the tears for sure then.

'Don't talk about it, Federigo. Never talk about that part of it. I *do* know!'

The words of a friend, but she knew he had taken them as the words of a lover bereaved like himself, still with some compassion to spare for him. Once she would have thought him absurd for believing she could love a boy of seventeen. But this was not a time for absurdity and laughter. She could not correct him now.

'I only want you to see that I understand,' he went on. 'I was only angry because you lied to me and you had no need to do it.'

She desperately wanted to make him see she had not, but at this moment it would have been a cruel thing to do. He believed they shared something and he needed to believe it; it was that belief which had let him open himself to a grief that until it was faced and raged at finally he would never be free of.

Cecilia felt her hand slide into his hair as she might comfort a child, and drew his forehead to rest against her own because she needed the comfort of it as much as he did. And yet she was, of the two of them, the most in control, the least damaged. She had lost her anger.

She felt him relax for a moment, then, even as she felt a soaring elation that she had once again, despite everything, succeeded in bringing him a little peace, she felt the tension building in him like the lava of a threatened eruption and knew that whatever it was it was beyond both his control and hers. She could only wait for the explosion.

It came in one abrupt, almost ferocious movement as he pulled her hard against him and kissed her mouth so fiercely that she felt that she must die from it, that she was drowning, that she could not breathe, that she wanted to drown, she wanted not to breathe. She wanted him.

Then just as abruptly he let her go. They stood facing each other, beyond thought, nothing but instinct and emotion; it was like being naked. Cecilia watched him watching her, beyond speech, beyond reaction. In a minute she would know what she felt, know why he had done it, but not now. Not yet.

For a full minute they watched each other, not even aware that they were doing so, then, as if in a dream, he said, 'Don't ever lie to me again, Cecilia, don't hide when I'm the only one who can ever really understand!' And he was gone.

It was five minutes before she understood what had happened. That some raw masculine instinct had made him want—no, *have* to show her just what it was Giulio had wanted in her. And that another instinct, his own denial of grief, had melded with his need to make her face her own, and erupted in a kiss that was part for her and part for Parisina Mansini.

Oddly, just in that moment, because he did not know the truth of it, Cecilia did not mind that she had shared what was perhaps the only truly perfect moment of her life with a woman who had died eight years before. But an instant later she did resent it, more bitterly than she had ever resented anything. Cecilia flung herself down on her bed and cried. She was feeling all the grief he suspected her of but she was feeling it because she could never help him, nor ever have him.

Piggy heard the sound she had always dreaded and peeped round the door that joined her own room with Cecilia's. She would have given anything to be able to go to her and help but she knew that not even she could do that now. There were some agonies one had to face all alone.

Piggy closed the door, and Cecilia heard her. She was all alone with this pain and she could not bear it. It was a full hour before she had cried herself into a fitful, empty slumber.

CHAPTER SEVEN

AT THIRTY-FIVE minutes past eight o'clock Cecilia rose, undressed and washed herself. Piggy brought in the black taffeta gown she had last worn when her father had died. Now more than ever before she knew she must attend Giulio Mansini's interment.

At half-past nine, with the sun faded and the sky turned to deepest violet, Federigo himself came to fetch her to the chapel. They did not speak to one another. It felt in that moment that it would be a long time before they ever did again.

Cecilia was the only woman present as the incense drifted across the cold marble floors and wreathed towards the arching ceiling. She was glad that the coffin was covered; she would feel an intruder to see Giulio, who had loved her, now. Sigismondo Vialli, who had first found the letters, smiled at her with a grace of understanding she had not expected, and she felt a disgust at herself for ever having doubted his decency at all. As he bowed and those amber eyes showed careful sympathy she smiled at him, wanting him to know she was sorry she had ever been so brusque and cold.

She barely listened to the words of the mass, but she did not need to. There was poetry for Giulio, she thought, then was scornful of herself for such easy sentimentality. A phrase from one of Lord Byron's letters came into her head; he had been speaking of the death of a mutual friend. He had said, 'We shall all miss him—we liked it so much when he was here.' It was the simplicity of it that was so perfect; this tiny chapel was full of young men, some not even as old as Giulio, openly crying, openly angry. They missed him; they had liked

120

it when he was here. But Federigo had been right; none of them knew who she was; Giulio had kept his own secrets.

Outside it was dark as the coffin was lifted by Giulio's closest friends on to a gun carriage decked by the women of the *castello* in the sweetest flowers and herbs. Cecilia noticed the jasmine and wondered if she would ever feel the same about her favourite scent again. The carriage moved off, pulled not by horses but again by Giulio's friends. The mausoleum was a mile away and by the time they reached it the sky was completely dark, their procession guided only by the flaming torches of the servants walking respectfully alongside. A faint mustiness no longer emanated from the mausoleum, but Cecilia did not want to go in. The velvet cover was drawn back from the coffin for his friends to lift Giulio out of it and to carry him into the marble tomb beyond.

Cecilia never knew what made her do it. Just as she had swept through the crowd in the square to get to him as he was dying, she went to Giulio now, knowing he would have wanted her to do it. The friars of San Franceso had done their work well; Giulio was as beautiful as ever, his wounds hidden—he really might just as well have been sleeping. Cecilia reached out and laid a finger against the lips whose last act had been to whisper urgently against her skin. Then she thought, I owed you something then, not beginning to know how much I *really* did owe you. I promised you justice. I meant it. I meant revenge. Cecilia had never taken off the green stone ring the Irish soldier had given her, the shamrock his mother had carved him for luck. She felt he would understand that she now had to pass it on. She laid it carefully in the folds of the velvet shroud that wrapped Giulio Mansini.

'Take care of that. . .of him.' She heard her voice ring clearly back from the mausoleum walls. Every friend of his, everyone present understood that gesture, when a woman appeared at a grave and left a token. They knew she had been in this country long enough; now she had made herself part of it. She had openly declared that revenge for this death was hers, was to be sought in her name; it was a gesture as old as Italy itself. And she meant it. She, the little English spinster from Wiltshire, had declared the *vendetta*. And she knew—she *felt*—that somewhere behind her, among the hundred or so gathered on the rise above the lake, was the person to whom that promise would mean disaster. She felt the stirrings of surprise; she felt their amusement that a mere woman should challenge them. Then their hatred. The air was so thick with that hatred that she did not even notice that Giulio was gone. Prince Massimo d'Aquilano-Mansini followed behind the poet's other friends, carrying the silk standard of the Mansini to be draped over Giulio before the marble tomb was closed.

All Cecilia was aware of was Federigo taking her hand for a moment and his voice, seemingly far away.

'That was insanity!'

Her own hand closed on his in recognition of his admiration.

'Yes. But I mean for it to happen. There must be revenge!'

The only other thing she noticed was the reflection, as she turned back to walk alone down the rise, of the gold of the torches in Vialli's amber eyes. It was the oddest thing to notice, she thought as she walked away, though perhaps not so odd, for he had been watching her so intently that she could hardly have failed to be aware of it.

Later she would think about what she had done. Later still she would sleep, then wake again and think about everything that had happened. About Federigo. And what his final words had meant. 'That was insanity!' She still did not know if he had spoken as her enemy or her friend, or as both. If he was guilty or innocent. She

knew nothing except that she had lost him completely—
to his eyes, she had declard her love for another man at
the graveside—and yet bound herself to his city; she
could not leave here until Giulio was avenged. She did
not want to. Had she ever had the urge to run from the
misery being close to Federigo would cause her, it had
been buried alongside Giulio in his sister's tomb.

She noticed as she looked from her window just before
closing the shutters that Federigo was the last to leave
the mausoleum, that he had stayed there. She knew why,
and what he had seen. Inside the mausoleum his ancestors rested on marble shelves; on many the seals were
broken. Parisina was with them. He would take a very
long time to recover from being forced to look at that.

She saw a smaller figure greet him—Gulliver. Saw
Federigo pitch himself down on the grass beside the dog.
Saw him do what she had done so often in the past, tell
Gulliver his most painful secrets because he could never
tell them to any human being. No more than he had had
the right to read Giulio Mansini's letter had she the right
to watch him now. Loving him, she had even less right
than any other.

Cecilia closed the shutters and crossed the room. The
letter was still on the floor where he had kicked it aside.
If he ever remembered he had done that he would hate
himself. She hoped that he had been too angry to do
anything but forget. Cecilia bent and picked it up,
smoothed it out. She now felt she had the right to look
at it.

The words hurt and yet she found herself marvelling.
A man could feel these things for *me*? He might just have
been a boy, but Giulio had been no callow youth.
Federigo had told her as much the first time they had
really spoken of him. As she read the words she found
she was hearing Federigo say them, in the voice in which
he had told her she should believe them, because she
was beautiful, and silly, and deserved it. It was strange

how that tone so perfectly fitted these passionate words. Strange when Federigo did not love her.

Sleep was out of the question; thought was even more unbearable. Cecilia did the thing she always did when she felt so confused and so lonely: she wrote to her friend. George Byron would listen—she could tell him everything. All of it. She so badly needed someone to know. Federigo would never know she loved him, so she needed to tell that she did to somebody who would understand her. She felt better even as she trimmed her pen and began to write the direction and the date on top of the letter. There had been part of a poem in Giulio's letter too; she would copy that out and Byron would comment on it. He would have the sense to say it was a good one, that Giulio showed promise. He would not even have to lie, because Giulio had been good. 'You are rather like one another,' she found she had written to Byron. She had not known Giulio Mansini before he had died, but she was coming to know him very closely now.

Footsteps sounded outside her door. Then there was a tapping, faint lest she had gone to sleep. But he must have seen the candle-light through the keyhole. Cecilia could hear that Gulliver was with him, for the mongrel was snuffling at the gap beneath the door. Federigo had brought her dog back, but she could not open the door to let him in. Poor Gulliver would never understand.

'Cecilia!' Federigo made it sound urgent. Still she could not bear to let him enter.

She might have known he would come anyway.

The door opened a fraction and Gulliver was able to wriggle through. Federigo began to close the door as Cecilia let out her breath in relief. Then he changed his mind. The door opened again and he came in.

Since Cecilia was dressed only in her softest lawn nightgown, she felt at a considerable disadvantage, but only for a moment. Until she saw his face. He needed her. At least, he needed the fact that he had learned to talk to her. He did not want to talk any more; but neither could he be alone.

Cecilia set down her pen and rose to meet him. With the briefest gesture she showed him to sit by the fire. It was unlit because the night had seemed so hot before. Now suddenly she saw that it had grown very cold. There was a storm rising.

'Do you know how to light it?' She came a little closer to him.

'Yes.' And for the first time since. . .well, since—she would not think of that—he smiled as he had smiled at breakfast this morning. 'A good thing I do, since the servants would never approve this!'

She smiled back, a little unsure of how long this lighter mood of his would last.

'No, I don't suppose they would.'

'Do you?'

'Why shouldn't I?'

For a fleeting moment she saw real laughter flare in his eyes before he turned away, took off his coat and made rather a point of stacking the fire and kindling a flame. He said in a tone that was deceptively casual, 'Most women would.'

She found she was saying, rather caustically, even before she realised she should not, 'I don't imagine all that many females fainting away or barring the door to you!'

'Perhaps not.' His voice was even more expressionless. 'There, that is alight. For all I know, it will actually burn now!'

Cecilia knelt beside him then and said drily, 'If it doesn't you may always take my blanket.'

Still he watched the flame as if only by the fiercest concentration would it flourish at all.

'Are you as generous with your wine, *madonna*?'

It was almost as if he was deliberately keeping his being here just a childish game, a midnight feast such as

the twins might have revelled in. That was the reason
Cecilia blew out the candle anyway.

'Is that conspiratorial enough for you, Your
Highness?' She felt the strangest excitement arcing
through her as she said it. She was mocking him again.
Whatever it was they had had to face today, they had
come through it and she thought that they were friends
again.

'I think so. What is in that basket?'

'English toffee—Piggy makes it.'

'Perfect!'

Cecilia found she had knelt again on the floor, the
basket between them, and Federigo was pouring wine
into the only glass she had.

'We'll have to share.' Again that tone of studied
indifference in his voice, and Cecilia knew that this was
something she could not do. This was something far too
intimate.

'No. . . I shan't have any. . .thank you. These toffees
are horribly stuck together; they are quite disgusting.
Perhaps I had best save them for the twins.' It was her
turn to feign a casualness that was far from what she was
feeling. She knew that he guessed it.

Federigo took the basket from her and investigated
the quite bewildering contents. 'I think perhaps you're
right. They look revolting.'

'They taste wonderful, when one can separate them.
No, Gulliver! No, you may not have any. Take your
nose away!'

'Yes, go away, Gulliver!'

And Cecilia knew that when he said it he meant, This
is between Cecilia and me. Even Gulliver did not belong
here at this moment. It frightened her a little. Something
was happening and she could not begin to understand it.

'Who were you writing to?' he asked.

'Lord Byron.'

Any other man would have been more than a little

jealous—she had yet to meet the man who could be completely at ease with the poet's extraordinary attraction for women. But Federigo was.

'I met him once. I rather liked him. Is he ever serious about anything, do you suppose?'

'Yes—but never in public. And perhaps he does not always know when he is and when he is not.'

'I see you know him well.'

'From his letters, mostly. And because he understands that it is good to talk about the things that matter. He has not the slightest inhibition about saying anything.'

'You think talking answers everything? That if one can just talk, and tell the real truth about a thing out loud, that that will make a difference? Talk as to a confessor and the pain will go away?'

'No.' They had come to it at last; if she deserved to keep him as a friend she must not fail him now. 'But it will lessen; it will never be quite so bad again.'

'Even Parisina. . .even if I were to talk about her?'

'Yes.' He was never to know just how terribly it hurt her to hear such devotion to another woman.

'I'd like to tell you about her, because I think you would have liked her.'

Cecilia had to turn away lest he see her smile; it was a cynical, unjust thing but she could not help it. She have liked Parisina. . .and loved him—impossible! But again he was not to know it.

'Was she like the twins?'

'I think so. Very like them. They have her spirit. . .her life.'

'Then I should have liked her very much indeed.' It was not quite untrue. She would have admired a woman such as that, even while she envied her bitterly.

'I wish she could have known them. She did not even live to know she had one daughter, let alone two.'

Cecilia knew then to let him talk. She filled the wine glass, knowing that he had emptied it without being aware he had drunk anything at all. It was almost as if he were back there on the night Parisina had died, deep in the shock of it again. Only this time, maybe, there was someone to help him.

'She must have been happy, Federigo, don't you think so? Looking forward to them, wondering what they would be and whom they would resemble. Knowing they were yours. She was happy and never knew anything but that happiness. It was you who was left behind. Parisina can't know what was lost; she can't suffer for it as you do.'

'I feel I took it all away. She. . .'

So that was it; he felt guilty for her death. It was not uncommon, any more than it was uncommon for women to die in childbirth. Cecilia had sat all night once with the husband of a friend raging at himself because he had the son he so desperately wanted but his wife was gone.

'Are you really going to be foolish and blame yourself because she died? You know better than that.'

She could feel how badly he wanted to believe her. He had never spoken of his guilt to anyone, and he had done it now because he half believed that Cecilia could make it go away. He turned to watch her, sure she was looking away from him into the fire—he was wrong; he met her eyes and saw that she really wanted to help him. Why she did when he had been so cruel to her, so thoughtless, so selfish. . . But he knew why; Cecilia did not have it in her to turn away anyone's unhappiness—she would always help. She could even make you believe it was all for you, you alone who mattered. . .

'I *want* to know better than that, but I so wanted a child. . .'

Cecilia knew what he was saying. Not just a child with the woman he loved, but his first child. Massimo was not his son and he had needed his own to feel cleansed of the marriage that had stolen everything from him. He

had needed a real son, a son who could be declared
legitimate and heir.

'Oh, Federigo, don't be such a fool! You speak as if
Parisina did not want the child, and only you did.'

The hardest part was that he had always half suspected
this was true. 'She was so frightened. Terrified.'

'Most women are frightened—there is reason to be.
Do you really believe she was so afraid that she was glad
to be with child only to please you?'

'No. . .' Now that Cecilia said it like that, he knew
how wrong he had been.

'Of course not.' He looked so tired in that
moment. . .no, not tired, exhausted, almost vulnerable,
that Cecilia reached out and touched his shoulder. He
was so tired that it was a second or two before he felt it.
'You should try to sleep, Federigo. You need to sleep.
Today has been. . .today has been so terrible that I don't
think either of us would ever want to repeat it. Too
much has happened. Giulio's housekeeper murdered,
the letters. . .the funeral. Giulio was Parisina's half-
brother, after all; how can you feel anything but shocked
and exhausted?'

How? Because he had to. He was born to be one of
those who was never to be shocked, never to be tired,
but always to function, never to escape his duty.

'Because I *must* not be. *I* must not be! I am the Duke
of Aquila Romana, and I will rule this state alone one
day. I can't be weak, Cecilia, I can't be tired. . .I. . .'

'Can't be a human creature and feel pain like all the
rest of us?' Even as she heard the smile in her voice, she
knew he was right this time. He could not, he was not
like the rest of us; he must accept that burden or give up
his heritage. He always had accepted it. He had become
so much the ice-cold, insensate figure-head that he was
feared and not loved, respected and set apart from all the
world. But that was only in public. He had to learn that

in private, with his family, he had the right to be as any other man.

'Maybe that's all true,' she was speaking her thoughts aloud as they came, 'but not now, not here. You don't have to be anything but who you really are, not with me. I'd never want to put such a burden on anybody. There's nothing weak about grief and feeling one has borne too much. If you would only stop believing the same things others need to believe of you to let you lead them you *could* be free.'

She heard him stir slightly, heard the wine glass set down; he moved to throw another log on the fire and watch as its halo of light engulfed the two of them, but only them. There was nothing beyond this warmth or this moment. If he could just believe what she said, trust it. . .

'Federigo, let go. Stop pretending. In the morning pretend, for Signor Vialli and all the others, but not now. Now you don't have to. Not when you're alone. . .'

'Or with you?'

'Or with me.'

Anything might have happened next and Cecilia knew it. Absolutely anything. She found that she was tensed against it, waiting, wondering. . .hoping perhaps. . . She did not really understand what she wanted him to do. None of the things she needed to hear would ever be said; he would never love her. Or even trust her completely. But that did not stop her wanting him to say that he did, even if he did not really mean it.

What he did say was, 'I *am* very tired.' And he found that for the first time ever he did not mind admitting it. Parisina had been closer in age to him than this quiet, unconventional English girl, and he had known her most of his life; even so, he had never told her how exhausting it was, how alone he felt with the burden of being the heir to the Aquilan Princes. Parisina belonged here in Aquila Romana, where the Dukes had for centuries been all-powerful; she would never have understood. To Parisina such power spelt doing exactly as one pleased, as it had to the less vulnerable Mansini. Cecilia, who was the stranger, understood.

'I am *so* tired!' It was such a relief to say it again.

'I know.'

'But I can't be alone!'

Cecilia knew that too. 'You don't have to be. You can stay here.'

Federigo looked at her then. Had she been any other woman she would have been offering him her bed, herself. In a way she was, but not as any other woman would have meant it. He almost wondered if she understood he was so tired that he was even grateful for that—that he would not have to pretend he wanted her, that she would not feel offended that he did not. Not now. He would never, *could* never, insult this girl with the real truth about that.

Cecilia was so sure she was safe from his advances that he almost laughed at her even as she said, 'There is plenty of room for two, and even Gulliver!'

'No Gulliver!'

'But he always——'

'Not tonight.'

Cecilia was not at all sure what was happening, or what she was doing, only that she was glad—even though he had not so much as pretended he wanted her—that at least he would stay with her. In fact she was glad he had not pretended. That would have been a pain she could never have borne. As it was, somehow, in this strange state of shock and exhaustion to which they had driven themselves, she could be with him tonight. It was all she would ever have of him. That too hurt like nothing else had ever done, and yet at the same time she knew that what she had now was more than anyone had ever had of him. More even than Parisina. She was certain of it.

Cecilia had trouble with Gulliver. He would not get

down from the bed when she asked him to. Indeed, he took one look at Federigo and growled.

'Has he been trained particularly to protect your virtue?'

'You would think so, wouldn't you? And yet. . .it is the strangest thing, but last night when the window flew open, and I was sure I had locked it, he did not utter a sound!'

Federigo crossed the room so fast then that Cecilia was almost jolted out of her dream-like languor.

'What did you say?'

Why were his eyes like that, as urgent and alert as when she had first told him about the Mansini secret? Something she had said had struck a chord with him.

'It was nothing, really. Only that I was certain I had not even opened that window, and yet it woke me by banging back against the casement.'

As quickly as it had come the urgency seemed to leave him. But only seemed to. She could sense in the firelight a tension that had not been there before.

'I take it you locked your door?'

'Of course not—why should I? How would the maid bring my chocolate if. . .?'

But he was not listening. He had gone to the door and locked it. Then he locked the door between this room and Piggy's too. He made light of both actions but Cecilia was not quite certain he felt quite so easy about it.

'Better the servents and your poor nurse do not discover us!'

He meant more by locking out the world than that, she was sure of it, and she felt oddly frightened by it. He saw her shudder as he tossed the keys down on the chest beside the bed. With a single gesture he dismissed poor Gulliver to the fire. Then knelt down and removed Cecilia's slippers for her. He was right—his fingers deliberately brushed her skin—she was terrified of something; her feet had turned to blocks of ice, and the fingers in her lap were caught together so tightly that the knuckles showed white.

Can I bear to have him touch me? she thought. Can I bear it? But she would have to, for his sake, because he could not be alone.

'Get into bed, Cecilia,' he ordered as he might have directed the twins. Even while her nerves reeled, she found that she was smiling.

Cecilia tucked her feet down beneath the sheets but would not lie down.

'Don't be absurd, child; you can't sleep sitting up!'

Lest he should touch her again Cecilia meekly did as she was told.

'That's better.'

The tension was still there in him; she could feel it even from where he was at the fireside, rescuing the bottle of wine from a delighted Gulliver.

'No—*no*, you do not like it! No more do I like drunken animals.'

Cecilia laughed in what she knew to be a very silly fashion. 'He did get a little foxed once. . .on brandy. When Perry Savernake found him he was next to death. Perry thought a little cognac might buck him up. . .'

'And. . .'

'It knocked him quite out. You would have thought someone had hit him on the head with a mallet!'

'Poor Gulliver. Yes, very well, you may have the toffee. But chew quietly, or we shall never get to sleep.'

He said 'we' so easily, she thought, as if he were used to being here, as if. . . She wasn't going to let herself think like that. Cecilia hugged the sheets around her and found that she was still shaking badly.

'You need a blanket.' He frowned at her. 'Good God, are you always such trouble at bedtime?'

'Piggy would say so.'

'Then my respect for Piggy knows no bounds. I shall

never understand how she has managed you all this time without finishing her days in a lunatic asylum.'

'She sleeps through most of it. . .' Unbelievably Cecilia felt herself getting sleepy, and she yawned even as she laughed at it. It was very warm now; he had spread the blanket over her, the softest French wool. She thought she heard thunder outside again but she could not heed it.

She looked so fragile there in the firelight, he thought, her gold hair and stubborn little nose all that was visible as she huddled into the covers for warmth. So beautiful. He knew then that this was a very bad idea. He had always known it. He must leave. Yet even as he thought it he knew that he was not going to. Gently he sat on the edge of the bed and plumped her pillow a little where it seemed to cause discomfort to her.

'Is that better?'

'Much.' She really was incredibly sleepy.

It was shock, of course; he recognised it. The shock of everything. . .but most of all, he thought, of Giulio Mansini's letter. He could remember every word of it as if it were still before his eyes. He did not want to remember, or ever think of it again. To avoid thinking he lay down at her side.

'You will be cold like that,' she murmured.

'No, I shan't; only the English are ever cold!' He could not be any closer to her than this; he could not risk it.

But in her half-sleep Cecilia defied him; without realising she had done so, drawn by the warmth of him so close to her, she curled against his side, and he found that he had put an arm about her and her head was resting against his shoulder.

Almost it would be easier to be alone.

Federigo lay quite still and watched the firelight, concentrated on it, lulled a little by her quiet, even breathing, hoping that this tension would leave him, as it should never have come, and he too could sleep.

Cecilia was not quite asleep, but almost. Almost she *had* to be. Yet a part of her wanted to stay awake all through the night, to watch over him while he slept, to be certain that he did and that he was safe and free from that grinding unhappiness and care, if only for a while. I wonder, she thought, if it is possible to love someone too much? Then she thought, Yes, it is, he did—does—love Parisina Mansini too much. Cecilia could do nothing about the tears after all. Federigo felt them soaking into his shirt, hot and silent, and hated them as even he could never have imagined he would hate it. She was crying for Giulio.

'Try not to think, sweetheart.' He turned his head and buried his face in her hair.

'I don't know how!'

I do, he thought, by God I do, and I wish that I could show you! But it would not be right, it would not help anyone. Not while there was Giulio Mansini between them, so desperately loved and unavenged. Maybe not even after the truth about his murder was known. Maybe it would never be right.

'Just by being quiet,' he murmured, staggered that in the grip of such an overwhelming frustration he could still sound so calm that it would comfort her.

It did calm her; he felt her relaxing slowly against him as the tears came to an end. He found that he had put his other arm around her and was holding her closer, willing her to sleep, because if she did not. . .

Dear God, he did not want her to sleep!

Cecilia slept.

But she did wake again, when the fire had all but burned down and Gulliver had snatched his opportunity to climb up on to the far side of the bed. For a moment she almost laughed at it, sandwiched as she was between the scruffiest mongrel in the world and the Duke of

Aquila Romana. Federigo was really here. And now he was asleep she could marvel at it.

His hold on her had relaxed, everything about him had relaxed. He was so much more beautiful even than she had realised. Cecilia raised herself on her elbow and gazed down at him. All I shall ever have of him, she thought, but just at that moment it was enough.

Because she had earned the right, because no one, whatever had been or whatever was to come, however much suspicion, however much distrust, could be closer than they were now, or better friends, or even belong to each other more than they did in this moment, she leaned over and kissed him softly on the mouth. He would never know she had done it.

Federigo stirred at her touch and she held her breath in a terror of hope, wanting him to wake and yet not to. He did not stir again and so Cecilia lay down close against him and thought, a little sadly, Whatever happens, nobody can ever take away this one, strange night. It belonged to them alone, and nobody could ever change it. As if by holding him close she could hold back the dawn that would end it, Cecilia curled her arms about him then and waited, wide awake. She wanted to be awake. She did not want to miss one moment of this too-short time with Federigo.

So she knew when Federigo, thinking she was sleeping, turned to her and kissed her even more gently than she had done. Whatever it was he said, she did not hear it; his voice had been too soft, too husky for that. It did not matter. She would feel that kiss for as long as she had to live.

Neither knowing the other was not sleeping, both wanting so much to say something, but knowing it would be misunderstood, unwanted, they saw the dawn rise above the Castello d'Aquilano, neither ever guessing how close they had come to telling each other the truth.

CHAPTER EIGHT

CECILIA woke just before sunrise, knowing that Federigo would be gone. Their closeness had been born of the protection of darkness and in a moment of absolute pain. Such moments never lasted. Cecilia was left alone, smiling a little that he had taken the care to lock the door from the outside and push the key underneath it: whatever the all-seeing servants might think they had seen last night, this locked door could only prove them wrong. Federigo had plainly taken the greatest care not to be observed—and she thought again of his most natural movement, the silent, lithe grace of a cat. If anyone could walk these corridors undetected he could do so. He had better have done so! was her first thought; her second was, I do not really care at all.

On this reckless decision Cecilia hurried back to bed to discover that Gulliver, jealous and determined to win back his sole right to Cecilia's affections, had usurped Federigo's place against the pillows. Cecilia ruffled his ears and laughed at him. His stubbly grey nose was glued and matted with toffee, and she knew from experience that the only way to remove it would be with the scissors—leave the toffee and he would be plagued with insects. Cecilia sought out her sewing scissors and began the task of persuading her mongrel that he really would be better off after a trimming.

Since she had opened the door so that the maid might bring her chocolate, she was not too surprised to hear it open; from halfway under the great bed and murmuring, 'Come along, Gulliver, you know it doesn't hurt,' she heard footsteps. Two sets, small but infinitely louder than any adult could possibly produce. The twins.

Dear God, but thank heaven their father was gone! But how long had they been awake? It would be the last thing in the world she wanted that the twins had seen Federigo leaving her room. She had the most certain feeling that they would view such matters with an open-eyed robustness that would outrage sensibilities back in England, and she would be left attempting to deny what they would feel contemptuous of her for denying at all. Figi and Talia were exactly keyhole-height—there was little they would not know about the castle; but they could never understand, least of all the extraordinary innocence of last night. Cecilia held her breath, and held her dog, and waited.

'What are you doing on the floor?'

She knew the moment it was asked that they had seen nothing, that everything was perfectly well. So she answered, somewhat muffled by Gulliver's tail under her nose and no little relief, 'Chasing Gulliver with my scissors.'

'Are you trying to kill him?' asked Talia rather anxiously. Cecilia heard a concerted thump, and both twins wriggled under the bed to join her.

'Not,' spluttered Cecilia as Gulliver licked her in the eye, 'unless he does that again! Do come out, Gulliver. What is Piggy going to say if she finds us all in this position?'

Naturally Gulliver could not care in the slightest what Miss Pigg might say; Gulliver had discovered his new best friends come to play, and that was all that counted with a dog, after all. Overjoyed, he let out an excited yip. Then he slithered out of hiding and began the chase, barking loudly enough to disturb even Piggy. Inevitably it was Cecilia's and the twins' stifled laughter and hisses of 'Sshh!' that brought Piggy to the adjoining door.

'Really, Cecilia, as if last night were not enough!'

Cecilia stopped in her tracks, a blush of pure horror

sweeping through her face. Piggy was looking at her most intently. What had Piggy heard—or seen?

'What on earth can you mean?' Cecilia's protesting question was little more than a shaken breath.

Now what in the world, I wonder, has got into the silly child? puzzled Miss Pigg, adjusting her nightcap as if by doing so she might adjust her early-morning thoughts. Never had she seen Cecilia look quite so anxiously guilty. It was quite beyond her to fathom.

Piggy blinked away a yawn. 'Well, Gulliver, child; what else could I mean? He behaved so disgracefully last afternoon that I had to send him out into the gardens.'

Cecilia felt almost dizzy with relief. Gulliver, however, felt that his name was being blackened unjustly and barked loudly. Liking the effect of its ringing back at him off the stone walls, he did it again. He was so enjoying making this infernal clamour that he was caught off his guard by Figi and Talia, pounced upon and held down for his barbering.

'Do you suppose, children,' and plainly Miss Pigg meant all three of them, 'you might take poor Gulliver out into the gardens again if you mean to assault him? I believe it is not even quite yet five o'clock.'

Indeed it was not, and Cecilia felt very guilty.

'I'm so sorry, Piggy, we have woken you up!' If the state Miss Pigg was in could quite be called awoken.

'Do not trouble about it,' returned Piggy politely. She was already soothed by the fact she might have another hour or so in bed.

'I know,' hissed Talia in what she imagined was an attempt to keep her voice down, 'let's go to the haunted garden.'

'Do let's! Please, Cecilia, you have never seen it.'

Cecilia had not even heard of it. She was more than intrigued.

'I have heard of houses being haunted before, but never gardens. Is it a gruesome ghost?'

'Would you like it to be?' Figi asked it as if she might, if the answer was in the affirmative, arrange for the apparition to be particularly alarming.

'I don't know. I've never seen a ghost before. Maybe just an ordinary ghost would be quite sufficient to begin with.'

'Well, the garden does give one bumps and shivers.'

'I think bumps and shivers sound quite grim enough. Where is this garden?' Cecilia was presuming it to be a part of the *castello* grounds not visited before.

'It is the Mansini Garden. Behind the Palazzo Mansini and the cathedral. It is very beautiful.'

Mansini again. The name alone made Cecilia shudder. It seemed to come into everything that happened here in Aquila Romana.

'Look, Figi, she's shaking already. This is going to be the greatest fun!'

There was just the faintest suggestion of a note of bravado in that whispered voice. Cecilia heard it and thought idly, They really believe in this haunting; somebody they trust must have told them about it.

'How would you like to help me dress my hair? Then you can tell me all about it. After that we can dress and have breakfast sensibly, and then we can go and see it.'

It was hard to tell which excited the twins more, the prospect of ghouls and spectres or or dressing Cecilia's very elegant curls.

'I'll brush them, you can hold the pins,' decided Figi, who was fifteen minutes older than Atalanta.

'No—I want to brush!'

Cecilia heard fisticuffs in the making and interrupted imperiously, 'You will take it in turns. I shall wear my blue ribbons this morning and you may tie one each, if you are quiet and sensible.'

For the second time since she had known them she saw the twins obey at once, and felt that she would have liked their father to have seen them; they were almost as charming when they were good as when they were naughty.

In the end it was decided that Talia might take the hairbrush first. Cecilia sat at her mirror, trying not to laugh at the solemn expression of the twins as they applied themselves with loving dedication to their task.

'Your hair is really pretty. Our mama had hair just like yours.'

Parisina had had golden hair? That had never occurred to Cecilia. Oddly it gave her a very unpleasant sensation; it added to the half-formed feeling that the woman Federigo had half believed he was with last night was Parisina. Added to the suspicion that whatever it was drew him to her—and he was drawn—had been some unadmitted likeness in her to Parisina. But she would not want the twins to sense her disquiet, so she said as easily as she could, 'Your papa told me that your mother was very beautiful.'

'She was.' The twins spoke about Parisina a little with awe, but nothing more than that; she meant little more to them than an icon, a lovely and comforting guardian angel that their father told them about to soothe them when they were frightened.

'Would you like to see a picture of her?'

Cecilia knew even as she dreaded it that this was what she had wanted to do—needed to do—for what seemed a very long time. Almost she needed to see not quite her rival, but the reason Federigo could never be hers.

Her voice was quite steady. 'I should like to very much.'

'Shall I fetch it now?' offered Figi, who was the one holding the pins and ribbons.

Cecilia was not quite ready for it.

'Not just now; I should like to look at it properly when I am a little more awake. You may show it to me before we go for our walk.'

Her hesitation—and her feeble excuse for it—seemed to satisfy the children.

'Very well. Shall we tell you all about the ghost instead?'

'Yes, please.'

'Well. . .shall I tell it, Figi, or shall you?'

'You do stories better; let me have the brush and then you can tell it properly.'

Figi, it seemed, was well set to becoming a very shrewd young lady indeed. She had successfully got her own way even as her sister swelled with bursting pride and imagined that she had in fact got hers.

'Of course.' Talia was actually polite to her sister when she handed over the brush. Then she sat beside Cecilia on the long brocaded stool, put on her most solemn face—carefully corrected in the mirror—and began.

'Grandpapa told us of it. It is a little bit a story about our Grandmama, only we don't remember her, do we, Figi? Grandmama was a Mansini, you see, and had grown up at the Palazzo Mansini. Her mother was an English lady and she had made such a beautiful garden that when Grandmama married Grandpapa she still used to go there every day, to sit and look at the flowers and to see her cousins. After a while she became the only person to sit in the garden—I think she must have been rather sad about something because nobody else liked to interrupt her when she was thinking. Then somebody said it was not because Grandmama was sad that the garden did not want anyone else to go into it but because the ghost was sad too. . .the ghost only liked Grandmama to see it. Nobody else has seen it, but everybody knows it's there because someone heard Grandmama talking to it one day. She called it Federigo. That is Papa's name too.'

'I know.' Why was it that as Cecilia listened she began to feel a very real creeping of her skin? Then she thought that it was because this story was so recent. She had expected a medieval ghost at the very least. There was something too immediate about the twins' own grand-mother—Federigo's mother—crying in a garden and talking to someone called Federigo. It was far too real.

'Grandmama died ten years ago—she was very old—and nobody has ever gone into the garden since, not even the gardeners. She would not let them tend it while she was alive either. Think of that. . .' Atalanta's voice was steeped in awe '. . .for a whole twenty years she sat in the garden every day, and nobody else went into it at all!'

'So nobody has ever been there for thirty years. Grandpapa owned Palazzo Mansini after Grandmama married him. When she died he kept the garden locked.' Figi handed Talia a hairpin, glad to have been able to play her part in the tale.

'Papa keeps it locked too and nobody is supposed to visit it.'

Of all that surprised and disturbed Cecilia most this last information was most disquieting. Federigo was neither a superstitious nor a sentimental man. What possible reason could he have for keeping the garden closed? She knew that there must be a reason, and a very good one. She also knew—as she saw Figi stare franti-cally at Talia and Talia clap a hand to her mouth in guilty horror—that she had almost let herself be tricked into taking them where they might not go.

She wanted to laugh at them but she said sternly, 'If your papa keeps the garden locked we can't visit it, now, can we?'

Figi stared daggers at the over-talkative Talia. Then she rallied to their cause.

'He hasn't actually said *we* may not go, only other people. We are Mansini too, after all; it is almost *our* garden. It *is* Papa's garden, and I can't see, if we are not frightened and only want to see the ghost *once*, why he should not let us have the key.'

'We know where he keeps it.'

This time Talia had said far too much for Iphigenia's short-fused temper. Atalanta received a very unladylike cuff about the ear.

Cecilia's voice froze.

'That will do, Iphigenia! You will apologise to your sister at once.'

Habit made Iphigenia's lips move to form the word 'shan't'. But she could not say it. There was something about Cecilia, even while she was the greatest fun to play with, that made one know one absolutely had to do as one was told.

'Sorry!' she muttered. And Atalanta stared at her in disbelief. But Cecilia's instinctive air of command had worked its spell on her too.

'That's perfectly all right,' she replied, a little sulkily. Iphigenia blinked.

'Papa would let us go if *you* asked him, *madonna*.' Figi was certain of this the moment the idea struck her. 'If *you* come with us he will know we'll be good and he wouldn't mind you going there at all.'

Just what it was could make the child say that with such confidence, Cecilia never knew. All she knew was that she could not ask him. She did not yet know how she was going to feel when she saw him this morning, she was only sure that she wanted to put that moment off for as long as she could.

'*Please*,' begged Talia, 'he really *would*; he'd let you do anything you liked.'

Cecilia's nerves trembled as she listened—how could they not? And yet even as she thought, I can't. . .what I can't do is test out their conviction and find that they are wrong, she knew that the reason was that she half believed it too. If anything, Federigo as much as Piggy had bracketed her with the twins, almost as if she were a child as well; certainly he had done everything so that she might feel at home here.

Something in her reflection must have shown that she was wavering.

'*Please!*' the twins begged in passionate unison.

Cecilia heard her voice say, 'Oh, very well, I shall ask him. But don't be at all surprised if he says no.'

She had not meant to say that at all! For her foolhardiness she found herself buried in a flurry of hugs and kisses. With the twins at least she was the most perfect person on the planet.

'May I speak with you, Federigo?'

After all, it was quite easy. Cecilia found herself on the stairs behind him as she hurried down to breakfast. He turned, and for a long moment she knew her heart had stopped completely. She did not know what to do or say; he was the man of the world, the one who understood these things—let him show her how to act now.

She might have known he would make it easy. Simply he smiled.

'*Buon giorno.* You look very wide awake this morning. What was all that barking and squealing I heard?'

Cecilia's hand fled to her mouth in guilt just as Talia's had done.

'Oh, lord, you did not hear it too? It must have awakened the whole castle.'

'I was awake already, remember?'

It was the only allusion he was ever to make to their long, healing night together.

'Of course,' was all Cecilia ever said about it. She learned in that moment that there were some things that never had to be expressed in words. This man and she were friends now, indissolubly—whatever happened—and as such they had no need to speak of it. 'Gulliver didn't want his whiskers trimmed.'

'I'm not entirely sure I blame him.'

'It was Piggy's toffee, you see; it was stuck to him and he knows he hates it when his whiskers grow all hard

and the wasps and bees chase him round the garden. He
has not the least sense at all.'

'Had anyone ever suggested that he had?'

Cecilia found herself half stamping her foot at his
insult, smiling as easily as he was. When he held out his
hand, took hers and tucked it through his arm, she was
quite comfortable about it. More than that, quite happy.

'Now, what did you want to ask? I suspect from your
expression it is something terrible and you are about to
shock me.'

'I doubt that I could! It is the twins, Federigo; they
have been telling me all about the haunted garden—they
so want to see it. Rather, they have convinced themselves
my life will be blighted forever if I am not permitted to
go there.'

She felt it then, the momentary tremor of tension, the
dipping wing of some dark emotion shadowing them for
a second, but then it was gone. Whatever had been the
cause of it, he was smiling quite easily again.

'Is that all? Why could they not ask me themselves?'

'I rather suspect they weren't going to ask at all. They
say they know where you keep the key.'

'Do they, now? Then I must remedy that.' The words
were light but the look about his mouth was grim.

'Don't let yourself be bullied because they insist that
they will fall into a decline if they can't go!'

'I haven't let them overpower me yet. But when are
they proposing you go on your ghost hunt?'

'After breakfast. You might even hold it over them to
make them drink their milk!'

'I am not a tyrant, Cecilia! I hated milk myself, didn't
you?'

'Horribly!'

'Surely ghosts are night creatures, though? It seems a
little unintelligent to go looking for it this morning.'

Cecilia spoke without thinking. 'But surely, they told

me, your mother used to sit there by day and that she was the only one who ever saw it.'

She knew the magnitude of her mistake the minute she had spoken. She felt his whole body stiffen, the arm beneath her fingers went rigid, his face expressionless.

'My mother saw nothing! The whole stupid tale began because the servants did not understand that she liked to be alone there. In her later years—for most of my life, in fact—my mother was not quite well. . .'

Cecilia knew at once what he was saying. She had had an aunt who was 'not quite well, poor Maria, but dearest Cecil is so wonderfully patient with her'.

'Oh. . .!'

Federigo heard her horror, the pity in her voice, and could not bear it. Not from anyone, least of all from her.

'She was not mad!' He almost snapped it at her. Then said more calmly, 'She had had some great grief. I am not even certain my father knew what it was. It was never spoken of. He cared for her very much and took pains that she was protected from any foolish gossip. I never really saw her. When I did. . . I suppose to a boy of five she seemed a little strange. She was so devoted to me, so overwhelming with it, that when she did see me I think I was even a little frightened of her. At other times she seemed almost remote, from the whole world. Whatever this ghost was, it was in her mind. Only the superstition of the servants made it into a legend.'

Cecilia knew he was angry with her, and even though she knew she had not deserved it, except for her carelessness, she accepted it. Every day she heard something new about his past life, and every time she did it was something terrible. So she said quickly, 'Might it not have been better not to lock up the garden? By making it such a secret place you have only strengthened the beliefs about it.'

Even as he smiled again, a little cynically, and said, 'Perhaps you're right,' Cecilia knew that again she had angered him. She had touched on something else that was hidden, something else he was not telling her. It was rather shocking after last night, when they had been so very close and had had no secrets, that today, returned to normal, he was as closed as ever. He still had things he wanted to keep from her. He would not completely trust her with them.

'At least let the twins play there—it is the only way to evict this nonsense from their heads.'

He was silent for a very long time then, as if he had something particular to decide upon. Then, as he seemed at last to relax again, he answered, 'Yes. They may go. But only if you go with them and Toro and your own groom escort you.'

Cecilia's eyes widened in near shock. In daylight, in the middle of the city. . .why should they need such obvious protection when they could not be more safe?

Federigo saw her expression, and the suggestion of rebellion about her always-stubborn mouth. He really did smile at her then, but his voice was quite serious.

'Just do this one thing, to please me. I should not ask it without a reason. Indeed I am *not* asking, Cecilia; this time it is an order and I expect you to obey it.' Then, guessing her response to such an autocratic tone to almost certainly be obstinacy, he added, with devastating innocence, 'I *need* you to obey it.'

Cecilia was completely disarmed even as she knew exactly how he had achieved it. He was insufferable, he knew far too much about women, about her, and was not the slightest bit averse to employing what he knew against her! What was most galling was that, even while she knew that he manipulated her, she let him do it.

She managed just enough face-saving irony in her tone when she replied, 'Very well, sir. Of course.'

Any further discussion was drowned out in squeals of triumph as the twins, creeping down the stairs behind them to eavesdrop, overheard that they were to be allowed their expedition and as near exploded in delight as made no difference.

Breakfast was short and mutinous; it was all Cecilia could do to keep them in their chairs. Fifteen minutes later she was being dragged bodily back up the staircase, then still more stairs, deep into the heart of the fortress to the twins' apartments. Bonnets were collected, Talia chased off to her father to collect the key. Just as they were ready to leave Figi remembered something.

'Oh, we promised to show you our picture of Mama.'

Cecilia had almost been hoping they had forgotten, yet even as she was guided towards the little portrait on the wall between their beds she knew she had to see it, she had to know.

What she had never expected was that she and Parisina Mansini would look so alike. Enough alike to rock the foundations of Cecilia's confidence in her friendship with Parisina's lover. Maybe none of his feeling was for her at all? Maybe it was all for memories of Parisina? The only real difference she could detect between them was that Parisina was so exquisitely, so ethereally beautiful.

Cecilia needed the visit to the garden so badly that she could not have believed it. She needed to be free of the *castello* and away from any chance of meeting Federigo. She needed something to do to occupy her mind completely. Governing the twins and Gulliver would keep a large army well and truly occupied. The twins were almost impossible to get into order; they were encouraged in their bouncing and skipping by a giddy Gulliver.

Cecilia had once seen Wellington bellowing at his troops. It was a lesson usefully taken to heart.

'Into line at once! All four of you. Sorry about this, Jemmy, Toro, but perhaps if you set an example. . .'

With the most angelic of smiles the two grooms fell into military formation.

'Now you two. And Gulliver.'

The twins decided to like the new game. It might be

fun to march like the soldiers they saw every day crossing the square. And if they remained amused by it Cecilia might just succeed in getting them to comport themselves in public in a manner befitting the daughters of His Highness the Duke of Aquila Romana.

Certainly they drew many eyes as they stepped briskly out into the sunlight. Talia had to be prevented from shouting 'quick march' and 'left, right, left', but that was the sum of their misbehaviour. Toro was laughing so much that he missed his step and had to hop and skip back into line. The maid Arietta, strolling home from the market, stood stock still and stared, and Prince Massimo, lounging with his closest cronies beside the fountain, felt obliged to peer through his quizzing-glass to be certain that these models of decorum were the twins at all. A great many citizens paused about their business and smiled.

The alley from which Giulio Mansini had fled to die was formed by the towering height of the cathedral on one side and the walls enclosing the Mansini Garden on the other. At the far end of this dark and mossy alley was another smaller square fringed by the garden and the Bishop's residence. All windows on to the square were shuttered at that moment; there was nothing to be seen but the sunlight and an idling cat. It was very peaceful. Jemmy laid hold of Gulliver lest he shatter the silence and pursue the kitten, and at last they came to the gates of the Mansini Garden.

These were tall and heavy, made of skilfully wrought iron, the gilding on the Mansini crest of a dolphin faded and peeling away. A clear layer of dust caked every surface, the fingerprints of the more adventurous small boys of the town clear for all to see. Beyond, a wilderness of tumbling roses and ivy and vines, lay the garden, walls gritty and crumbling in places, statues green and featureless with age and weathering. There had been rain the night before and much of the area about the gate was mud and puddles.

They all saw it at once. Beyond the locked gate, unmistakably, the clearest footprints in the mud. Someone had already been here. And yet Federigo kept the only key.

Without a word Toro slipped away from the party, heading towards the *castello* to give the Duke the news. Gingerly, and followed by a pair of twins more than a little subdued, Cecilia set the key in the lock. It was a struggle to turn, it was so rusted, but at last the gates swung open.

The twins hung back.

'Don't be frightened, children; no ghost I ever heard of left his footprints!' Jemmy Pigg had ever a practical approach to the unusual.

The sun burst suddenly through the cloud and flooded down on to a mass of dying lilac, and the smell of fertility and decay was almost overpowering. Ghosts don't leave footprints, repeated Cecilia to herself. Even so, she shivered as at last they went in.

CHAPTER NINE

THERE was not the least doubt that someone had been here before them, for more than one clear path had been thrust through the tangled undergrowth and plants were trodden down all over the garden. Among the tiny English daisies and the delicate wild irises Cecilia found more and more footprints, all seeming to her to be the same. The twins were so excited about detecting that they had almost forgotten the ghost. Cecilia was left staring about her, trying to understand how anybody could have got in without the key.

The walls were far too high, and anybody attempting to climb them with a ladder would almost certainly have been caught by one or other of the military patrols, either the Austrians, Federigo's or the Bishop's. On the other side of the garden lay the Mansini palace itself, but here the windows had long been boarded up and the place deserted. Giulio had lived in a small set of apartments overlooking the main city square; the rest was locked, impenetrable. There was no getting into the garden from there. Cecilia pushed her way towards a stone bench, now half fallen with age, and sat warily. The sooner Federigo came, the better.

When he did arrive, not ten minutes later, it was in a hurry, on horseback and with Sigismondo Vialli and the Austrian Governor. Cecilia was glad she had taken care to make sure the twins avoided the footprints. The men needed to see where this strange visitor had gone to even begin to guess what he had been doing.

'Good morning, *madonna*.' Vialli bowed with his usual almost ironic elegance that was, even so, infinitely charming.

'I have never seen the twins schooled so precisely as you managed them this morning, *madonna*,' put in Governor von Regensberg. 'I am more than tempted to put my troops under your command.'

'Thank you, Count, but I'm afraid I don't see such obedience lasting. And I own I would almost be sorry if it did!'

'And so would the whole of Aquila Romana,' laughed Vialli, turning to fend off the over-boisterous greetings of the ecstatic twins. 'We like them as they are; the good God alone could tell us why!'

'The ghost's left footprints all over the place!' bellowed Atalanta.

'Lots and lots, in the mud,' confirmed Iphigenia.

They were far too excited, and Cecilia sought out their father at once, certain that he would want the pair removed. He had followed a trail towards the furthest wall, where the climbing roses poured down into the garden in fall upon fall of translucent pink-white petals. There was another stone bench here beside a dried and empty pool. Federigo seemed to be intent on the tiny gecko sunning itself on the cracked fountain rim, but she knew he was not; this must be where his mother had come to sit, every day for twenty years, mourning something nobody had ever understood and believing, in the peace of this almost enchanted place, that she had no cause to grieve at all.

She almost did not want to interrupt him.

'Federigo, do you wish me to take the twins home? They are far too excited and getting very noisy. They will be sadly underfoot.'

For a moment it was as if he had not heard her. Then he said, so softly that she barely heard it, 'If I knew why she came here I'd know the answer to everything that's happening. I have to *know*; I *must* find what it was Giulio discovered. . .'

'Federigo!' Cecilia was forced to touch his sleeve to claim his attention. 'The twins. . .'

He almost spun round then; certainly she had startled him back from thoughts that were very far away from his daughters and their infectious nonsense. As he did so there was a particularly piercing howl. He came round completely at that.

'I think perhaps you better had.'

'I shall only be able to get them to come away if I promise they can come again!'

'Of course they may. I hear you had them well in hand until they found the footprints.'

Cecilia coloured up; she was aware by now that the whole of the city must be talking.

'Only by making a game of it, I'm afraid.'

'Even so, it's more than anyone else has ever done. As we passed I heard Brother Luigi telling Brother Andrea that he had not thought it possible to see them so quiet and disciplined without the use of laudanum.'

'Heavens, are they *so* notorious for their high spirits?'

She could not quite keep the pride out of her tone. Federigo could not have missed it but he did not seem to mind that she was becoming almost as attached to the twins as if they had been her own.

Whatever he thought about it, he smiled ruefully. 'I'm afraid so. And always will be if people like Sigi encourage them in their silliness. Vialli, can you not silence Atalanta?'

'You want me to smother her?'

'Both of them, if you feel you can manage it!'

Slowly Federigo and Cecilia were making their way back to the rioting mass of dog and children by the gates. Cecilia was so taken up with laughing at Figi desperately fleeing Signor Vialli's most convincing ogre that she almost missed it. Only by chance did the sun's flashing on the tiny piece of metal catch her notice. Cecilia bent, curious, picked it up and brushed off the mud with her fingers.

'What is it?' Federigo stopped to see what she was doing.

'I'm not entirely sure. A button of some kind perhaps.'

'Let me see. . .'

Cecilia handed it to him. The button seemed to have a crest on it but it was rubbed and worn and she could not make it out. But all too plainly Federigo did so. As she stood up she looked at him to see what he would say and felt her throat go dry, her whole body dissolved with flooding alarm. Never had she seen anyone so pale before. Never had she seen his face so hard, so closed; he stood looking down at the button in his palm as if transfixed. Then she saw his mouth twist as his hand closed quickly on the fragment of silver and he put it in his pocket. His mouth was set in so harsh a line that she felt she had never really known him before. She had forgotten that only three days ago they had met and he had badly frightened her, she who had never been afraid of anything in her life. He frightened her again now.

'What is it?' She heard her voice catching on her nerves.

He took a moment to answer, and in that moment he gave a brief, satisfied smile. Cecilia thought she had never seen anyone look so dangerous, but a second later the impression was gone.

'A coat button, very old. It cannot have anything to do with our mysterious footprints.'

And as he turned to lead the way back to the gates Cecilia thought, He lied. That button explained a great deal to him. I know that it did! Yet again her friend of last night had shown that he was not prepared to trust her.

Cecilia was glad the twins had so exhausted themselves as to have fallen asleep almost the moment they had eaten their fruit at luncheon. She was tired herself but she knew she could not sleep. There was thunder in the air again, heavy and oppressive, and it had always made her restless. What she would do was continue her letter to Lord Byron.

She had been certain she had left it on her writing table but it seemed that she must be mistaken. Cecilia shuffled papers impatiently about in the hope it had become buried beneath the unused sheets, but there was nothing to be found. Had it disappeared, then? And, if so, who had taken it? Letters could not wander off by themselves.

She stood rooted to the spot then, trying with every drop of concentration to remember what she had done. She had been writing when Federigo had arrived. No, she was certain she had not put the letter away. Could he have taken it? Why?

Then she began to panic. What had she written in it? She knew what she had been going to write, but how far had she actually got with it? She could not remember. All she knew was that she had been intending to tell her wise friend everything—about Federigo—all of it, her lingering suspicions, her feeling she must do something to avenge Giulio Mansini. . .the fact that she was completely in love with the Prince d'Aquilano. Dear God, but if she had written that and Federigo had seen it!

But she could not let herself believe that he would pry. Federigo would never be so vulgar as to read her private correspondence.

Only—he was also the Duke of Aquila Romana and something dangerous was happening in his city. He needed to know what was behind it all and he had suspected her no little involvement from the first. Under those circumstances might he not have read it—given that he would first have had to imagine her stupid enough to commit her guilt to paper? Yes, under those circumstances he would do anything, for the future of his people was at stake.

Yet even that did not quite make sense. . .

Then perhaps she had accidentally put it into the box of Lord Byron's letters to Papa? The heavy inlaid cedarwood box of Persian origin—a birthday gift from the poet two years ago—sat in all its elegance on the corner of the table, buried beneath all the papers through which she had been rooting. Cecilia brushed the papers off the box and opened the lid. Had Gulliver not that instant barked an unmistakable warning, a few moments later she would almost certainly have been dead.

Curled in the bottom of the box, hidden beneath the letters, a viper stirred, angry to be woken from its slumbers. The deadly tongue forked out, and only just in time Cecilia stepped backwards. But the danger was not yet over. Awake and enraged, the snake twisted out of the box with a speed she would not have believed possible and uncoiled its way across the table towards her. The mongrel, hackles high and teeth bared, circled round it as it dropped to the flagstones, and suddenly Cecilia came round from her shock.

'No, Gulliver. *No!*' He would be killed if he tried to attack the snake and he was just brave, and stupid, enough to try it.

Beside the fire lay a large and heavy metal rod that was used for the purpose of dislodging soot from the chimney mouth. Whichever maid had been here this morning had by some miracle forgotten to take it when she had gone away again. Cecilia snatched it up and raced back to the viper. Even armed as she was, she knew it was infinitely more dangerous than she would ever be. It could move so much faster than she could.

Gulliver seemed to understand just enough of her danger to begin his growling again, almost as if he knew he could help her by distracting the snake's attention. The minute the bright-eyed head swung towards Gulliver

Cecilia struck. For one long, sickening moment the snake writhed and she had to strike it again, but at last it was dead.

Cecilia flung herself to her knees and took the dog in her arms.

'Oh, Gulliver. Darling, darling, Gulliver. . .brave boy!'

For the second time since she had been here Cecilia broke into a flood of calming tears.

The snake had to be removed quickly—she did not want anyone to see it. Especially not Piggy, who had a particular horror of the creatures. Cecilia was so busy hurrying the remains into the garden and out of sight behind a laurel bush that she had not time to think until she was back in her room again how the snake could have come to be in the box in the first place.

It was not, she knew, something she wanted to think about. Even as she tried the lid of the box she remembered how it had always been stiff and awkward and needed two hands to open it at all. The snake could not have crawled in by itself. Someone had to have put it there.

It would have been all too easy. Everyone had seen her leaving for the Mansini Garden with the twins. Anyone might have put it there.

It was only when a message was brought to her from Federigo that he hoped very much that she would accompany him to a long-standing engagement at the opera that evening that she realised what had been at the back of her mind ever since the viper had attacked her. This was something she could not tell him. He had too many things to think about, and this could only be a practical joke that had gone wrong. She knew even as she made up these excuses for her reluctance to tell him that her reasons for keeping the matter to herself were far more complicated. The only way she could explain it to herself was that she would feel safer if nobody knew. Particularly the perpetrator; tell Federigo and he would have the whole castle in uproar until he discovered who had done it. No, let the perpetrator, whoever he or she was, think that she had not opened the box yet and perhaps she would be able to guess, from the way someone was watching her, who it was responsible, and why. Whatever her reason—and she would not admit to the other darker motive clamouring into her head—she would deal with this herself. It was the only way.

Cecilia had but one gown that she felt would stand up to scrutiny at the opera, that would not let Federigo down. She owned no jewellery, for her father had sold off everything her mother had left her to pay his gaming debts, so she had chosen this gown because it needed no adornment. It was a fine yellow net that was as gold as corn and almost perfectly matched her hair. It had the most delicate little upstanding collar of lawn trimmed with lace and pearls, and a satin underdress which showed at the hem in the most exquisite silk embroidery. Tiny buttercups picked out on the pale butter satin, a theme that she carried to her hair, for Piggy had fashioned a band of buttercups from the best Venetian silk. Her darker yellow ribbons twisted into her curls and she was almost satisfied with her appearance. Her gloves were a little threadbare, but nobody could say that this gown was not as good as new, for all it must be the best part of seven years old. Over it she flung her one remaining evening cloak, a simple dull gold velvet, and then hurried quickly down the stairs to where Federigo was waiting in the *castello* hall.

She supposed she should have thought of it before that for the opera, where he would be at his most public, he would also be his most formal. The stark black and white of his court dress suited his harsh beauty to perfection; unlike other men, he spurned all jewellery and decoration, except for the one thing she had seen and admired so much in the portraits running along the gallery outside her chambers—his badge of office, the red and white ribbon from which depended the flawless diamond d'Aquilano cross. Cecilia did not think she had ever seen a man look so elegant, so noble. He carried his rank with such indifference that he was magnificent.

She could not help herself saying so.

'Oh, you make me feel so very pallid! I had never imagined that you could look so grand!'

He knew to take it as a compliment.

'And I have never seen you look *less* pallid. That gown suits you to perfection. . .the twins have begged to stay out of bed to see you; they said you would put us all to shame.'

Without another word he took her hand and led her across the hall to where the twins were sitting neatly on a sofa before the fireplace. They both had their hands behind their backs as if they were hiding something, but the minute they saw her they burst out, 'You look so *beautiful*!'

'Much more beautiful than *anybody*!'

'We've got a present for you.'

And almost shyly they presented their booty, a tiny basket of fresh white violets they had picked from the gardens not half an hour before. The scent was violet at its purest, delicate, honeyed, sweet but never cloying. Cecilia breathed in the freshness of them, the dark tang of the leaves, and thought, Why is it I feel I want to cry? But she knew the answer. Just for a moment she was part of this family and she wanted so much to be forever that she wondered how she would bear it when the moment was gone.

'Thank you.' She knew Federigo would hear the trouble she was having schooling her voice.

He did. He took her elbow lightly and laughed her

emotions away. 'How they managed to pick these and remain clean I shall never know.'

'Because we had to.'

'It's special. . .so we didn't want to be grubby.'

'Cecilia won't let us kiss her if we're dirty.'

'I was not aware,' drawled their parent, 'that such considerations had ever deterred you from kissing your victims in the past.'

The twins were scornful. 'Oh, *you* don't count! You don't wear pretty dresses that would be spoiled!'

'And I'm very glad to hear it!' Cecilia pulled herself together and joined in their laughter. She might as well enjoy it while she could. Carefully she kissed each twin on the not so clean as their father had suggested cheek.

'Mud, Talia, behind your ear,' she whispered.

Atalanta spoiled the conspiracy at once by uttering a most unacceptable word and scrubbing at the mud with her elbow.

But tonight Federigo was not in the mood to scold them. They knew perfectly well when they were in the wrong, he had no need to remind them.

'Sorry!' Talia proved their father knew them very well indeed.

'Good girl,' he smiled at her. 'Now, if you can persuade Gulliver that he really would not enjoy the opera we can be gone and you two can go to bed.'

Cecilia's last view of the twins before stepping into the carriage was of the two of them tugging Gulliver away; the mongrel turned pleading eyes to his mistress but she could not help him. With a sad droop of the shoulders he turned and walked away. She had deserted him. Cecilia found that she was laughing.

Watching her closely in the darkness as he had been doing for some minutes, Federigo said, 'I'm glad you have come to live with us, Cecilia; it has been such a different place since you came. . .so much laughter in it.' If he was not careful he would say what he really meant. To ensure that he did not, and lose her completely, he turned away and looked out of the carriage window. Cecilia was glad that he did, because he did not see her crying.

The opera house occupied one whole side of the third famous square of Aquila Romana. Indeed it was the only side, for it stood majestic and dominant, alive with the light pouring through its tall windows, flooding the square with its warmth and welcome and not a little of the excitement of the enthusiastic patrons of its halls. It had been built on the lines of St Peter's of the Vatican, if, fortunately, a little smaller, and was the pride and joy of Federigo's great-grandfather, who had three-quarters bankrupted the treasury to provide it. The rest of the square, again following St Peter's, was formed of elegant marble colannades, and here and there stood carts of flowers, and wine sellers, a man with a brazier offering early chestnuts, an itinerant clown. Cecilia gazed out at it all with delight; it was why she loved Italy so much on these velvet summer evenings; she loved the bustle, she loved the noise, she loved the way these people so adored to enjoy themselves. And, of course, like every other city all over Italy, there was at the centre of its enjoyment the opera house, with its own resident company and orchestra. Tonight they were to hear Monsieur Gluck's exquisite '*Orfeo ed Euridice*', and Cecilia, who had fallen in love with it when she had heard it years ago in London, could not have been more excited had the event been planned especially to please her.

For all the deference and burning curiosity her appearance at Federigo's side engendered it might just as well have been.

'This is your evening, *madonna*,' smiled Sigismondo Vialli, who could say such things and make them sound quite careless. 'I hope you will accept a small present. . .you have to like it: Axel and I have spent all afternoon deciding on it.'

The most dangerous thing about the extraordinary Vialli was that he had all the true enthusiasm of a little boy.

'Indeed we have, *madame*.' As always, the elegant Count von Regensberg was smiling. Alongside him was another, older, Austrian gentleman and his very pretty and young Italian wife.

'You will adore it!' cried the young wife, who was called the Baroness Luneburg, and the party burst out laughing at her exuberance.

'Then if you keep me waiting a moment longer, Count, Signor Vialli, I shall never forgive you!' Cecilia had long since caught their happy mood and was exhilarated by it. It had been such a long time since she had been out into society that she had forgotten how much she had used to enjoy it.

Vialli promptly produced a package from behind his back, and Count von Regensberg complained at him.

'*Signor*, I told you you should have let me have care of it—I knew that you would squash it!'

'I dropped it, I'm afraid.' Vialli was unrepentant and irresistible.

Cecilia opened the package and was met by the most delicious smell imaginable. Chestnut, champagne, orange, even a little brandy. Inside the pretty silk box were the most luxurious comfits she had ever seen.

'These are wonderful! Dropping them ten times would not have made them any less delicious. I have never seen them before. . .'

'The friars make them, at San Francesco,' put in the Baroness. 'When Franz and I return to Vienna I shan't go until they let me have the receipt.'

'They would go to the stake rather, Diana, and you know it!' Federigo too seemed to have relaxed completely. But then this was more his element than hers—

this was his city, and tonight the fact was acknowledged by all around him.

So much was it acknowledged, with the deep bows and curtsies commanded by royalty alone, that Cecilia was almost surprised when the first thing the orchestra struck up was the Austrian national anthem. There was just the barest breath of dissent among the well-bred Italians present; even so, she knew that, had not Federigo politely stood respectfully throughout it, not one of them would have done so and no Governor, however much they liked him, could make them. It was the first time Cecilia had sensed their patriotism *en masse*, trapped and somehow heightened by the gardenia-scented heat of the dark blue velvet and gilded opera house. From her position between Federigo and the Governor at the front of the flower-bedecked box she felt almost as if she were lifted up by the power of their sentiments. She knew from the way in which the faintest smile never left Federigo's face that he knew it and that it amused him. It was all he needed to know, after all. One day soon he would be ready to take back this city for them all, and they would support him.

The opera began, and it was so well performed that Cecilia completely forgot even the avid glances cast her way. She knew why everyone was curious; she knew what they were asking each other. She was even aware that had the night not been so perfect she would have been angry with Federigo for putting her in such a difficult position. He had singled her out for attention so publicly that everyone in the opera house was convinced they knew the reason why. Not all of them prognosticated marriage, but without a doubt they believed they were witnessing the birth of a very grand liaison indeed. All of it embarrassed Cecilia, came too close to the truth about her feelings, feelings she needed not worry others might see simply because they assumed she felt them anyway, yet tonight, as the ethereal strains of the grief-

stricken '*Che farò*' rose up from the stage and she felt as
she always did the hairs on the back of her neck rise in
an almost primitive response to the sorrow of the music,
nothing could challenge her pleasure or her happiness.
She could feel Federigo, indulgent and amused, beside
her. They had for the moment both been able to forget
the world outside, and the unhappiness within. And that
was all that mattered. He wanted her to enjoy her
evening and she was enjoying it; he wanted her to be
happy, so whatever came next she would be. The
heartbroken chorus lifted again and it seemed every
breath in the place was silenced. The aria was performed
so perfectly that it was some moments before anyone felt
able to respond. Then in a storm of cheering and a hail
of flowers the mezzo-soprano who had sung it was
obliged to sing it again, and again, and again. Cecilia
thought then that nothing in her life would be more
perfect.

When the opera was over and she had found herself
being led by Federigo to join him with the Governor in
congratulating the performers they remained for a while
in the vast entrance hall beneath its chandeliers, Cecilia
trying her best to remember the names of all the people
who were presented to her. By the end of the evening
the heat and the pleasure of it all were just enough to
make her a little sleepy.

'I think,' she heard Federigo say drily at her elbow, 'I
had better take you home before I find myself obliged to
carry you.'

Cecilia smiled sleepily up at him and laughed. 'I'm
afraid you will, any moment.'

'Come, then.' She thought nothing at all of the fact
that he took her hand. That the crowd saw it and burst
out into a flurry of fascinated whispers could not have
mattered less. It was as if they were not really there at
all.

The carriage was waiting as they descended the steps,

and Toro leapt down to open the door for her, encased, rather than dressed, in his black and silver livery—and looking very resentful; even so, he managed his most dazzling smile.

Cecilia sank back against the silver-grey leather squabs, and Federigo, sitting opposite, smiled at her again.

'Are you so very sleepy or can we play truant a little while longer?'

'Truant?' Cecilia tried her best not to yawn.

'Yes. I have something I want to show you.'

There was something in his voice, close to excitement, yet more than that, that brought Cecilia awake in an instant; it was almost as if he had physically transferred his mood to her. She sat up, eyes suddenly burning with delight that the evening was not quite over. There was to be more of it, alone with Federigo.

'Will not everybody be gossiping about us?'

'They already are, so what can it matter? To the Devil with all scandalmongers, I say.'

'To the Devil it is!' Cecilia curled her feet childishly up on to the seat beneath her gown, and asked, 'Where are we going?'

'You'll see.'

He had been so sure she would agree—she knew it the moment the carriage moved off—that Toro had already been told where they were headed. They were obliged to make several stops, however, as the flower sellers and the chestnut man craved sales as an excuse to get a closer look at the English lady who had caused such a stir since her arrival. Loaded with carnations and jasmine and a cup of scorching chestnuts, the carriage at last made its way towards the town gates; these were opened automatically on sight of the d'Aquilano crest, and the carriage bowled out along the straight cypress-lined road that led back into Tuscany, away from the city and out into the wild surrounding hills.

For a quarter of an hour they drove without exchanging a word. Federigo wanted only to watch her childlike pleasure at her illicit adventure; Cecilia wanted only to feel that pleasure and to hug it to herself. It would one day, when she had nothing left, make up her most precious memories. At last, after a testing climb up a steep incline, the team of bays, steaming and grumbling, drew to a halt and Federigo handed her down from the carriage, out on to a path of grass dried to the scent of straw by the sun, and all about the air was loud with the sound of the cicadas, the rustle in the undergrowth of sleepy birds and the spicy scent of verbena, olive bark, wild thyme.

'It's only a little way—we'll walk from here. Are those slippers up to it, do you think?'

Cecilia was lost in a word all of her own. 'If they are not I can always take them off.'

'And when you cut yourself I am meant to carry you, I suppose?'

'Oh, I shan't cut myself. I have feet like cowhide— Piggy says so. I used never to wear shoes. . .'

Somehow he felt that he was not surprised that she had not. There was about her all the time, but tonight especially, the untamed spontaneity of a wild creature. Her elemental nature, her complete lack of inhibition in the teeth of all convention, was so alien to what he had had to train himself to be that he responded to it as if she were showing him the way back to the undisciplined boy he had once been. With Cecilia he almost forgot he had left such carefree ways behind him.

Cecilia did kick off her slippers and Federigo put them in his pocket so she would not lose them. Then he took her hand again and they walked in silence once more until they came out on to a small plateau at the top of the hill, and there below, as he had wanted her to see it, alive still with the lights of the taverns and the opera house, as clear in the moonlight as ever it was by day, lay Aquila Romana. His city. His home. He wanted her to see just what it was at stake, just what it was he had to fight for. . .so she could decide for herself, knowing all the dangers, if she really wanted to stay, not just for now, but for always. Then maybe. . .

Cecilia, caught by a sudden breeze whipping at her cloak, swayed slightly, and he caught her against him, wrapped her closely into the warming velvet, holding her steady. So perfectly matched was their breathing, she thought suddenly, that they might just as well have been one.

'There.'

He had no need to say anything more.

Cecilia looked down on the city that had by accident become her home—it *felt* like home—and knew that it already mattered greatly to her. Its future, its fate, all that was important to her. Almost she believed, as she gazed down on the tiny carriage lights weaving through the streets, It matters as much to me as it does to Federigo.

'It's beautiful. Quite perfect.'

He knew from the slight tremor in her voice that she meant it. She had been in exile so long that she had never had a real home. He let himself hope in that moment that she had at last found one here. Why he did he was not yet ready to admit to himself. Only that since she had come he had felt so much more optimistic, that he needed her to stay, he needed whatever it was about her made him feel closer to finding peace than he had ever believed he could come. He needed, he supposed, his first and only true friend.

Still thinking this, he took her by the shoulders and turned her to face him.

'Are you going to stay with us, Cecilia, *never* leave?'

If only he had said 'stay with me'!

But somehow even that could not matter at this

moment. It was so easy to look up into those eyes that had once frightened her and smile.

'Of course—I feel. . . I almost feel I have to.'

Something in him broke in that moment. He let himself understand his feelings. But he only understood at last what he had always expected; it had been inevitable, he had always known. Could he tell them to her?

'You *have* to stay!' It was not what he meant, but perhaps it was better that she did not realise.

Cecilia could have told him the truth in that moment. How he could not see it in her eyes, feel it where he held her, she never knew. Here, alone, she wanted him to know. Whether or not he could ever love her, she wanted him to know she loved him. She would never leave him—not while she could do him any good.

'I. . .' But she stopped, because she did not know what she was saying.

She felt his hand touch her cheek then, delicately, as if his fingertips were trying to read her meaning from the line of her bones, her lips and her shaded eyes. She felt herself pulled a little closer to him. She went unresistingly, so he moved, and she felt their bodies meet in a slow, expectant beating of her pulse through his. She could feel his breath against her cheek, smell the clean, sunburnt scent of his skin; she felt his hair, soft against her forehead. So she waited. Because she thought she knew what he was going to do.

Federigo did do it. Slowly, almost as if unsure of his welcome, he kissed first her hair, then the flush of her cheek. It was Cecilia's instinctive movement that brought his mouth to hers. Please kiss me, she prayed; if he did not kiss her now she knew he never would.

So often had she imagined what it would be like if he did that she almost did not realise that at last it had happened. Federigo really was here, holding her, his lips moving gently over hers, still unsure, still wary. There was so much to lose. . .

Cecilia heard her breath escape in a tiny, dazzled gasp, and it was all he needed. Slowly, rhythmically, but with sure purpose at last, Federigo began to kiss her, light kisses no longer, but deeper, more insistent until before she realised it her lips had parted and she was kissing him back. How anything could be so gentle and yet rock her so completely off her feet, she could not understand. . .but then, she could not think at all, nor did she want to. Helpless, fascinated by the liquid disintegration of her bones, Cecilia slid her arms about his neck, her fingers deep into his hair, and gave out the softest, most ecstatic breath as his arms tightened about her and she felt, building inside him, inside both of them, what she now knew they had denied themselves last night. She knew it absolutely. That both of them had wanted this—wanted each other—whatever the reason. Last night was gone forever, but by a miracle she had this little time now.

They neither of them heard Toro at first, even though he shouted. He had to shout again, twice, before the spell was broken, and even then it was almost, thought the groom, as if his master did not understand what he was saying.

Toro understood, though, exactly what was happening; he knew to speak slowly to make himself clear until Federigo had a chance to pull himself out of this trance of desire and attend to him. Any other servant might have smiled. Toro approved of what he was seeing, so he kept his silence and his face was mute.

'Repeat that, Toro.' Cecilia heard Federigo speaking as if from a long way off. His voice sounded indistinct, almost slurred; she curled closer against his side because she did not want this intimacy to be destroyed. He held her, Toro thought, almost defiantly, as if challenging Toro to have something so important to say that it would make him let her go. Toro was sorry, but he believed he had seen something.

'Look behind you, Altezza, the *castello* square. Look! Too many lights. And also down there, by the barracks. There is a fire, a bonfire. . .'

He said this last word as if it were particularly significant, thought Cecilia, still lost in a dream. Then she felt in the stiffening of every muscle in Federigo's body that it was significant. The dream was ended. Even as she drew herself reluctantly away he had taken her hand to hurry her back to the carriage. He had not even bothered to glance down at the city; he knew that Toro was right.

Bonfire, thought Cecilia; what on earth can a bonfire mean that is so urgent? Then she knew. The city was stirring. The uprising had begun. Too soon. If he could not stop this now it would destroy Federigo and he knew it. Without a thought for her bared feet Cecilia broke into a run beside him; ten seconds later the carriage was racing for the city gates. Somehow in the next ten minutes Federigo had to decide what to do. If it was not—she could barely stand to think of it—already far too late.

CHAPTER TEN

THE Austrian guard on the gate almost made the mistake
of forbidding the carriage to pass, then he saw it was the
Duke and waved them urgently through. Only the Prince
d'Aquilano could avert the conflagration now.

The barracks as they sped past were alive with activity;
the clamour of horses and armory was deafening. They
swung into the *castello* square to the sight of a crowd of
several hundred, many armed with rifles they had got
from the lord knew where, a sweating, hostile mass
beneath the acid flare of torches; facing the crowd with
Prince Massimo at their head was the *castello* garrison,
the fifty men the Governor had permitted Federigo to
retain. Their faces were impassive and they were, Cecilia
knew it, where Federigo's one chance lay. He had to
remind them that they could liberate the city with their
Duke but never without him; they were pledged to him
and not some surge of patriotic lunacy.

As the carriage reached the drawbridge Federigo saw
that against all his most explicit instructions it had been
raised. There was no time to get it lowered again before
the Austrians came. His only thought in that moment
was to keep Cecilia safe. Then he would find out who
had disobeyed his orders and raised the bridge, so
effectively cutting her off from the security of the *castello*
fortress.

'Toro, take the Lady Cecilia to the cathedral. Now!'

'No!' Cecilia would not stand to leave him now.

But Federigo had other things to contend with than
her stubbornness.

'You, Cecilia, will damned well do as you are told!'
Then, incredibly, he smiled. 'If only this once try to do

172

as I say!' Then he was gone and Toro was racing the
carriage the two hundred yards to the cathedral.

The groom could drive her there but he could not
make her go inside. No more could the Bishop, hovering
ineffectually on the steps, far more nervous than she
was. It was when she watched the old man huddling in
his cloak, murmuring that God must bring the rabble to
their senses, that she knew she really was not frightened.
She believed too much in Federigo for that. Toro knew
when he was beaten. But then, she could no more stop
his standing beside her with a loaded pistol. . .

Even from this distance the reek of the bonfires was
choking, smarting in her eyes, and the fervour of the
crowd contagious. And yet. . .and yet there was something wrong with it. How had this risen out of nowhere,
when only a few hours since she had seen these same
Italians at the opera house content to follow Federigo's
peaceful lead? And why tonight? Why, most of all, while
Federigo was out of the city? Everybody would have
known that he was gone. For all Massimo seemed to
have the *castello* guard in hand, he was little more than a
boy, after all, and his nerve not entirely to be trusted.

Even as she thought this she saw Massimo jump down
from his horse, gesticulating furiously, explaining something to Federigo. She saw Federigo nod, but she knew
he was not listening. He was waiting for the sound of the
Governor's men; he had until they came to disperse the
would-be rebels. After that. . .after that he would have
to decide which side he was on. And there was no choice
at all. If he could not quash this patriotic madness he
was finished.

Cecilia half held her breath, straining to hear what he
would do. What he did do took her breath away, it was
so daringly simple.

At the very moment that he was as much in danger
from the crowd as from the Austrians—he had only to
show he was not with them for them to move against

him and put Massimo in his place—he showed not the least sign of fear or that he even knew he had reason to be afraid of them. Quite calmly, almost casually, he stood back, using the steps of a small drinking fountain to give him height so the whole crowd might see him, and he raised a hand for silence. One hand. One man alone. And yet they were afraid enough of him to obey it. When he knew he had their attention he spoke.

'If each and every one of you leaves this square—now—I shall do nothing to find out who is the fool stupid enough to bring us right to the edge of destruction. He will remain a fool, of course, but a fool in private. He would do well to leave my city—not, I think, by the Tuscan gate, I shouldn't like the Governor to see him, but he may leave unhindered. If you do not clear the square I think you know that I will discover who the insurgent is, and he will be punished. By letting him goad you now you have destroyed everything I and my father—and *you*—have ever worked for. Unless you leave the square now we have no hope of freedom at all.'

Cecilia could just hear his words, and marvel at them, conversational, almost quiet, but deadly. But could he make them heed him?

It seemed that an infinity went by before the first heavily cloaked shape broke away from the outskirts of the crowd, then a second. Then three more. There were exclamations and grumbles, but not many, and never in the same voice twice. He had succeeded in doing the only thing that would disperse them: he had reminded them that he was by far more dangerous than the Austrians. Even so, a group of some twenty remained. Cecilia felt her heart twisting into her throat even as she realised to her relief that Federigo had kept them there deliberately. Then she saw him gesture to two of his soldiers. Instantly they jumped from their horses and—on his laconic instruction—began to fight. The crowd roared its approval and took passionate sides. Cecilia almost hugged Toro in her excitement. Federigo was an even shrewder strategist than she had expected.

Just as the sound of the approaching Austrian troops cut through the air, echoing off the high walls of the narrow city streets, Federigo leapt on to one of the vacated horses and rode forward at the crowd. As the Count von Regensberg rode into the square at the head of his men and waved them to a halt the first sound that met his ears was a shot fired into the air by Massimo, following Federigo's instructions.

Obedient to his every order, the crowd played their part and fell into theatrically startled silence.

'What is going on here?' Federigo demanded, quite as if he had not the least idea already.

Massimo, sounding really nervous, answered him quickly. 'A fight, Father. Lodovico Braccio and Stefano il Genovese. . .'

'Again?' Federigo's tone was quite awful.

As the Governor approached the sordid spectacle the two offending soldiers trotted meekly from the crowd, one with a bleeding ear and the other nursing two broken fingers. Both hung their heads in convincing shame.

'I believe I have had reason to speak to you before. My streets are not for brawling in. No more are they for the rest of you to disturb honest citizens from their sleep by encouraging these imbeciles with your vulgar howling. This is the last time I intend to witness such a disgraceful exhibition. Do I make myself absolutely clear?'

Everyone shuffled and nodded and muttered, 'Yes, Your Highness, of course, Your Highness,' and the other *castello* guards struggled to stifle their laughter.

Consequently everybody looked suitably chastened by the time the Governor enquired, 'Dear me, I had been led to expect violent insurrection! Are you telling me all that commotion was but a common mill?'

'It was over a lady, sir,' defended one of the putative miscreants.

'Some lady!' retorted the other, and they snarled at each other with a great deal of threat.

'Is that so? And you have had cause to speak to them about this before, Prince?'

Federigo's tone held just the right degree of embarrassed annoyance to be convincing. 'Frequently, I am ashamed to admit it.'

'I imagine you would be,' drawled the Count von Regensberg, and Cecilia knew in that moment that he had not been fooled at all.

But then, he was not supposed to be. Simply, neither he nor Federigo needed trouble, and they were entering into a sophisticated conspiracy to obscure the fact that there had ever been any real danger of it at all. She could see from the way the two men looked at one another that each was sardonically admiring of the other's tactics.

'Well, Prince, if you will allow me to suggest, a full twenty-four hours' sentry duty should see them properly repentant. What say you?'

'I had been thinking exactly that myself, Count.'

'And perhaps a personal apology to His Grace the Bishop for waking him so rudely from his slumbers.'

The miscreants sulked because it would not do to take their punishment too gracefully. Cecilia saw Federigo hiding a smile and silently applauded them; certainly if those two young men ever decided to make their livelihood upon the stage the very greatest actors in the world would do well to lay guard to their histrionic laurels. Almost as suddenly as it had begun the danger was over. The Count was bowing to Federigo, and Federigo bowing back. Massimo slapped one gaping peasant loudly about the ear to good effect and the Austrians were gone.

The moment they were out of earshot Federigo raised his hand.

'The first man to laugh really will do that sentry duty! Braccio, Genovese, take it that you have our heartfelt congratulations. We applaud you—silently! Now, if you would be so good, go home! And remember, the first one fool enough to repeat such lunatic behaviour answers to me, and I promise you he will not enjoy it.'

For all the crowd were laughing and patting each other on the back and gloating over their cleverness, his final words struck home. In a huddle that was almost wary, they broke up and departed. The drawbridge grated back into place and the *castello* guard made their way back to their quarters. Federigo remained looking down at Massimo, and said, 'It seems I have to thank you for your so prompt action, Massimo.'

It was the tone in which he said it that sent Prince Massimo storming across the square and out of sight in the wake of the last of his cronies, burning with an unforgiving rage. Federigo smiled after him. Federigo was beginning, he thought, to understand.

Shaking off the thought, he wheeled the borrowed horse around and trotted over to Cecilia on the cathedral steps. He dealt with the quailing Bishop in one single sentence.

'Your Grace must go indoors at once; you know how the night air does not agree with you—I promise you, the danger is past.'

Bobbing, nodding, still terrified, the old man scurried away. Federigo jumped down from the horse.

'Let Braccio have his mare back, Toro.' And the groom too was dismissed. He had to speak to Cecilia quite alone. But how to start it?

For a long while Cecilia looked up at him in silence, puzzling what it was she felt was wrong. Then she knew. As if the intimacy of the hillside had never been, he was beyond her reach again. The time for amusement, for the unimportant, for seeking the oblivion of mindless pleasure was over. . .and she had known, even so close to him, that that was all she could ever have been to him. Whatever it had felt—and it had felt so much more— she had known deep inside that it was only because she had come close to believing that she could love enough for both of them that she had let him kiss her at all. But she knew now that, however tempted he had been, his need for her had passed now; simply he had other things too urgent to waste his time on grieving for the past, and without that pain he had no need of her to try to obliterate it. If anything, now he would feel that she was in his way.

She was sure she was right the moment he spoke.

'You have to leave Aquila Romana, Cecilia. Go back to Siena.'

'No!'

He seemed to hesitate for a moment as if aware that his dismissal was too abrupt. 'Only until all this is over.'

It was his hesitation that found her her voice. He *must* care a little for her feelings to still be gentle with them now, when all he really wanted to do was find Sigismondo Vialli and get to the bottom of what had happened here tonight. With her voice she found her old resentment.

'Until what is over?' she demanded, almost indignantly. 'The real insurrection, and you have got yourself killed?'

He sounded tired then—and cold. 'Do I look like a man meaning suicide?'

He had some right to be angry with her in that moment; he had risked his life to fend off violence not ten minutes ago, and he would hardly go looking for it now.

Because, even now, Cecilia could not quite accept that their time together was gone, that his need for her was ended, she tried to laugh him out of this obdurate mood so that he would talk to her and tell her what he was really meaning.

'You did it very well. It was quite as good as any Drury Lane production.'

But Federigo was not to be deflected. He was too caught up with his own most immediate problems even to sense her bewilderment or her growing anger. If he was right Cecilia was in particular danger now. . .because she herself was the most particular danger to someone else. Or so whoever it was had raised the ill-assorted rebels tonight believed. Whoever that was had made a serious error. . .

Just because he was in love with Cecilia did not mean she would ever love him. Just because he would give anything to be able to ask her to marry him did not mean she would accept. He knew that she was his friend, that she had responded to him tonight as if she could let him be so much more than that; but she was just a child after all, and she had been in the dizzying grip of her first real evening of frivolous pleasure in years. Her life with the late Duke of Downside had been grim and lonely. She had responded because it had all been part of an illusion of freedom. That and, he knew, just a little from kindness, because she knew his life to be grim and lonely too and she was sorry for him. That was all. If he ever tried to fool himself she could love him he needed only remember Giulio Mansini. She had loved Giulio completely—he did not think he would ever forget the way she ran to the boy across the *castello* square, heedless of his pouring blood, heedless of death, of everything but her need to get to him. There was her grief for Giulio, too, behind what had passed between the two of them on the hillside tonight—just as much as he had been, Cecilia too had been reaching for oblivion. Only he had been running from the fact that he could never have her; not be loved by her, not the way he wanted it—needed it—as she had loved Giulio, with her whole being and without any doubts at all. That was what he wanted from her; nothing less would do. The mistake the man who was his enemy—who had brought him within an inch of defeat tonight—had made was that he had assumed where one loved so must the other, and thereby lay the danger to Cecilia.

Federigo knew the gossip. From the moment Cecilia had come to the *castello* he had heard it and been angered by it. They all assumed because he was a wealthy Prince and she impoverished and alone that she must want him, that she must be as dazzled by him as he was by her. They were wrong—but it was a mistake that could cost Cecilia her life. There was no doubt whatever that to whoever it was meant to destroy him any chance that he might marry and consolidate his family's hold on power would be the most immediate threat. He knew that for certain, because he now knew exactly who it was.

So he would have to make her go away. Only how to make such a stubborn, reckless girl obey him?

Then he knew. He must be angry with her, suspicious, no longer recognisable as her friend of yesterday. In the end it was perhaps best for both of them if she believed him; she would go away and he could—try to—forget her. It was most certainly best for her if she left tonight.

'By the way, Cecilia,' it came to him without thinking what he must say to anger her, 'Toro tells me that you killed a snake.'

From the moment he had heard about it he had wanted her to tell him. That had been when he had first realised her danger—as he should have done before when she had told him of the mysteriously opened window and he had known someone had been in her room that night without her waking. He had been waiting for her to tell him, only somehow, in the gentle pleasure of this evening, even her continuing distrust of him had ceased to matter.

Cecilia, as he had guessed she would, lied. She had to—she could not trouble him with such a petty matter now.

'Snake. Oh, that! Gulliver found it and brought it to me, if you would believe anything so foolish! Fortunately it was drugged with the heat and I was able to kill it.'

He had meant to feign his anger but when he heard her lying again, refusing to trust him, the wound was all too real. Icy, hurt, but sounding only contemptuous, he replied, 'No, I shall not believe anything so foolish. Because I am not quite so stupid as you think me! One day, Cecilia, perhaps you will be finished with your lying!'

He turned quickly to walk away from her before he saw the hurt inflicted; he knew it would hurt her and he knew himself in danger of relenting if he saw it. For her sake, her safety, he must not waver. She might not love him but she believed herself his friend—the fact that he so plainly rejected that friendship, distrusted it, would cut her deeply.

It did a great deal more than that. Cecilia could not believe it. It was so impossible to believe that she almost saw what he was really doing. Had her own welling up of pain and frustration not been so fierce in that moment she might have heard the voice in her head that told her, He wants you to go away because ʜe wants to protect you. All she thought now was, He wants you gone and he will do anything to make certain you leave. He does not want you here; your use to him is ended. Why he should have swung from that almost passionate declaration out there on the safety of the hillside of his need for her to stay, to this, a cold dismissal of everything she might have given him, she should have understood, but loss and misery were not emotions to make one rational.

He had expected her to fight, to argue. . .run after him and force him into saying things that were even more contemptuous and cruel. That she ran right past him, as if she could not bear to look at him, he could never have expected.

Simply she wanted to be away from him, hidden in

the safety of her rooms. She was shocked beyond defending herself because incredibly, even now, he could repeat
the same old charge that she did nothing but lie to him.
She had thought he had no longer cared if she did at all.
Now she knew he disdained it, and knew as well that
nothing she could do would make him believe her, or
understand why she had kept the truth about the viper
to herself. She had to get away because she knew that
for the first time his accusation was a just one. She had
not meant to tell him about it; she had not meant to ask
for his help. She really had acted as if she still did not
trust him.

Who was really at fault now mattered little. It was
only as she raced across the drawbridge and caught her
foot painfully on the uneven planking that she realised
she was still in her stockinged feet. At the very same
moment she noticed it Federigo remembered the satin
shoes still in his pocket, mocking, like some insulting
parody of the tale of Cinderella and her Prince. In a rage
of anger at her for believing what he needed her to
believe—that he ever could despise her—Federigo
hurled the shoes into the fountain where Giulio Mansini
had died. They disappeared silently beneath the icy
water.

To the Devil with all of it! He almost hated her in that
moment.

I almost hate him, thought Cecilia as she stood on
bleeding feet on the drawbridge. She was beginning to
be angry.

Rage, pain and loathing boiled over then, even before
she realised she was speaking. He was a long way off,
but she knew that he would hear her.

Defiant, 'I am going nowhere, Federigo, and not even
you can make me! And you know it! I, *I* have declared
the vendetta—you know that I must stay. For Giulio!'
Even as she spat the last word at him she almost
understood the agony it would inflict. Her instincts

understood enough that she almost wanted to hurt him to make her repeat it, more quietly, coldly, 'I stay because of Giulio, and the whole city knows it!' Only her shocked and whirling brain failed to see what she had done to him.

She saw him, rigid in the moonlight, felt his fury even from where she stood, and she was satisfied. Cecilia threw a look at him that was almost a mocking laugh— he was too far away to see that she was crying.

If it was possible to hate and love at the very same moment, both she and Federigo hated—and loved— now.

CHAPTER ELEVEN

'GULLIVER! Wicked dog!'

It was only as she shouted at him that Cecilia saw that
he was accompanied by two equally wicked children.
Perched on her bed, the comfits Signor Vialli and the
Count had given to her—and which Toro had found on
the seat of the carriage and handed to Arietta with the
severest instructions that the twins were not to open
them—Figi and Talia. . .and Gulliver. . .huddled
together in the face of wrath, the tell-tale signs of sugar
about mouth and whiskers.

Cecilia, precipitated within the frame of a single
second from absolute despair to justified parental fury,
inevitably felt her grip on her emotions slipping and
knew that if they did not leave the room at once they
would see her crying. And the twins must never see it—
how could anyone begin to explain? And yet not to
explain would mean more lying.

She might have known that all deception was useless.
Leaping to their feet, comfits spilling unheeded—except
by Gulliver—to the floor, the twins ran to her side and
threw their arms about her.

'Please don't cry!'

'What's the matter?'

Carefully, solicitously, they led her unresisting
towards the fire that had been lit for her return from the
opera and sat her on the gilded sofa. Talia found some
extra cushions for her back and Figi sat down beside
her, holding her hand and looking very serious.

'It is Papa's fault you are crying, isn't it?' she
demanded in a tone that boded ill for her absent parent.

Cecilia, because she had suddenly understood how

much more than Federigo she had to lose if ever she left this place, shook her head but had to tell the truth.

'A little.'

'Was he horrid to you?' Talia sounded as if she had already planned his painful punishment.

'No. . .no, not really. It was all the fighting in the square—the soldiers. I suppose it frightened me a little. . .'

Figi looked at Talia, and Talia at Figi. Such evasions would not be allowed to do.

'Pooh!' they chorused. 'As if you would ever be scared of anything. You even followed the ghost when *we* were frightened!'

It was a display of confidence as absurd as it was touching.

'Well, I was, just the same. Because your papa. . .' What was it she was saying? Could she not be more careful than to alarm the children by letting them know their father had been in danger?

'Papa would not be frightened either. Massimo was.' Neither sounded the least bit surprised or even ashamed of their step-brother. 'He told us we had to go to bed. But we heard them raise the drawbridge and knew there was going to be trouble, so we went up on to the battlements to watch. . .only Arietta fetched us down. . .'

'I don't like Arietta. She spoils things.'

Cecilia should have known it would take a good deal more than imminent war to upset these twins.

'Arietta was only doing what your father would have told her had he been here. And don't say "pooh" again, it isn't elegant.'

But they were not to be chastened.

'Did you quarrel with Papa?' She had not, after all, diverted their attention from her foolish tears.

'Because if you did Papa will be very unhappy. Won't he, Talia?'

'He wouldn't *cry*, of course. . .' Talia rushed to the defence of his masculinity '. . .but he would be miserable. We don't like it when you quarrel either. You might go away.'

They had come so close to the truth of how she was feeling—that, despite her defiance to his face, she would have to leave the *castello*—that Cecilia started and they knew at once. Silent with horror, Talia gripped her hand and Figi flung her arms about her neck and whispered, 'You're not to go! We'll tell Papa you're not to go and he won't let you!'

'What,' said Cecilia gently, putting an arm round each of the twins and holding them close, 'if it were Papa who wanted me to leave?' They were bound to discover what had passed in the square from someone; there was no hope at all that she and Federigo had been unobserved.

Figi shook her head in frantic denial and Talia cried, 'He never would! He would never want you to go! We asked him. . .if you were going to live with us for always and he asked us if we wanted you to and we said yes, and. . .'

'And he said he did too.'

Cecilia froze then, her heart stopped dead, her nerves suddenly alive to the most stupid hope. . .he had said that to the children, and he would never lie to them. He couldn't. They would know it the moment that he tried. If he had not lied. . .

'We asked if he liked you and he said he did, so he couldn't possibly want you to go away. . .'

Cecilia's heart began to stir again, erratically; she felt as if she were not able to breathe.

'So, you see, you can't leave us. We want you to stay *forever*. You, and Gulliver, and Signorina Piggy. Everything has been so lovely since you came. Please. . .'

'Please don't ever leave us!'

How had she ever allowed them to become so fond of her when she had always known that one day she must

go back to England and their father would find someone
else to be their mother? How was it that just the thought
of it—not just losing Federigo but the twins to someone
else—was so unbearable? It had been so inevitable that
she could not even say when she had come to love them
too. She did love them, with a fierce possessiveness that
almost frightened her. It was not even just because they
were his daughters and so very like him; Cecilia loved
the twins as if they were her children too. Now whatever
was she to do about that? Other than stay?

Their happiness counted above everything. Talia was
sobbing into her lap, so near to heartbroken as to make
no difference, and Figi was clinging to her as if she could
physically prevent her from leaving. She would never
go, not if it hurt them like this. She raged again against
Federigo's selfishness; just because he had no need of
her now he had quite overlooked that to the twins she
was their special friend. Well, she would not allow him
to forget it! If she was to leave, let *him* try to explain it
to them, and face, if he could, their near-hysterical tears.

'Don't *you* cry,' she gave their comfort back to them,
'I'm not going anywhere, I promise it!'

A promise she would keep if it was to kill her, as she
felt that staying near Federigo surely would.

It was a good few minutes before the twins eventually
started to believe her, dug around for their handker-
chiefs, remembered they were in their nightgowns and
were not carrying any, and looked about to wipe their
eyes on their sleeves.

Cecilia fetched two silk and lace squares of her own.
The way the twins took them from her, one would have
thought they were made of gold.

Talia blew her nose loudly. 'Will you come and sit
with us while we go to sleep?'

'Gulliver can come too.' Figi blew her nose still more
loudly.

'Very well. . .but I think you will find Gulliver is too busy finishing my comfits!'

Reminded of their crime, the twins flushed hotly.

'We didn't mean. . .'

'Only they smelt so lovely. . .'

'We only had *one*. . .'

'Well, *two*. . .'

'Perhaps three. . .'

'Each.'

'Are you very cross? They were your special present.'

Cecilia looked down at them, wondering if what she was feeling now was any different at all to what a mother felt, her throat dry and constricted, caring so much about them that it hurt.

'Did you enjoy them?'

The twins exchanged a look and decided to be honest.

'Oh, yes, they were wonderful!'

'In that case,' said Cecilia, taking one hand of each to lead them off to bed, 'I don't mind in the least that you had them. All I want is that next time you ask me first.'

'Next time. . .' Talia repeated the words ecstatically. Words like 'next time' meant Cecilia was really staying.

They took a very long time to clamber into bed, what with saying their prayers and being so excited and sleepy that they kept getting them wrong and having to start again. By the time God had been invoked to bless and watch over even Gulliver Cecilia decided it was time to call a halt. Blowing out their candles, she tucked them carefully back beneath the sheets and rescued ill-used pillows from the floor. Moonlight streamed into the room as she sat down to watch them.

'Goodnight. . .' murmured Talia vaguely.

'I love you. . .' whispered Figi.

'I do too.' Talia was not to be outdone.

Cecilia rose and bent to kiss them. 'And I love you too.'

Almost before she had said it they were fast asleep.

* * *

'*Madonna, madonna*! Come quickly. Oh, please, *please*
hurry!'

Cecilia woke to Arietta pounding on her door. The
sound woke Piggy too, and she hurried into Cecilia's
room to let the frantic nursemaid in.

'Now, now. . .don't take on so!' Piggy began, but
Arietta was quite hysterical.

'The twins. . .oh, please hurry!'

Cecilia needed no other warning. Spurred out of bed
by a terrible sense of foreboding, she ran without slippers
or candle into the passage and raced as fast as she could
for the twins' apartments. At the door she turned to the
stricken Arietta.

'Tell me, slowly, what is wrong. Then go at once for
their father.'

As it always did, the quiet command of her tone got
through to Arietta, calming her just enough for her to
speak.

'They are so sick, *madonna*! So terribly sick. . . I
cannot think what it is; they must have eaten something.'

'But what? Surely they have eaten nothing that the
rest of us. . .?' And then she stopped abruptly, for she
knew. 'My comfits!'

It was as if the very last drop of blood had drained
from Arietta's face. She looked almost as if she were no
longer alive, no longer beautiful.

Her voice came out harshly, almost ugly. 'No. . .that
is impossible! *No*! Nobody could ever have meant. . .'

Even as she realised what she was saying—and Cecilia
heard it and reached out to hold her back—Arietta fled.
Cecilia was left with her head spinning. . . 'Nobody
could ever have meant'. Those words she knew to be so
very important, but she had no time for them now.

'Piggy, Arietta is hysterical. I must go for His
Highness. Go to the twins; if anyone knows what to do
it is you, Piggy.'

She was running for Federigo's apartments even as

she was speaking. As she passed her own door something made her look in; Gulliver lay shaking and whimpering by the fire, unable to move. The empty box of comfits lay beside him and she knew that, unless Jemmy could come to help him, her dog was dying.

'You, there,' she rapped out at a footman disturbed by the noise and come to investigate the source of it, 'fetch my groom and Toro; bring them to my rooms—they will know what to do.'

'*Subito, madonna!*' But she was gone.

Cecilia burst in upon Federigo without hesitation. Whatever unresolved enmity lay between them, there was no place for it now.

'Federigo—come with me now!'

He was out of bed even before she had finished speaking. She could not even care that he was naked.

'Throw me my dressing-gown. And, Cecilia,' his hands gripped her shoulders for a moment, 'calm down.'

'The twins. . .!'

'I know.' And she could hear in his voice that he must already have heard her giving instructions to Piggy. 'But you must be calm. Come, gently, now.'

For the briefest moment, long enough for the blood to stop pounding in her head and the very real nausea of fear to begin to subside, he held her. She felt the still, steady beat of his heart beneath her cheek, the comforting warmth of his skin beneath her palms where she clung to him, burning through the fragility of her nightgown. Then he said, even more quietly, 'It was Vialli's comfits, wasn't it? They are what has made my children ill?'

Meant for her, of course, for Cecilia, and when she was calmer she would realise it. Federigo wanted there to be time to go on holding her, to keep her close by his side to be sure she was safe, but even as he was thinking it he was taking his dressing-gown from her shaking fingers. 'Come with me. . .it's well now, Cecilia; come.'

Anyone would think, she mused confusedly as she ran after him, that I really were their mother, the way he is talking to me. Then she understood—that all her feelings for them were written in horror on her face. He knows I love them. And he isn't even angry with me.

On that irrelevant thought Cecilia followed him into the twins' room. Federigo took one look at them, his face ashen, and sent the footman running for the *castello* physician.

'Do you know what it can be has made them sick?' Cecilia whispered.

'No,' and she heard at last the anxiety creeping into his voice, 'but I know that it is poison.'

Poison? What kind of poison? Meant to kill, or meant to frighten her away? Someone else other than Federigo does not want me here, she thought, but do they want rid of me enough to kill me? All she knew at this moment was that, if it had not been for Gulliver and his terrible greed in taking most of the comfits for himself, Atalanta and Iphigenia might be dead already. Even now she knew they would be more than lucky to survive.

The twins did survive, but only after four long days and nights of pain and fear as Cecilia, Piggy and the physician worked to save them. Cecilia had thought she was used to sickness after Waterloo, but nothing had prepared her for the ordeal of watching two such little children quite so terrified. Through it all Federigo drifted like a ghost, refusing to sleep, refusing to accept he could be no help at all beyond holding the twins close and whispering to them softly in the short periods when their pain would let anyone touch them at all. On the night the physician finally pronounced that the twins would live Cecilia forced Federigo from the room. He was exhausted and could not go on like this.

He went as he was guided, uncomplaining. Until they reached the door to his chambers and he said, as if she were not there, 'Until you came. . .everything was well, until you came.'

He meant he knew everything that had happened had happened because of her, that it was she under the greatest threat, and he would protect her. That was not how Cecilia heard it. Nothing he was ever going to be able to say could ever make her stay here now. Nor could she ever forgive him. What he had said was true, but he had no right to blame her for what had happened. Cecilia, absolutely silent, walked away.

The twins were sleeping peacefully, Figi with her pillows thrown carelessly to the floor as usual, Talia with her head completely buried in her blankets; Cecilia watched them through the shaded candle-light and wondered why it was she could not cry. She knew that she was going to have to leave them. She could not stay here—whatever she had promised the children—not now that she knew Federigo blamed her for everything. She had thought over and over about his words and was sure now that he had meant even more than he had actually said; he still believed that she knew more than she was telling about the death of Giulio Mansini, or why else should two attempts have been made, if not on her life, to frighten her into leaving? Yet how could he believe she had loved Giulio and still imagine she would keep her silence if she knew who had killed him? How could he imagine such cowardice at all? Such a betrayal, not only of Giulio now but of himself and the children too. How could he ever have believed she could be so selfish?

Not that it mattered really, not any more. Cecilia had never been so tired in all her life. She had been trying to read but could not concentrate; when she had picked up one of the children's muslins and started to mend the inevitable rips and tears she had found her hands were shaking so much that all she was doing was pricking herself and drawing blood. It was an exhaustion such as she had never believed possible; she was completely numb. So she really did not care what Federigo had meant, who it was had tried so determinedly to harm her, or even that tomorrow she must leave the *castello* forever. It was almost as if she had never cared at all. She was not sad: she felt nothing; it was, while it lasted, the greatest imaginable relief.

Federigo watched the fire dying in the grate and felt the cool stone walls of his bedchamber begin to give off the ice chill of dawn. He had stood here all night and still he had got nowhere. He knew what he had done wrong, he knew that he had hurt Cecilia, he knew this final damage to their friendship to be irreparable. But he could not accept it, he could not accept that there was nothing he could do. It had to be possible to save it. If only he knew how.

Just as the first shards of morning light seeped through the cracks of the old wooden shutters he made up his mind. The only thing he could do was tell Cecilia the truth. All of it. That he loved her and that he wanted her to stay, nothing else counted for him but that. It would anger her, almost certainly disgust her, and he would lose her, but at least she would understand everything he had done. She would leave Aquila Romana, but perhaps as she went she would at last begin to forgive him. Before he could lose his resolve he left the room and ran for the stairs leading to the twins' apartments.

'May I come in?'

Cecilia looked up from where she had been half asleep over her sewing, and her heart stood still. Even as it did so, and she felt the chilling flood of anger and betrayal curling through her veins again, she recognised that it was almost as if she felt it from a distance, as if it were happening to someone else. She was tired to the point that she had no real feelings at all. She looked at Federigo, knowing that he hated her and that she would always love him, and it could not matter—her whole being was dead. All she was aware of in that moment was how tired he looked, and how terrible these past few days had been for him. Setting her work aside, she shook her head quickly for him to be as quiet as possible and rose to lead the way into the nursery beyond. Federigo hesitated, wanting to see his daughters but afraid to disturb them; Cecilia found she had smiled.

'A minute, then, but as quiet as you can; they must sleep.'

Federigo could hardly believe she could be so kind to him after all he had done—he understood, though; she knew how afraid he had been that he would lose the twins, afraid enough that, now they were mended again, he could almost not see enough of them to satisfy himself that they really were quite safe. But then, Cecilia had always seemed to be able to do this, set aside her own feelings for the sake of other people's. It was one of the reasons he had fallen so completely in love with her. Federigo found the tiny wooden elephant that was Talia's favourite toy lost among the bottles and potions the physician had ordered, and tucked the battered creature under the sheets to where he guessed Talia's nose would be. Then he rescued Figi's pillows, knowing that within a second of his putting them back on the bed she would fling them to the floor again. Then he kissed her cheek, and what could be seen of Talia's head, and turned to follow Cecilia into the nursery. Had Cecilia only known it, it was the normality of such a scene that hurt him the most. Perfect domesticity, such as he and the twins had never known. Only tomorrow Cecilia was going to leave them.

It was hard for him to know where to begin—almost he did not want to when he saw in the early light of the nursery windows her drawn, drained face and the way every movement of hers seemed automatic in her exhaustion.

'You should go to bed, Cecilia.'

Cecilia had not known what she expected him to say, other than to tell her that he had made arrangements for her to leave later that morning, and the gentleness of his words surprised her.

'I shall, as soon as Arietta comes to take my place with the twins. . .'

The fact that it *was* her place, that she had felt all the time she had watched over them that it was for her to keep them safe, it was she they wanted—it was her name they had called when they were frightened—almost had the power to hurt then. Certainly a faint frown of pain touched her brow, and Federigo saw it.

'I don't think I shall ever be able to thank you for what you have done.' Surely she would at least accept his gratitude, if nothing more?

Cecilia knew that she had done little to deserve it, so she said, 'I have done nothing. . .your own physician, Piggy. . .'

And Federigo began to feel angry. 'Can you not even accept my thanks, Cecilia? Have we become so far estranged as that?'

Estranged? It was the oddest word, thought Cecilia, and yet it was true. The gulf between them now was too wide ever to be crossed, and both would want to have to bridge it, not just one of them. Both would have to love equally to heal a rift as final as this was. Because she could not think what to say, could not deny it, she shook her head, careful to turn away from him, to go to the window and look out into the softness of the early sun above the rose gardens. She saw nothing through the blinding sting of tears.

Federigo thought he understood that gesture—that he was being dismissed. It was his helplessness to fight the fact she could not care enough even to listen to him that made him so angry now. She must not turn away until he had finished what he had come to say. Even before

she knew he had moved, he was beside her, eyes fixed
on the sun rising above the far hills, too close—she could
hear, almost feel his taut, jagged breathing; certainly she
could feel every wave of tension that ran through him.
She noticed that where his hand rested on the casement
the knuckles were rigid and white. She knew he was
angry with her again. But why now? Why waste anger
on someone already despised?

His voice was as remote as the hills beyond, almost
cold in his efforts to steady it.

'So you don't forgive me? You know I didn't mean
anything by those foolish words I said; you know it and
you still don't forgive it.'

He had accused her all along of lying to him. So, even
though it spelt the end of everything, she found herself
telling the truth.

'No. . . I don't know why, but I can't forgive it.'

She saw his smile then, the cynical, hurtful smile she
had first seen and that had frightened her; it seemed so
long ago now but it was little above a week. He believed
her now.

He turned to her then and she could see his eyes, the
coldness of the laughter in them; he was laughing at
himself.

'I deserved that, I suppose. The truth at last! Thank
you at least for that, Cecilia *mia*!'

There was something more to his tone than his
habitual irony. There was a bitterness she could not
begin to understand. It made her flare back, 'I have
always told you the truth. You demanded it. You cannot
blame me now if you don't like it!'

Almost, she thought, the laugh that came into his eyes
now was a real laugh, there was true humour, appreci-
ation in the burning darkness before his eyes shaded
beneath those heavy lashes and he shut her out.

'I wonder if you like the truth any better than I do.'

Again his words were bitter and spoken almost to himself.

Cecilia felt suddenly too tired to bear this any longer. Too tired to maintain her protective shell of numbness; if he did not leave soon she knew that she was going to cry and she would die rather than let him see he could hurt her any more. Struggling to keep her voice even, she answered, 'This is getting us nowhere, sir. Please say what it is you came to say and then leave. I am very tired. . .' Tell me what arrangements you have made for me to leave and then go! she thought. Why must he drag this out when he knew how badly it must hurt her?

She was almost sure now that he did know—that he had read what she had written about him to Lord Byron. Nothing else would explain the strange interlude on the hillside above the city the night of the opera when he had almost taken advantage of her feelings to salve his own hurt. Nothing but his knowing how much she loved him could explain how close he had come to forcing her to show it. But back in the real world it was an inconvenience. . .what else to explain his abrupt dismissal of her in the *castello* square, when he had had no more time for games, however quaintly amusing her helpless devotion might be, and wanted her out of his way, no longer his responsibility? He must have seen her letter. . .so why hurt her any more now?

For a long minute Federigo wondered if there was any point in going on at all; in the colourlessness of her voice there was only dismissal. If he spoke now there could only be rejection. But if he did not speak. . .by this afternoon she would be gone from Aquila Romana and his chance would be lost. Not his chance to win her, of course—he had never had any hope of that. Just his chance to honour their friendship with the truth. Only— he was almost as tired as she was.

'I came to say that I don't want you to leave.' It was

nothing less than the truth, but after all that had happened it sounded so very stupid.

He expected her to laugh. Instead he saw the very last of the blood drain from her face and her eyes close against any more of this. She did not believe him; she had had enough.

It was the fact that she could ever have really believed he would have turned against her so savagely in the square that gave him the anger to fight for the little that could be salvaged. Cecilia saw his fingers tense against the casement again and felt the rage behind that unconscious gesture. Felt too the first of her own tears and turned away to lean against the furthest window-frame, looking out, away from him; the smell from the roses below was overpowering and a little sickly. All she wanted was for him to stop whatever he was doing to her and go away.

She knew that he was watching her, so she kept her eyes closed to fend off the words as he said, 'It was for your own safety that I wanted you to go, Cecilia—can't you see that? You must see that now, after what has happened to the twins. I needed you away from here. . . I needed to be sure that you were safe.'

It was her tired, cynical smile that broke him. Before she knew what was happening Federigo had pulled her upright by the shoulders, roughly, almost as if he could shake the numbness out of her—if she would only be angry with him it would be better than this.

Cecilia was, suddenly—very angry.

'You said all the things you did say and then you expect me to believe you, that you were concerned only for my safety? Now who is it will not tell the truth?'

Federigo's fingers tensed painfully against her shoulders. 'Who is it will not recognise the truth when they hear it? It's you who has never trusted me, Cecilia! Anyone less stupidly obstinate would have the sense to see that I'm not lying now. Why should I bother?'

There was that, certainly, thought Cecilia, spinning between the confusion of her numbness and her growing anger—why bother?

'Perhaps it is just a habit with you.' The bitterness of her own voice shocked her. 'How am I to say when I don't really know you at all?'

Of all the things she could have said to hurt, she had said it now, and almost she knew it. It had taken a very particular kind of courage for him to confide in her as he had done over the past few days; to throw that back at him was the cruellest thing she could ever have done.

Federigo reacted as if she had struck him. Almost as if he might strike her.

'Do not know me? No, that is going too far even for you, *madonna*! And you know it! You know that you know me better than anyone has ever done—you *know* it—it is you who is the one who has secrets, Cecilia *mia*, who won't even admit to loving Giulio Mansini. You believe he deserved that of you, to have loved you so desperately only for you to deny him?'

Cecilia had to get away from him now. He could not mean what he said; even now he must be playing some cruel game, because he must have seen her letter to Byron and know that it was not Giulio she loved. She caught at his wrist to pull his hands away from her. She might just as well have tried to snap a bar of iron.

'Oh, no, Cecilia. You are going to listen! You hate the truth, don't you? I think it almost frightens you. Giulio frightened you. What were you afraid of, *madonna mia*, what is so very frightening about being loved?'

But I never have been loved! Cecilia wanted to shout it back at him but he would not listen. She had never been granted the opportunity to discover whether being loved in return was frightening. But to love as she did, alone, unwanted, and faced with such bitter contempt, almost hatred—that was the very worst mockery of love in the world. She had to make him let go of her.

'Let go of me, Federigo!' Her voice was almost purring with threat. She was afraid of him, of what he might make her say, and in her fear she was dangerously angry.

'Oh, no. And don't think you can make me, Cecilia—you know you can't. You are going to hear me out. Why does it make you so afraid that I want you to stay? You tried to run from me from the very beginning. Why, Cecilia? Why don't you like it when I tell you I *need* you to stay?'

He could break her if he went on like this, she knew it; she could feel, as if it was a compulsion she could not fight, the need to shout the truth back at him—because I love you even though you hate me. Anger spilled over into helpless tears and she tried again to force his hands away.

'Stop lying, Federigo! Stop putting the blame for what has happened to us on me! You wanted me to go, you. . .'

What had happened? Why was he suddenly so still? Cecilia stood absolutely motionless, her tears unheeded—almost she had stopped breathing.

Federigo was watching her so closely that it was as if he could see into her very soul. Just for a moment he almost wondered if he could. Just for a moment. . .but that was impossible!

He acted on it just the same. His hands came quickly to her face, fingers catching into her hair so she could not turn away from him. There was more than distrust of him here.

She had never heard his voice like this before, so very soft yet so utterly compelling. 'No. . . I never *wanted* you to leave, except for your sake. And I think you *do* know it. I have always wanted you to stay. I want you to marry me.'

Cecilia did not even hear him say it at first, because he could not possibly have done so. Then she knew that he had said it; Federigo was saying that he wanted to marry her—she felt then as if she had just gone mad. It was impossible—she half believed him—she wanted to believe it. . . he must not mean it; why should he want her?

She had never understood just how much her eyes mirrored every last shadow of her thoughts. Federigo watched, the intensity of his own eyes burning against her own, looking for what he needed to see, her expected anger, her horrified rejection—because she loved Giulio and he had spoken far too soon—but he was looking for something else too, that infinitesimal pause before she rejected him that might mean that, one day, he might have a chance.

He saw it.

Cecilia sensed something in him then that she was never going to understand, an excitement, almost an elation; against her cheek she felt his pulse quicken, she heard his breath silenced as if he might never breathe again, then it came, harsh suddenly, electrifying. But why?

Then she understood. In her stunned silence he had verified the truth, he knew that what he had read in Byron's letter was what she felt, he knew how much she loved hm. He believed that all he had to do was fight her anger and her hurt and she would be his. She knew why he wanted her too.

Whatever was happening here in Aquila Romana, it was out of hand; it was getting far too dangerous. *She* was getting far too dangerous. But if he married her he could buy her silence.

Federigo saw only her hesitation. He saw the first, fragile reason to hope. Even as she stood as if unaware even of the tears pouring down her face his arms came about her more gently and he was leaning closer, as if he could not control his voice enough for her to hear its urgent whisper.

'I know I should not have spoken yet. I know you have no thought for anyone but Giulio. But I couldn't let you go. . . I *can't* let you go! You have a home here,

Cecilia, and while the world was shut out of it you were happy, I know you were. I was happy. I know you don't care for me; I'm not asking for that, I am not even asking you for an answer. . .not now.' Then he knew that he was asking, that he had to know; he almost laughed at himself. 'No, that's a lie, Cecilia. I do want to know. I want you to marry me and I want you to say yes, now!'

So sure of her that he could even laugh—no wonder he was excited, when he was so close to trapping her completely where she could be no threat to him at all! As his wife she could not hurt him; anything she knew about Giulio's death could no longer be used against him. As his wife she could only hurt herself if she ever told the dangerous truths he believed she knew. What was it he believed? That because she had been fool enough to love him she would accept him whatever he had done, and however much he would not trust her or she could not trust him? Did he think, as the whole city thought, that he could buy her silence—from impoverished, unmarriageable spinster to Duchess of Aquila Romana in one night, and whoever it was he was protecting would be safe forever?

Cecilia had been almost certain when she had handed him the silver button in the Mansini Garden that he knew who it was behind the plots against him, who had killed Giulio, and who had tried to kill her. Did he believe she had recognised the crest on that button? Did he still believe Giulio had said more than she had admitted before he died? Did he believe that she was lying—was it Federigo all along behind the death of the poet Mansini? And did he really think he could marry her into silence if she knew it?

Obviously he did, or why marry her at all? How convincing he was—he could almost have meant it that he wanted her to stay, that he needed her, that he could not bear to lose what they had found together. It would be so easy to believe it—if she did not know for sure he was lying. For it to be true he would have to love her. And who knew better than she did that he loved only Parisina Mansini?

So who was it he was protecting now? Himself? It had been Sigismondo Vialli who had given her the comfits. Would he protect even Vialli after what had happened to the children?

Even as she felt certain that he never would, she knew that he might have to—there was more at stake than the safety even of his family; there was the whole future of Aquila Romana. And the twins had not been meant to eat the comfits. She had.

So that was it. They had failed to frighten her away, they had failed even in an attempt to kill her—only somehow she could never really believe this; it was too impossible, too frightening; one more mysterious incident involving her might cause comment, investigation by the Governor. But marry her into silence. . .a small price to pay for the city that he loved.

Why even now, when she knew how much he despised her, could she look into those molten eyes and still want to believe that he had spoken nothing but the truth?

She had been silent too long. Federigo knew what was wrong.

'I'm sorry, *carina*. Sorry about Giulio. Sorry that it is I and not he asking you to marry him. I *do* know. But Giulio is gone, and we could be happy—you know we could, Cecilia.'

And at last something in Cecilia snapped. He talked of happiness and Giulio Mansini, he dared to pretend that what he felt for her was as that boy had done! Pretend it because he had to be sure of her silence; marry her to imprison her where she could never do Aquila Romana any more harm.

Her voice was so cold that she barely recognised it. Cold and final.

'You dare to even speak Giulio's name! Dare to ask me to marry you, after all you have said and done! You imagine that I should *want* you!' She was hurt, and hurt had the bitterest of tongues.

'Cecilia——'

'No, it is you who will listen to me, Federigo. And understand that I would not marry you were you the last man on this earth! I would not marry you if you could prove every day for the rest of our lives that you loved me, or even cared for my friendship even a little!' She had stopped crying now. Everything she had ever had to cry about was over. 'What is it you think I saw, Federigo? What is it you think I heard? What do you think I know? What is it makes me so dangerous to you that the only way to silence me is to marry me even when you hate me so badly?'

Federigo believed he had thought of everything, every possible reaction she might have to his proposal. But not this. How could he ever have thought of this? How could *she* have ever thought it? He was almost too appalled to be angry.

Had he been angry with her, had he denied it, shouted back at her, anything but this frozen silence, Cecilia might almost have begun to believe him. She might have given him a chance. But in his silence she knew that she had spoken the truth. He was not even going to deny it.

'I am going to bed now,' she said, almost easily. 'When I wake up I shall leave the *castello*. But not the city, Federigo. You will never make me leave Aquila Romana until I know the truth about what happened to Giulio. Only then will I go back to England. I shall return to the hotel later. *You* explain to the twins why I have gone—you will think of a lie so much better than I could ever do!'

He was still holding her, though the hands that gripped her shoulders now might as well have been stone. There was no feeling in them at all. And now, as he seemed to notice them, he let her go.

He had always known really that he could never have her. But he had never realised she hated him as much as this. The last man on earth, she had said, and she had meant it.

There was nothing to fight for any more, so it was almost easy to be civil.

'Not the hotel. I shall arrange for you to stay with His Grace the Bishop.'

'No!'

Of all the things she had done, it was her obstinacy in this one small matter that enraged him completely.

'You forget your position here, Cecilia! You forget who it is owns this town! You are a guest here, and you will remember that—and just this once you will do exactly as I say!'

Cecilia had to fight him—the part of her brain that was working knew exactly how such a move would be interpreted.

'I cannot go to His Grace, because people will say it is because we are to be married and I can no longer remain under your roof because of it.'

Federigo flung her away from him as he turned to leave the room.

'Us? Married? Why should anyone believe such a foolish thing? When I am the very last man on earth?'

Cecilia sat abruptly on the window-seat where he had thrust her. The only man on earth she had ever wanted, ever loved—she would always love him! All she needed to have done was keep her silence and she could have had him. But not on those terms. Not the way he had meant it. Better never to see Federigo again than to wake each morning beside him, knowing how badly he wished she were someone else. He had been willing to sacrifice his own future in marriage to her to protect Aquila Romana. Well, she had nothing to protect but herself, and the agony of watching his indifference and frustration grow with each passing day would be too great. She had done the right thing. She had thrown away everything she had ever wanted, but it was—it had to be—the right thing.

CHAPTER TWELVE

CECILIA was so exhausted by all that had happened that she slept right through that day and into the night, Piggy standing guard over her as if she would most certainly murder anyone with the least intention of disturbing her precious charge. When Federigo sent word that he needed to speak with Cecilia about her move to the Bishop's Palace the footman was sent away so briskly that he felt that his feet had barely paused on Cecilia's threshold; not even His Highness the Duke needed think he was getting past Piggy.

Eventually, as the moon rose high above the city and she began to yawn, the old nurse decided that her charge could safely be left alone. She had not stirred throughout the whole day and Piggy was not even the smallest bit surprised. She had not meant to overhear Cecilia's final quarrel with His Highness—it had just happened that she had come to the twins' apartments just at that moment to take over from Cecilia in nursing them; she had heard it all. She had even, for a moment, thought of hurrying after the Prince and telling him not to listen to Cecilia's foolishness, telling him that only hurt and exhaustion would ever make Cecilia deny her love for him, but she had known even as she had begun to follow where he had stormed down the stairs that she must not do it. Nothing could be done by anyone now, except Cecilia and Federigo themselves. But that would not stop Piggy lecturing Cecilia on her stupidity until her head rattled the moment the child was wakened enough to heed her! So thinking, Piggy kissed Cecilia gently on the cheek and, taking the candle with her, sought out her own much-needed slumbers. Within a minute of her head's touching the pillow Piggy was lost to the world completely.

Federigo was tired, and frustrated that he had not been able to speak with Cecilia. He knew that she would not want to see him—that she intended to leave without speaking to him again. But he had things he must say to her, if it was only to tell her what she must tell the twins about their illness.

Even while he made his way through the darkness to her chambers he knew that this was but an excuse; he *had* to see her—and see her now, while she was completely off her guard. Simply he could not let her go—however angry he was, however deeply her contemptuous rejection had hurt him, he would never let her go without trying one last time. His need for her was stronger than any pride.

He knew his way about the *castello* without light, and he could not risk being seen as he approached her door. Piggy had not thought to lock it—why should she? But the very first thing he did was to turn the key in the door between Cecilia's room and her nurse's.

Cecilia heard the faintest sound; someone was there, but it would only be Piggy. She was not even really awake. She felt the drift of moonlight against her eyelids from the open window just as she had been but vaguely aware of the sunlight of day. She wanted to sleep. The way she felt at the moment she never wanted to be conscious again.

There was someone there—she knew it now. Why she knew, she could not say, only that it was almost as if she could hear the effort it was costing the intruder to control his breathing so she would not hear him. In one abrupt, icy flash of fear Cecilia woke completely and sat up, reaching out for her tinder-box and candle. They were not there. Even as she realised Piggy must have taken them her eyes adjusted to the light and she saw him, just a shadow against the door to Piggy's room. She was more afraid then than she had ever been in her life, but more than anything she was angry.

Federigo saw her move, saw the quick, instinctive dart of her hand towards a small box she kept on the chest beside her bed; just in time he guessed what she was doing. He was across the room, one hand trapping hers, the other hard against her mouth to stop her calling out and waking Piggy. She struggled and fought like a cornered cat, but she had no chance against him. Even as she began to recognise who it was he wrested her father's pistol from her fingers.

Incredibly, even as he snatched his hand away from a particularly vicious bite, he was laughing at her. This was Cecilia as he had first seen her, too brave to pay heed to her terrors. She really would have killed him.

'Be quiet, you little fool—it's only me!'

Confused, still a little fogged with sleep, Cecilia reacted explosively. 'Good! I hope I hurt you!'

'You did.' He smiled ruefully down at his palm. 'I even think you would have shot me!'

'I would!'

'Even knowing who it was?' He was laughing again— she could hear it through his ragged breathing.

Cecilia jerked her wrist from his grasp and rubbed it furiously. 'Especially had I known!' She spat it back at him. 'Now get out of my room, Federigo! How dared you come here?'

He could see little of her in this light but the pallor of her skin, the soft oval of her face and the iciness of her shoulders where her nightgown had slipped aside; that and the hot glitter of her eyes, flashing with uninhibited anger. He had never seen her more beautiful.

'*Udolpho* again. . .listen to yourself, Cecilia *mia*—you sound like the most foolish of novels!'

Cecilia heard the mockery—heard the excitement behind it—and could have scratched his eyes out. To behave as he was now, after all he had done. . .

'And you behave *exactly* like a very bad melodrama!'

'Like the very worst of villains?'

Had she been even a little less angry she would have heard the challenge in his voice then. She should have felt it; she could certainly feel the tension of him even as he gripped her wrist again, in the erratic pulse beating through his fingers and his tightening muscles. Even as she failed to recognise it, she responded to it. Somewhere inside, almost fuelled by her rage at him, Cecilia felt the beginnings of the same excitement. She began to understand it.

Even so—half knowing what might happen—she challenged him back. 'The worst!'

And she knew by his laugh that he had accepted it. Anything that had gone before was irrelevant now. She saw his smile, almost insolent in its pleasure at his ability to goad her, that he knew what he was doing—what he could do—and Cecilia felt her throat go dry and her own heart beating deafeningly against her temples.

'I haven't behaved anywhere near badly enough for such an insult, Cecilia. . .but I think I'm going to.'

She understood.

'If you touch me ever again. . .!'

'Still the fluttering little heroine, *carina*!' Even as he said it, he silenced them both with the softest of kisses.

It had been born out of the darkness, the strangeness of their situation, his fascination with her beauty and her courage, but even as his lips met hers and he felt her twist helplessly away, not from him but from her own treacherous response to him, he knew that it had always been more than that. He knew why he had really come to her. Cecilia felt his hands slide about her waist, she felt the heat flood into her sensitised skin where they touched, and knew he felt it too. She felt the rush of quickened blood to her cheeks, catching her breath away; she knew he heard it; she knew he could feel the spiralling heat of desire erupting inside her. It was exactly that, like the inexorable gathering surge of lava, boiling to the surface. She felt him run the backs of his fingers along her throat, following the path of her blushes, and felt him laugh again. All the time he was barely holding her—he knew he did not have to more tightly—and his lips never left hers; he knew she did not want them to. Cecilia too knew why he had come.

She had to fight him—she had to fight now or he would know everything. She hated him, didn't she? She could never forgive him for all that had happened, she knew she couldn't! Federigo's fingers curled coaxingly about her neck and all her loathing of him dissolved in the tenderness of it.

But she must fight. 'Don't!'

But when she tried to turn her head away she had no strength to do it; it was as if all her muscles had melted into water.

'Don't what?'

She felt him smile against her cheek. She could almost believe then that she meant something to him. She knew without a doubt how much he wanted her. And she could so easily let him have her.

Her voice sounded almost pettish in its weakness. 'Don't do that. . .stop. . .!'

'Very well,' his tone was all husky innocence, 'I shall do this instead.'

'No!' It was a cry shocked from her, every last breath torn away and with it her resistance; with a gentleness that was so much more seductive than urgency Federigo's hand had slipped to cup her breast; she could feel the pulse of it quickening as he felt her own stunned response. All he did was hold her like that, no more, and she knew there was nothing she could do to stop him now.

'No!' She tried one last time.

'Quietly, Cecilia. . .do you want to wake Piggy? Do you want her to send me away?'

She could almost not bear it—no more could she

believe it. Just the barest caress of his hand, and he had
won the truth from her.

'*Yes*!'

Just a laugh, and the most languid, the most sensual
of smiles—she could never fight it.

'No. . .!'

'No!' he echoed with the barest ghost of a laugh. But
he did not want to talk. How could she ever know what
was happening to him now, that she was almost frightening him? He felt the ardent swelling of her breast into
his palm and it was almost too much for him to bear it.
She was too much. Certainly she was more than he had
ever known. All hate and anger were lost in a feeling
that came close to wonderment. Almost he convinced
himself that he must let her go. Almost. . .

He could not fight this, even though his conscience
knew he had to. He felt the unmistakable innocence of
her helpless response to him and knew he should never
abuse it. But he couldn't let her go.

Cecilia watched him, almost too dazed to be puzzled
by his sudden hesitation. Almost it frightened her. Was
he thinking of Parisina—had he remembered whom he
really loved? She could not bear to lose him now,
whatever the truth of that; he could love whom he liked,
so long as now—just this once—he was hers. In the
silence their eyes met, and she knew they said the same
things.

She felt his other hand at her neck still, gently stroking
aside her hair at the nape of it; she felt her spine dissolve
just at the slightest brushing of his skin against hers. She
felt so drugged by him that she could barely keep her
eyes open. He saw it and smiled. Then he lifted his hand
and rested one finger gently against her lips. Cecilia felt
the tenderness of it and swayed against him. This time it
was she who kissed him.

She felt his surprise, then his pleasure, all in the brief
second while she was still able to think at all. Even as

she knew it and exulted at it, her last consciousness was swept away; Federigo was kissing her again and with such a hunger that it was as if he needed her in order to live. Cecilia's arms curled about his neck and he caught her hard against him. She heard him murmur something, but she did not understand it. Her fingers twisted into his hair as if she would never let him go.

There was one more moment when he felt, I must not do this. One half-second when she thought, I must not let him. Then she thought, distantly, This is all I shall ever have, and I *will* have it! She shuddered as the intensity of her need swept through her—or was it through him?—and all hesitation was ended. She was but vaguely aware of the icy silk of the counterpane beneath her shoulders—of his brushing aside the fragile lawn nightgown, of her shaking fingers urgently tugging away his shirt. Aware of nothing else but him.

Please don't stop, she thought, for one second terrified it was only a dream.

As if they were one mind, he understood her. 'It's real. I'm here!'

'Don't leave. . .don't stop!'

Federigo didn't.

How had it happened—why? Cecilia lay in the silence of the moonlight, hardly daring to move lest she wake completely and find that he was gone, that he had never been here. While she remained asleep, held close in his arms, knowing only the scent of him, the feel of him, it was all true. So long as she kept her eyes shut and felt only where her limbs were entangled with his, the taut youthfulness of his body against her own, the softness of his hair, she could keep him. He was not really hers and she was going to have to be grown-up enough to accept it when morning came; but for what he had given her tonight—for what no one could ever take away—she would pay any price. He was here now; it was enough.

She felt him stir then, and thought again, Just for now he is mine. And he is going to know it. She had only instinct and love to guide her, but as he half woke to the soft breeze hushing through the windows Cecilia began to make love to him. Whatever happened, he would never forget it—that just this once he had belonged to her completely.

Dawn came softly, almost imperceptibly, heralding the full heat of another summer day, Cecilia could smell the promise of it on the breeze now stroking the curls back from her forehead.

She opened her eyes. It was not the breeze at all. Federigo. He had stayed with her!

He seemed to understand this too—as if they were not yet separate, as if they remained one being.

'Did you think I would be gone?'

There was something in the teasing behind his smile that made it impossible to answer him; something so infinitely tender in the rhythmic caressing of his hand that she could only gaze at him, her every emotion as naked to him as her body.

Federigo watched her, hoping for the impossible; he could not see it. He had wanted her to open her eyes warm with love for him—something that meant he could keep her. Something hovered in those uniquely blue depths, but it was not love. How could it be?

But to the Devil with Giulio for now—until he left this bed she was his!

Why is he looking at me like that? thought Cecilia. It was as if his eyes were meaning to burn her like a brand, mark her, stamp his ownership. Could he not see she had been his from the very beginning? She lifted her still-drugged hand to his cheek but was too languid to reach it; instead her fingers caught at his wrist and seemed to pull it away from her cheek. He withdrew his touch at once.

That had been too much, of course; to look at her like this was too intimate a thing, too possessive, to caress her back to wakefulness and love her so openly—of course she must reject it. Cecilia saw the almost ironic twist to these lips that had brought her unimagined pleasure and understood it; she saw the pale strands of her own gold hair slip from his fingers and knew that he was seeing Parisina's. But until he rose and left her it did not matter. Her fingers closed over his own where they rested now against her breast, seeking comfort. Federigo understood that too. He knew now that she believed at last that he loved her; in the reassurance of that regretful touch he knew that she was sorry he could not have her.

These things happened—two people, lonely, utterly confused by all the hurt they had inflicted on each other, desperately needing to be friends, even more desperate to forget grief and murdered love—they would not be the first to meet in bed because of it. But it should not have happened to them; he could not bear that—it had to be something more.

'Cecilia. . .'

But she could not listen. She wanted no explanation, only the serenity of this warmth between them. If he explained, her dreams would be gone forever; if he said why he had really come to her she would have nothing left. While he was silent she had this one memory. Gently she rested her fingers against his lips to stay him. Federigo felt the silencing touch and knew that it was hopeless. She would know, of course, that he wanted to tell her he loved her. . .that he *had* to keep her and that none of the cruel and bitter things they had said and done to each other counted for anything any more, or ever really had. She was not going to let him. Even as he felt the savage kick of despair inside him, he knew that she was being kind. He was almost grateful for it.

Even so, he said again, 'Cecilia. . .'

Dear God, don't let him apologise, don't let him say

this should never have happened! Cecilia reacted as if he were trying to snatch her sanity away.

'No! Don't!' It came out as the most passionate of whispers. Even as she said it, she curled herself frantically into his arms. Federigo caught her; she was within a second of remembering Giulio. Then the guilt would begin, and the anger, perhaps even shame. But she must never be allowed to regret this! Because he could not let her wish their loving undone he caught her hard against him and began to kiss her. Because she had to stop him raging at himself that he had made love to her at all, Cecilia whispered desperately for him to make love to her again.

When she woke this time the sun was bright across the flagstones, jewel-rich on the embroidered roses and violets of the crumpled counterpane, and Federigo was gone. Beneath her fingers the warm linen of the pillow still held the impression of his head. Cecilia caught the pillow hard against her and, stifling a scream of real agony, she cried.

Cecilia knew the moment that Piggy came to sit with her and share her morning chocolate that the old nurse knew. All she did not know was what Piggy thought.

Until Piggy saw her beloved charge's face she had not known what to think. Other than that she had expected this to happen. But when she saw Cecilia's face latticed with the stains of tears she knew she was glad of it, because behind the tears there was something else: there was real contentment.

Cecilia saw her nurse taking in her misery and put out a hand to hers.

'Don't mind about me, Piggy darling.'

It was all Miss Pigg could do not to cry herself then. She caught the hand to her cheek and promised, 'I don't mind, my angel.' Promised herself one other thing, too: that, if it killed her, she would make this foolish pair see their own terrible stupidity. But not just yet. Just at this moment she knew that neither of them could cope with it.

So she changed the subject.

'I have been speaking to Signor Vialli and he has been telling me what we are all to tell the twins. They had caught some nasty fever that is rife in the *castello*. . .that is why we are leaving for a while, of course, because His Highness does not want us to catch it.'

It was a clever notion, but Cecilia did not really hear it. She heard but one thing: Piggy had said they must leave, but only for a while.

'We shall be leaving for good, Piggy, once the Mansini secret is discovered and Giulio's murderer brought to justice.'

'If you say so, my angel,' replied Miss Margery Pigg carefully. But not, she added to herself grimly, if I can help it!

The twins were sitting hunched in blankets by the nursery fire when Cecilia was at last packed and ready to take her leave of them. The subdued and much thinner Gulliver at her heels, she closed the door to give them privacy. The twins still looked terrible, pale, fragile, neither could yet eat enough, and they were only able to remain out of bed an hour each day at most. Cecilia took in the harm done them again and wondered if she would ever feel such hatred as she now felt for the person who had caused it. Someone had nearly killed Figi and Talia, two of the most fascinating children she had ever known; the only children born of another she was ever going to feel were her own.

But she must not think about that or they would see her cry.

Figi peeped up out of her blanket and managed the most feeble of smiles.

'Papa says you are going away.' She succeeded in sounding more than accusing.

Cecilia smiled at it, her spirits lifted. 'Not very far, sweetheart, only to His Grace the Bishop.'

It twisted her heart intolerably to see the vivid light of real pleasure in their haunted little faces; it was almost as if most of their misery was that they were going to lose her.

'Oh, then we may see you every day?'

'You will come and play with us?'

Cecilia had already planned to ask Federigo that they be brought to her at the Bishop's Palace each morning.

'Of course.'

'And tell us more stories, about Napoleon, and Wellington and the man whose leg was shot away but he didn't notice it.'

'Lord Uxbridge? Yes.'

'And Gulliver can play too?'

Cecilia looked at her dog then and wondered however she was to explain his illness if the twins were never to know they had been poisoned. Then she saw it was obvious. Tell the truth.

'Well, Gulliver may not want to play,' she laughed ruefully, 'I'm sorry to say he ate every last one of those comfits you spilled on the floor and deserves it that he has been very sick indeed!'

The twins accepted this at once. 'Poor Gulliver!' They tried to get up from their sofa to cuddle him but none of the three was feeling up to such ruthless displays of affection. Gulliver scudded beneath the schoolroom table as if his life were in danger, and the twins subsided in an exhausted heap on Cecilia's lap.

'Papa says we can go to the haunted garden if we like. So long as you come too. He says we can't go anywhere without you. I'm glad.'

'Does that mean you and Papa aren't quarrelling any more?' Talia demanded.

Cecilia felt for the briefest second the echo of that indescribable closeness of this morning, felt almost that he touched her still, that she held him inside her again. No, they might have lost one another forever, but they were not quarrelling.

She smiled. 'No. We are being almost civil to each other!'

She might have known the children could not be fooled. After all, she knew now that they were looking for every last sign that she might remain with their father.

'Do you know,' Talia almost whispered it in awe, 'you looked so beautiful when you said that, even more beautiful than ever before. . .?'

'That's because she's in love with Papa. You are, aren't you, *madonna*?'

Cecilia hesitated only for a moment; she knew that, if she asked them to, the twins would keep anything she told them their special secret.

'Yes.' She took one hand of each. 'But it is the most important thing in the world you keep it a secret.'

'Even from Papa?' demanded Iphigenia, seeing right through her.

Cecilia laughed then. 'He knows already, *angelo*. So there is no need for you to tell him at all.'

The twins digested this in silence. Then Talia said, 'Well, I'm glad. Mama is dead and we never knew her. . .so Figi and I decided we could choose our own. . .'

'And we chose you.'

Cecilia never knew how she kept hold on the very fragile remnants of her self-control. She did, just. Enough to say, 'Well, I'm glad too. I think I love you two more than anything in the world.'

'Think?' They pounced upon this outrage.

'Well,' Cecilia rose to her feet with a smile, 'after all,

there is always Gulliver. He expects me to love him
best.'

Even as the twins were laughing raucously at this
Cecilia and her mongrel fled the room.

At the head of the stairs she stopped, unable to control
her tears. At first when she heard the footsteps she
thought it must be Federigo—certainly the figure
coming towards her was more than familiar. But it was
Massimo. Even as she puzzled again how she could keep
mistaking him for the man who was not his father at all,
she knew that he had seen her tears and was going to use
them against her.

She was certain of it the moment she saw his impeccable bow; and he spoke so elegantly.

'My dear *madonna*. . .you have tired yourself too
much! Have the twins been expecting you to entertain
them when you are so exhausted by your nursing?'

Had anyone else been speaking the words they would
have been kindly meant. Cecilia knew these to be acid
with venom. She pulled herself together—anything but
let the spiteful Massimo guess the cause of her
unhappiness.

'The twins are not yet fit to play with anyone, sir.' She
sounded even more cold than she had meant to.

'Oh?' He looked almost genuinely disappointed. 'And
I had been going to see if I might amuse them for the
morning.'

'They have Arietta; she will want to get them back to
their beds. They have been up quite long enough.'

For a moment when he smiled Cecilia would almost
have described it as seraphic. Certainly it was beautiful. . .oddly so very like Giulio, his cousin. Then he
said, 'Oh, but I don't think so, *madonna*. Had you not
heard that Arietta has disappeared?'

Even as he smiled still and he reminded her again of
Giulio Cecilia began to feel quite literally sick. Massimo
had meant so much more by that word 'disappeared' and

he meant that she should know it. Something had happened to Arietta and he was amused at it.

Cecilia understood his game—and that she was his quarry; she even knew why she was his victim; with the shrewd eyes of hatred he had seen her love for Federigo, and anything he could do to damage Federigo's possessions—however little they might really mean to Federigo—he would do it. Mustering the chilliest smile of her own, she said coolly, 'Then I must ask Piggy to see them to bed before we leave.'

'You are leaving us, *madonna*. What a pity!'

Cecilia nodded her head in what was plainly dismissal, and smiled back at him.

'Yes,' she replied. And you know it already, Prince Massimo, she thought, *and* you know why. As she made her way quickly down the stairs to her chambers and Piggy she heard him turn to watch her progress; he was laughing.

The carriage was at the door—it would not be the thing to walk to the Bishop's Palace for all it was but a few hundred yards away. In the great courtyard stood the Governor and Signor Vialli, arrived to discuss Arietta's disappearance with Federigo. Cecilia was glad they had come. With these men here, her taking leave of Federigo must be brief. And it was leave—a final goodbye. She would see the twins each day until she left for England, but she would never see Federigo again. Not in private, not as anything more than an acquaintance passing by her in the square. And it was best that way.

'Governor, Signor Vialli.' She nodded greeting to them.

It took her a full minute to realise why they were both looking so terribly sheepish. Then she understood and had to laugh at them.

'Good God, you foolish creatures! Anybody would have thought you had poisoned my comfits yourselves!'

Everybody laughed. But it was only when she heard Vialli laughing, the vivid amusement of it, that she looked at him and caught those eyes and realised that what she had said might so very easily be the truth.

'We are so sorry you intend to leave us, *madonna*.' He spoke for himself and his companion. And Cecilia thought again. . . But *are* you, or is it you who has wanted me gone all along? Is it one of you who has tried to kill me?

But she would not follow those thoughts because they led to Federigo. To the possibility he knew his friend Vialli to be involved and was willing to do anything to keep his guilt from the Governor. Even marry her. Even come to her as a lover. . .

No! That at least had been honest.

Even as she felt what she had never believed she could feel about it—doubt—she saw Federigo come out on to the steps, saw him pause on seeing her, saw his smile, and she knew that she was wrong. Whatever had happened between them last night, enough of the calm of it remained; so much so that she sensed even without looking at anyone but Federigo that the two other men had felt something of it and had hastily departed. Piggy too had hurried quickly into the carriage. For the last time she and Federigo were alone.

He came straight to her, and even as he reached for her hand she was holding hers out to him. Their fingers met and caught at each other, saying more than words were ever going to. He had one last chance now, one last try.

'Only for a while, Cecilia.' And in his voice she heard all the tenderness of the night that was gone.

She would have given anything to believe it was more than guilt, a feeling that in some way he might have harmed her by what he had done. Only he had done nothing she had not done; whatever had passed between them had been needed by both of them. He must not feel responsible.

So she shook her head. 'No. No, I cannot stay, Federigo. I think you know that I can't.'

Yes, he did know it. For her there would only ever be Giulio Mansini. He meant then to be the impeccable gentleman—he meant to make it easy for her. To kiss her fingers lightly and let her go away. He could not bear anything so cold. But he had to let her leave him; if to stay would only make her unhappy, he would never keep her.

'Very well, then.' It was all he said. Then, taking her gently by the shoulders, he kissed her fiercely on the lips, just once, and even as she snatched herself away and into the carriage, and Jemmy whipped the horses into motion, she knew that that one kiss had meant more than anything he had ever said or done. It had told her that, as much as he could ever love anyone but Parisina, he cared for her. Cecilia sank back against the sun-warmed squabs and closed her eyes. Now that she was leaving him she wanted to be gone. She did not want to see his face as she departed.

Five minutes later the carriage was drawing up in front of the Bishop's Palace. Cecilia stepped out into the midday sun of Aquila Romana and thought, He is only across the *castello* square. I can see the towers so clearly from here; only cross two squares and she could see him again. So close and so finally apart. Because it was impossible to bear it Cecilia stopped thinking at all. With a brisk smile at an unhappy Piggy she hurried up the steps and into the palace. Behind her Toro jumped down from the Downside carriage, shouted a vulgar farewell at Jemmy and was gone. The palace doors closed silently in the elegantly gloved hands of two richly liveried footmen and at last, quite undramatically, her dreams were ended. It would be for the best if she never thought of them again.

CHAPTER THIRTEEN

CECILIA awoke and for a moment wondered where she was. Wondered too what it was that made her reach out automatically across the bed as if she expected Federigo to be there. Then she understood why—that once he had been—and remembered at last that she was in the Bishop's Palace. Through the opened window she could hear the sad tolling of the cathedral bell, and beyond, fainter, muffled by the bulk of the cathedral itself, she thought she heard the sound of horsemen in the *castello* square. But she was too tired to wonder at it. Too tired—and she was thankful for it—to feel anything at all.

The door opened and Piggy entered, followed by a young nun carrying a tray of chocolate and hot bread and peaches. The nun smiled placidly at Cecilia, any natural curiosity she must feel politely veiled behind her friendly welcome. Piggy crossed the room to open the other shutters, and Cecilia sat up to take in her surroundings. She was so charmed by the calm whiteness of the room with its fading frescoes of Christ, St Peter and the fishermen of Galilee that at first she did not notice Piggy's real distress; then she saw it and said quickly, 'Piggy, what is it? Has something else happened?'

Piggy had not been meaning to tell her, but she had got to know.

'It is Arietta, my angel. The good Lord forgive me, for I could never abide that girl, but now she is dead. . .they found her this morning.'

Why was it that the only word that struck Cecilia in her shock was 'they'?

'They?'

'His Highness and Signor Vialli, just outside the city. . . I believe the Governor was with them.'

Cecilia knew then that she was never going to be able to eat her breakfast. More killings—Arietta this time. Why?

Then she remembered; Arietta running from her saying, 'Nobody could ever have meant. . .' Arietta had known something, about the poison in the comfits, and that was why Arietta was dead. Cecilia rose and dressed as quickly as she could; she must send for the twins at once. It was now more important than ever that she take charge of them during the day; they had not liked Arietta very much but she had been their nurse, after all, and the twins were going to be horribly upset by this.

The Bishop, a kindly man and even more distressed than Piggy, sent a footman hurrying to the *castello*, and within an hour the twins arrived, in the care of Toro. Cecilia was about to send the little groom back to his horses when she realised that Federigo had instructed him to remain there. Toro confirmed this seconds later when he asked for an audience in private.

'The Austrians have turned the city upside-down, *madonna*. Every known patriot has been rounded up. The Governor says this has all gone too far. . .'

'His Highness told you this, of course?'

'Yes. . .and what he doesn't tell me I listen to anyway, at doors.' Toro gave his most angelic smile, and Cecilia thought again how fortunate Federigo was to have this one man he could trust with his life. Toro was the only one.

'What else did you hear?'

Toro had expected nothing less; his master would never have fallen in love with a girl who would be squeamish now. Toro had always liked Madonna Cecilia. If he resented her just a little too it was only because Federigo had been so hurt by loving her. Toro did not know enough to understand it, but he hated it just the same to see his childhood friend so deeply unhappy. But, looking at Madonna Cecilia now, he more than understood it. He was halfway to being besotted with her himself. . .he knew that because his wife had said so.

Toro grinned again. 'I heard the Governor talking to His Highness. . .'

'And?' Cecilia heard the echo of Federigo in her tones even as Toro did, and they laughed together. In that moment Toro forgave her everything. She loved Federigo after all. Now all someone had to do was kick some sense into that blind, stubborn fool, the Duke of Aquila Romana!

'And he was giving His Highness warning. . .'

'Trying to!'

'*Si, si, madonna*, trying to! His Highness, he listened very nicely, of course. . .'

'To threats of what exactly?'

'Martial law. Curfew. The whole city is already under the Governor's sole control.'

'And Federigo will be deposed?'

'Yes, *madonna*.'

'And Federigo said what precisely?'

'That von Regensberg could go and. . . No, I shan't repeat that, *madonna*, it was not polite—but it was very original!' He beamed with pride at the memory.

Cecilia felt a shiver of pride run through her too; she could imagine very well exactly what Federigo had said.

'I see, von Regensberg was instructed to do something hideously uncomfortable. . .then what?'

'To leave everything to His Highness. That within forty-eight hours the trouble would be ended.'

'His Highness is certain of this?'

'Certain, *madonna*.'

'And in the meantime I am to keep the twins with me as much as possible?'

'Yes, *madonna*. And Jemmy Pigg. . .oh, that is a stupid name, but then, he is a stupid person! Jemmy

Pigg and I must be with you at all times. That was an order, *madonna*.' Toro took on his most stubborn demeanour, looking very bullish.

Cecilia could not resist teasing him. 'An order to you, Toro, or to me?'

Toro had the courage for anything. 'To you too, *madonna*,' he said firmly, 'especially to you. His Highness thinks it best that you do as you are told.'

Cecilia was to wonder later if that was the moment she decided she must find the answer herself—almost as if the Mansini secret were her problem; certainly she must show Federigo she could not be left out of what was happening now. Giulio had spoken to her, after all—and she wanted to find the truth for herself.

'Very well, Toro, I shall be good as gold.'

Toro knew that smile. The twins looked like that when they were about to be particularly disgraceful.

'Of course you will, *madonna*; I told His Highness so.' Toro almost sounded as if he really believed her. Surreptitiously he felt in his belt for the pistol he kept there. Cecilia saw it and said to herself that she must find her papa's pistol after supper. In Aquila Romana under martial law it would not be a bad idea to keep it with her.

The rest of the day she spent with the twins, picnicking in the Mansini Garden, the key to which Atalanta and Iphigenia now had charge of. The twins ghost-hunted while Gulliver snored and Piggy sewed, and Toro and Jemmy leaned on the gates and gambled recklessly with a grimy pack of playing cards. Cecilia went as if she were drawn to it to the crumbled stone seat beneath the climbing roses. This time a tiny song-bird was perched on the edge of the silent fountain. Cecilia closed her eyes and began to think. If only she could guess what it was Federigo's mother had been doing in this place, who it was had been her ghost, what had been her terrible grief. . .then she would know. As she dozed in the afternoon sun, her own grief soothed by the tranquillity of this lovely garden, Cecilia began to understand. By talking to an unseen Federigo the old Princess had not been imagining her son; and her husband's name had been Francesco. Cecilia, her heart aching for a Federigo of her own who was lost to her forever, knew the only possible answer then. There had been another Federigo and he had been the Princess Marfisa's lover.

In the silence, as the song-bird hopped closer and began to peck at the dried ground after the chuckling cicadas, Cecilia felt almost as if she could feel with the old Princess's senses; and understood at last that Giulio had come to the same conclusion. Of course he would have done, observant, sensitive Giulio—Giulio had also been in love and in despair. Had she been a more fanciful person Cecilia would have said that Giulio spoke to her then. Certainly the truth whispered into her head as if someone really had murmured it close against her ear. Enough that she opened her eyes with a start, almost surprised to find there was no one there. The answer remained, however. What was it a lover left behind him, or her, that could be discovered by those who came after? Letters. And where was the most likely place for letters to be if they had been written between Federigo's mother and her secret love? Here. Somewhere in the Mansini Garden. That was what Giulio had found. And—if she could somehow manage to steal the key from the children—this was where she was going to come to look for them. She knew that she would find them.

So thinking, Cecilia rose to her feet again and hurried to join in the twins' noisy tug-of-war with Gulliver and what was left of Toro's favourite neckerchief. Above the walls the cathedral bell ceased tolling for Arietta, and the city was silent.

* * *

The waiting was almost unbearable over the next two days before Cecilia at last found her opportunity as the twins fell into a careless heap just outside the garden gates one sundown and the key fell unnoticed from Atalanta's pocket. Nobody saw her pick it up, she was sure of it. That was the first part of her plan completed. Now to the second. Somehow she must get out of the Bishop's heavily guarded palace and into the gardens unnoticed. When she had found the letters she would hurry them straight to Federigo.

It seemed that evening that the Bishop would never go to bed. He had discovered in Cecilia a real talent for chess and, starved for years of a challenging opponent, he fought drooping eyelids and yawns until at last Piggy felt obliged to scold him, and send him to his sleep before he made himself unwell. Cecilia smiled at his obvious annoyance; he looked just like a little boy who wanted an exciting day to go on forever.

She spoke to him as if he were. 'We can play again tomorrow, Your Grace. After all, I must have my revenge, for I suspect that in one more move I would have been soundly defeated.'

The Bishop perked up at this and smiled. He had been most put out at the idea of entertaining a guest before Cecilia had come, but he was glad now that she was here and would miss her when she left. He wondered, not for the first time, if there was anything in the gathering rumours that she was to be the next Duchess of Aquila Romana. He hoped so. Then he would not have to be quite so lonely.

Once he was gone Cecilia made a pantomime of yawning indelicately. The more people were convinced of her innocent slumbers this evening, the better. Both Piggy and the nun who brought her bath-water remarked upon it, and Cecilia felt safe for her expedition. She had spent the last three nights watching the patrols in the square—the Bishop's men somewhat careless in their duties, for everyone loved the old man and no one would want to harm him. She knew that the sentries made a habit of sloping off into convenient shadows to share a bottle of wine and ribald conversation. She had heard them laughing beneath her window. She was going to have to find a less reckless exit.

There was also the problem of Toro. Defying the curfew and almost certainly on Federigo's orders, both Toro and Jemmy had passed each night since she had been here keeping watch on her windows. It should have amused her had she not been so annoyed at it. It was more than inconvenient because both of them were quite capable of braving her anger to send her ignominiously home to a startled Bishop. They were there again tonight. Moonlight shone brightly down on the square, leaving only its borders in shadow. Cecilia was about to disconcert them a little by waving at them when she saw a third moving shadow at the far side of the square by the gates of the Mansini Garden. The figure was bent as if searching for something. Even without the moonlight she would have known it was Federigo.

Even as she thought how it hurt to see him, she could not take her eyes from him for a moment. She wanted every second she could have of him; she knew what it was he was looking for. Her hand slipped into her pocket and she smiled. So Federigo knew the key had gone. He would never find it. She saw a gesture so explicit of frustration that she might just as well have heard him cursing. It was a strange thing to flood her heart with such a surge of love, and yet it was perhaps the mundanity of the gesture that so moved her. Federigo the Prince, just impatient enough to behave like an ordinary mortal!

She watched for the next five minutes as he gestured Toro and Jemmy to join him. He would leave soon, and then she would have her best chance to make her way across the square without their seeing her. Then she saw what he was doing. With Jemmy and Toro helping him up, Federigo had managed—somehow—to defy the forbidding height of the wall. He slung one leg over and reached down to help Toro up. Then the two of them disappeared out of sight into the garden and Jemmy was left to melt into the shadows by the gate out of sight of any Austrian patrol. This was a chance too good to be missed and Cecilia snatched it. Taking up the black woollen travelling cape she had purloined from Piggy, and dressed in the plain blue velvet of her darkest gown, she slipped out of her room, downstairs to the library, easily out of a window well hidden behind a high-backed chair and along the terrace to the small side-gate into the square. To one side she heard the Bishop's sentries sniggering. She heard a female voice with them. She smiled: safe from them too. Cecilia opened the gate and ran out into the moonlight. Just in time she reached the walls of the Mansini Garden, just as Federigo pulled himself up on to the height again, gave a hand to Toro and the two jumped down into the square below. Five minutes later he, Jemmy and Toro were gone. Cecilia waited another minute, holding her breath to catch every last sound in the tense and unlit city. Nothing. Taking the key from her pocket where it lay with her father's pistol, Cecilia unlocked the rusted gates and went in.

She had not been sure where to look before she entered the garden, but as she ran quickly in the moonlight along one of the overgrown paths she knew where she was going. Again it was almost as if she were not alone here, as if someone else were with her and knew just what she wanted. Her feeling of not being alone was so strong that she stopped abruptly and listened. But there was no one there.

Even so, she was certain she was not alone. Perhaps, here in the garden, safe from prying eyes, there could be ghosts; maybe people really did come back to the places they had never wanted to leave. She heard a voice say urgently, 'Giulio?' even before she realised it was her own; yesterday she would have been appalled at such superstition. Now it felt no superstition at all—as much as anyone could be, she was sure Giulio was with her now, if only in the fact she now understood him, and, understanding, she knew just what to look for.

In the letter he had written to her, how often had he talked of her serenity, the serenity of flowing water, soft, soothing, immortal? The gentleness of streams and fountains. The poem he had written to her, 'The Fountain'.

Cecilia made straight for it. It looked so huge, looming out of the darkness, the diving Mansini dolphin in lichened stone. The letters were here somewhere, but where? Where would they have been safe from the water while the fountain still ran as it had in Federigo's mother's day? Cecilia fell to her knees beside the fountain, disturbing the little gecko, which had been there before; he dashed quickly out of sight beneath the very foundations of the fountain. Only he could not have done. . .

He had. The gecko had shown her where to look. Carefully Cecilia slipped her hand beneath the stones. Yes, there was a gap, and something was in it. Even as she pulled the oilskin package out into the moonlight she knew that she had found them. She did not even have to open the package—she knew what would be there. In her hand she held the Mansini secret. Whatever was in these letters, four people had died for them already. The twins had almost died. She herself was meant to have been killed. Shaking with excitement, Cecilia pushed the letters safely into the pocket of her cape beside the pistol. Now she must get to Federigo.

When she turned round she saw him coming towards her through the spilling vines. She had been right, she hadn't been alone: Federigo was here. She was just about to run towards him when she stopped abruptly.

'So you have mistaken me for Father again, *madonna*!

Most extraordinary, is it not? And now,' added Massimo d'Aquilano-Mansini, 'you will give me what it is you have found. Letters, I imagine? And then—I am sorry to say it, but I must kill you.'

For a whole minute Cecilia stood rooted to the spot, completely unafraid, flooded with near-elation and thinking but one thought: it wasn't Federigo, none of this was Federigo! Massimo. Federigo had never lied. I should have believed in him. She was so drunk with the happiness of it that she saw she had disconcerted her opponent; certainly the pistol in Massimo's hand wavered a little. To get a grip on himself he began to talk.

'I knew that you would find them. Mansini told you, didn't he? I found his journals. I knew he would have tried to tell someone. I found his letter too. I took it when I searched his apartments after I killed him. Only I couldn't understand what he meant. You did, though; I knew if you were given the letter you would understand and lead me to the secret, so I put it back with Giulio's things where Father would certainly find it. . . It was all in the poem, wasn't it? The fountain. I was a fool not to have guessed it for myself.'

Cecilia saw two things then. That he had a button missing from the sleeve of this elegant black coat— Federigo had known for days that Massimo was responsible. Even at this distance, she would know that figured silver anywhere for the match to the button she had found here. Saw, most of all, her anger, her real rage at Massimo; this evil, perverted boy had read Giulio's letter that had been so private. . .and yet if she showed her disgust, how much she hated the idea of such defilement, it would only please him. Massimo would like to think he could have hurt Giulio even further.

Cecilia was not going to give him any satisfaction. Just in this moment she despised him so much that it was as if his pistol were not there at all. She heard the arctic contempt in her voice as she spoke, clearly, without a trace of the fear he so badly wanted to see, 'I always thought it was you.'

She knew that she had shaken him again. Even so, he managed a commendable sneer.

'Is that so, *madonna*? Then you will at least give me credit for trying to get rid of you without another murder.'

'By frightening me away? That trick with the opened window. The viper. . .'

'Yes.'

Her voice hardened. 'And the comfits.'

'I never meant for the twins. . .'

Cecilia took a step or two closer, clear into the moonlight. She knew as he saw her face that he was frightened of her. But then he was facing her rage about the children, and not even a mother could hate him more than she did for that.

'You thought of nothing at all—not the certainty that I would share my present with the children! Everyone is dispensible to you. How did you poison them?'

'A mild tincture of yew. Arietta did it for me; Toro found the comfits on the carriage seat where you had forgotten them in the excitement of the rioting, and gave them to her to bring to your rooms. We had been planning to poison your morning chocolate but this was an infinitely better plan. I didn't tell her what it really was, of course, only that it would make you very sick and you would be desperate to get away from Aquila Romana.'

'And Arietta knew too much, after what happened to the twins, so you had to kill her?'

'Of course.' His smile was so like Federigo's that it nauseated her—it was such a mockery of all that she loved. And still so very puzzling. 'I was always going to have to kill her; she was in love with me, you see.'

Cecilia did see, and had a moment to spare in her

anger for Arietta. No wonder the girl had been so set against her, as close to insolent as any servant had ever come.

'And you meant Federigo to believe Signor Vialli to be to blame—his closest friend?'

'It would have been an amusing touch, would it not?'

He told her all he had to tell—except why he wanted the letters, and why he wanted her gone. Once he had told her everything he would kill her. She had to keep him talking. Until she thought what was best to do.

'What are these letters to you?'

Yet again the pistol shook in his hand as he fought the very real fear her unnatural calmness fed in him.

But he retained his sarcasm. 'I rather imagine they might be from my mother. . .to my real father. Proof that I am not the d'Aquilano heir. The proof Father,' he spat out the hated word, 'needs to dispossess me. That is the Mansini secret Giulio discovered—how to prove who I really am.'

Even as he said it, Cecilia knew it did not make sense. Federigo needed no proof to disinherit Massimo; he was perfectly capable of doing it anyway. Again, just for a fleeting second, her new understanding of Giulio prompted her. . .almost as if he had spoken and said 'I had to tell him something while he murdered me; I had to lie to keep him from the truth'. That meant that the truth in her pockets was even more dangerous still— dangerous to Federigo, not Massimo, and Massimo must never see them. Giulio had died to make certain that they were safe.

Cecilia had to pretend to accept Massimo's explanation. He must not even guess that this was not the truth.

'Perhaps. . .you cannot expect me to know.' She had just the right tone to make him believe that she did know, and for certain. Then she asked the final question. . .the most puzzling of all.

'Why was so important to you to have me gone? Because I might reach the letters before you? And yet you have used me to find them. . .'

Massimo stirred then, as if he too felt the tension to be almost unbearable. When he answered her he would kill her. Cecilia had perhaps a minute in which to save her life. She spoke quickly then, buying herself more time.

'If you shoot me, Massimo, you will bring the soldiers. You cannot get away from here; you will be arrested, and Federigo will see that you are punished.'

It was a foolish speech—it could not save her; even less could he afford to let her live after what he had just told her.

So it surprised her that when he spoke now there was only pleasure in his voice, excitement. 'Ah, but it would be worth it, *madonna*, worth dying for it to kill you!'

Cecilia at last began to be afraid. This made no sense, this was too personal, and yet there was nothing he could possibly have against her as herself, nothing so bad that he must kill her for it. She responded to her fear as she always did, lifting her head, her eyes blazing, and demanded, 'Why? Why me?' There was not the slightest tremor in her voice.

It was her courage that finally lost Massimo his control, brought all his instinctive cruelty spilling out in all its ugliness.

'You think I want you dead because you are in love with Father? Aren't you going to deny it. . .beg me to believe it isn't true. . .swear that you will be silent if only I will let you go? Aren't you going to pretend you do not love him?'

Still it made no sense, but she almost laughed at him then. If he expected her to deny Federigo he was even more of a fool than she took him for.

Even though she knew that only fools were truly

dangerous, she flung back at him, '*I*, deny the truth to you? Why should I?'

She saw again the frown of bewilderment cross his features as she did not behave as he expected her to. It was an obvious struggle now to keep that casual cruelty in his tone.

'I knew you did. Everyone knew it but him, the fool. . .'

And at last she saw. He was afraid Federigo would marry her, marry her and produce a legitimate heir. And she could so easily have done so. She knew that she was close to losing her own control when she laughed then. The irony was real, the laughter was real, and yet she knew that close beyond it lay hysteria. To die because someone feared she would do what she had sworn she could never do if Federigo were the last man on earth! It was as if the most bitter part of their quarrel had come back to taunt her.

She defied that growing hysteria and with it Massimo again. 'If only you knew—you are the fool! The greatest fool who ever lived! I have refused to marry him. All this, and there was no threat to your ambitions at all!'

She shook him completely then. He strode across the grass as if he might strike her, grab her, anything to gain control over her. . .

'*Refused*?'

'Yes.' Cecilia stood her ground, though she was trembling with a disabling mixture of anger and excitement and dread. It made her stupid. 'Yes, but never again. If ever he can forgive me. . .if ever he was to ask me again, I should accept him! I love him and I *shall* be his wife!'

Massimo was so close to her then that she felt the brush of the pistol against her stomach. There was something so obscene about the gesture that she thought for a moment she might actually be sick. Certainly she felt dizzy—he was too close, too like Federigo. Only that could not be. . .

Even his voice was Federigo's in its harsh, ice-cold whisper.

'Oh, he would have you, *madonna*! Do you still not see that I don't want you to die because you love him, but because he loves you? He *wants* you, *madonna*, as he has never wanted anything in his life. Nor ever will. He would kill to have you. . .that is why you die, *madonna*. Because it will destroy him utterly to have to live without you!'

It was almost as if he had known how to break Cecilia. To lie about such a thing now, to taunt her with her most precious hopes. . .and then she saw it. He was not lying. He believed every word he said. Even as she began to shake uncontrollably, fighting away his words and the evil behind them, she began to burn with something else. He believed what he said. It might even be true.

The pistol grazed her breast then, and she understood even more how much he hated her. In that last moment she knew he had wanted her too. Massimo had wanted her for himself, and she had chosen Federigo. Now he had come close to her, was touching her, and as she heard the hard, disjointed breathing she knew that for Massimo his thwarted lust for her was the most important reason that she must die. She felt his hand then, reaching beneath her cloak. . .for herself or for the letters? Cecilia thrust her hand into her pocket to protect the letters and found her own gun. It was her only chance. Lowering her eyes so he would not see the spring of hope in them her fingers closed round the comforting metal and she knew she was going to kill him.

She never saw the shadow move across the garden but she felt it. She never heard anything until Massimo froze, his hands dropped away from her and his pistol fell to the ground at her feet. Then she saw the glitter of moonlight along a vicious blade of a sword. And then she saw Federigo.

She thought she moved towards him, but maybe he

pulled her into his side, his arm tight about her until she could feel every muscle of his body, taut, angry and infinitely comforting. No one else moved at all. Federigo watched the boy he had brought up as his son as Massimo at last turned to face him and Federigo kicked the pistol lazily away from his reach and lowered the sword with contempt that would have goaded a stronger man than Massimo. Massimo exploded.

'*You*! You think. . .!' But all Federigo needed to do was smile at him and he was silent. It was a smile that promised death. Cecilia, looking up at Federigo, saw it and shuddered. He felt it and held her even closer; he even rested his cheek against her hair for a moment. He was as unafraid as that.

Then he spoke. 'I think nothing, Massimo, I only know. I know that you have killed four people. I know that my children almost died. Most of all I know what you meant to do to Cecilia. Did you really think I did not know all along? All along, Massimo. Who else could it have been but you?'

'You know nothing!' Massimo was speaking through teeth gritted against the chattering of fear; he was ashen with it. More than fear, he had lost everything, and to the very man at whose hands humiliation was most impossible to bear. Never had Cecilia seen such naked hatred, such impotence. She could almost have pitied him then. If it had not been for the twins and for Giulio she might have done.

'You know nothing!' he repeated, and the poison was back in his eyes. He was finished, but he would take Federigo down with him if he could. 'You do not know about your precious Cecilia. . .or do you? Do you know that she will never love you? Do you know that you will never have her, not as Mansini did? You hold her so closely now—can't you *feel* she doesn't want you? That once she has stopped being afraid of me she will be sick at just the thought of your touching you? You are not

Giulio, *Father*, and never will be! I saw the journals. . .
I still have papers I did not put back in his apartments
for you to find. I know that if she has told you he was
not her lover she is lying. I read it! I read what Giulio
wrote about it. . .shall I quote it to you? Would you like
to hear what they did together. . .how much she wanted
it, *craved* it, so that even if you took her it would be
Mansini she was thinking of? She would blot out your
face with his even as you. . .'

It was not anything that Federigo did, but somehow
Massimo could not go on. Then he knew why. It was
not working. Federigo smiled, not the tight, desperate
smile of one who was engulfed by jealousy; he smiled as
if he was amused, as if he did not care at all, whatever
was true. He loved her as much as that; so he would
never care what she had done or who she had loved. He
loved her so much that Massimo could barely grasp such
feelings were possible.

Federigo waited for it to dawn on Massimo, then
smiled again. 'That's right, Massimo. I don't care. Not
now.' Not after what she had said to Massimo just now;
even when it could have brought her instant death, she
had flung back at her tormentor that she loved him,
Federigo. She had not been lying in that moment;
nobody ever would. He understood everything now and
he was never going to lose her.

Massimo heard that 'not now' and misunderstood it.

'So the servants were right. They are saying you have
been with her already. . .'

Cecilia felt herself released abruptly, and came round
from her shock of relief to the knowledge that unless she
stopped him Federigo would kill Massimo for what he
had just said. Instinctively she caught at his arm; she felt
him tense to shake her off and dug her nails hard into
his flesh until he heeded her. Nothing Massimo could do
could hurt them now and he had to see it.

Federigo seemed to. She felt him pause, then relax.

She drew close against him again, knowing that while he could feel the warmth of her she could control his anger.

Massimo was almost defeated. 'What are you going to do?' A dying note of defiance was there. 'Tell von Regensberg I was responsible? And have the whole city up in arms for the poor motherless boy you would make your scapegoat? Who would ever believe you?'

'Oh, they will believe it.'

'Then you would take the risk of the Austrians deciding we little Princes are too corrupt, too dangerous to be tolerated? That the d'Aquilano family is so divided that we——?'

'You are not my family.' It was the final disowning.

Massimo flared just once more. . . 'But they don't know that! And you cannot risk that they know it. No one must know, you can never disinherit me! If you do you have no heir and von Regensberg will take the opportunity he has always been looking for to force you out completely. Perhaps you are going to kill me!'

'Perhaps. But I should prefer not to—oddly, I don't enjoy it as much as you do.' As if to emphasise the point Federigo tossed his sword aside, then added casually, 'But you are right, the truth must not come out. You have brought Aquila Romana to the brink of disaster already with your abortive little rebellion. I can risk no more scandal. You will leave. . .a broken heart would be a nice touch. . .you are going to leave, Massimo, because you cannot bear to watch Cecilia marry your father; you are going to—er—travel to forget.'

'And if I refuse?'

'You won't.'

'You cannot keep me away!'

'You think not? Then understand that this is your only chance to live. You will leave tonight, and should you ever return I will kill you. You know that I will. And somehow, Massimo, I don't imagine the courage of a martyr in you, not even for your greediest ambitions.

You are a born killer, and killers are always cowards. No, you won't ever come back.'

For a long minute Massimo stared at him then, and Cecilia looked from one to the other, the identical frozen smile, the identical cast of the head. All but the eyes were the same. But that was quite impossible. Then Massimo was gone. Behind her she heard at last Jemmy and Toro move out of the tangled roses, move to follow Massimo and escort him on his way. Federigo had already forgotten all of them.

'Now, Cecilia, if you would kindly stop pointing that pistol at me. . .in fact, throw it down over there—you can be such a careless creature. . . I think we have a great deal to discuss, you and I.'

Taking the pistol from her unresisting fingers and tossing it into the grass, he took her hand and led her back through the roses to the fountain. There he pulled her down beside him on the bench to which his mother had come for twenty years in search of her lost love. He had found his. Just for the moment, the Mansini secret was irrelevant.

CHAPTER FOURTEEN

THEY were silent for so long that the tiny gecko came bustling out of his hiding place and out on to the very edge of the bench where they were sitting. Cecilia watched the little lizard, fascinated by how beautiful he seemed; everything seemed beautiful in this strange, almost enchanted garden in the moonlight. Now that Federigo was here. She was tired—almost exhausted— and she knew that soon they must speak of Giulio, and his mother and secrets. But first they must talk of something else, and now that it came to it she did not want to listen. What if that one moment of certainty under threat of murder had been wrong? What if Massimo had been, in his jealousy, totally deluded? What if Federigo did not love her after all?

He knew Massimo could have been wrong, the whole world could have been wrong—he had not even believed the twins' most unsubtle hints that Cecilia loved him. But he knew to believe her; Cecilia herself, laughing the defiant truth at Massimo. The reason he was silent now was that it was so impossible to believe it.

Though perhaps not so impossible. Why could she not love two people when he did? The fact that he loved Cecilia more than he had ever loved in his life did not mean he had forgotten Parisina, nor ever would. He had loved the twins' mother; he had believed at the time he could never want any other woman; when he thought of her it would always be with sadness and gratitude and real affection. So why could Cecilia not feel the same now? She loved Giulio—perhaps she loved him more than she would ever love again—but she loved him too, maybe only a little, yet it was enough.

'Why didn't you believe how much I loved you, Cecilia?' He could not quite look at her, looking instead at her hand where it rested in his. So he never saw her smile. Cecilia finally grew up in that moment. She was able to laugh at him.

'Because,' she whispered with all the dryness of tone he had loved from the first, 'you never told me. You never said anything of love at all!' Then her poise deserted her and she turned to him, desperate to know. . . 'Why? *Why* did you not say? Oh, so much more than that! Why me at all?'

Federigo saw the tears on her lashes and knew that she was not even aware of them. So he reached up and touched them away with the tip of his finger. He felt her lashes dust against his skin and smiled at it. Such a little thing, and yet it rocked him to the core with love. This was more than he had ever known was possible—it was more than need, and companionship; more than desire. It was almost as if, from the very beginning, he was part of her. As if he had become her and she him. As if there was no barrier of flesh between them. Just a tear against his fingers and she bound him to her forever. But how to make her see it?

'I. . .' He shook his head on his helplessness, how to find words for something as absolute as this? He tried again. 'I didn't have to tell you. . . I *was* telling you, all the time—you wouldn't see it. Everything I did should have told you. My God, I even arrested you that first night you tried to leave the city because I couldn't think of any other way to make you stay! I *couldn't* lose you!'

The tears were coming faster now, but all Cecilia heard was the near-impatience in his voice at the lengths to which she had driven him in her blindness. That was the old Federigo, the one she had loved from the start. That was what at last made her believe.

'But you were so angry with me all the time. . .'

'For trying to run away. And for—Giulio Mansini.' It had to come to this.

When she withdrew her hand he could not believe it. Not now. Then he saw. She too was battling to find words. And in her frown he saw a mirrored exasperation with his own stupidity, his own blindness, the same fury he had felt at hers, and he too knew. She had never lied at all.

'I never knew him, Federigo. But you wouldn't listen. You wouldn't believe me. You were so impossibly obstinate ——'

'Jealous!'

'. . .*stupid* that I could happily have murdered you!'

'The letter——'

'I *didn't know him*! He wrote. . . I suppose he wrote it because that is what he did—he wrote things, he was a poet. Perhaps it eased him to at least have written those things, even though I would never see them.'

'And I showed them to you!' She could hear in his voice the pain of having so betrayed Parisina's half-brother.

'You didn't know.' Cecilia laid her head against his shoulder as if to comfort him. It did. He caught her hand again and kissed it.

'I wish I had never done it.'

Cecilia knew what she said now was true. 'I think, you know, that he would have been glad that you did. I think he would have been proud that I should know it. I am proud he wrote such things for me. To have been loved by such as Giulio. . .'

'You, who cannot understand why any man should love you at all!'

'Don't laugh at it, Federigo!' Cecilia turned away then, her face hot with confusion; it was not a thing she could ever comfortably be teased about.

That had never stopped him in the past. 'Oh, you little fool! How can I be expected to think you anything but absurd? Piggy has told me you were endlessly fending off the most passionate horde of suitors. In fact I believe a distant cousin of mine shot himself because you so callously broke his heart.'

'Pietro? Oh, but he didn't! Well, he *did*, but. . .'

'He can't have done both—which was it?'

'Well, he *did* shoot himself, but only in the foot. It was a romantic gesture, you understand!'

'Damned lunatic! But that was always Pietro.'

'So you can see that I could never take any man's declaration seriously. All that effusive sentiment, all that gushing nonsense!'

'So why not believe me? I was never sentimental in my life, nor have I ever gushed at you!'

He felt at last that she was beginning to laugh at it. 'I suppose I should have known you loved me,' she mused half seriously, 'you were so completely horrid, and so rude. . .'

'Very. But you still refused to understand it!'

'But. . .why me?' She had to know. If it was her or her likeness to Parisina.

Perhaps it was because of the moonlight, pouring from behind a cloud then soaking her golden hair with brilliant silver, that he read her thoughts. Parisina's hair. They were very like each other. It had never occurred to him before.

'Why not you?' He had to make her say it, so all was in the open between them finally and they were free of the past.

'Parisina. You still love Parisina.'

It was easy now. He caught a strand of her hair between his fingers and watched the light play through its filaments. He could almost hear that she held her breath. That was when he knew for certain she would never be anyone's but his. She could almost not bear to hear he had ever been Parisina's. She would bear it only when she believed Parisina was finally gone.

'Yes, I still love her. She never gave me reason not to

love her. But she is a long way away, Cecilia, and, though it does hurt, and perhaps I don't feel easy saying this yet, if she were here now and I had to choose there would be no choice at all. . .there is only you. I never loved her the way I love you.'

Cecilia could not let him say that. She lifted a hand quickly to his lips and whispered, 'I don't need that. I'm not asking that! It isn't fair. . .'

'To her? She would want me to say it. Do you think she would want me to live on without her, dead inside, never love again? Had you loved Giulio as he loved you would he have wanted you to be lonely? As I have been, desperately, until you came.'

She knew no other person in the world would admit to loneliness, nobody else was that brave. Her hand met his and she let him pull her closer. 'No. Giulio would never have wanted that.'

She felt him smile then against her hair. 'We are all there is, Cecilia. Even in this haunted garden. There's no one but us here, no Giulio, no Parisina. . .'

'And yet for a moment. . .' She wanted to tell him, but would he understand? 'It must have been you, because you were here all along, but I really did believe for a moment I wasn't alone here. That maybe Giulio. . .'

He did understand. 'It is this garden, *carina*. Something about this place is so timeless, almost as if past and present do not matter. I think that's why my mother needed it.'

'I felt him here —as if he was the one telling me where to look for those letters.'

'He did. In the letter to you. He knew if anything happened to him I must see it. You understood him better than I, that is all.'

'I did, didn't I? I'm glad I did. I owed it to him. . .'

She felt his other arm come about her then, felt the

rich smoothness of his coat against her cheek and his quiet breathing.

'And what do you owe me, Cecilia? Because I love you more than Giulio ever could?'

She believed it now. Just as she knew he believed she loved him.

'Anything you want. . .always.'

'Stay. And marry me. Be a mother to the twins. That is only the beginning. . .'

'Yes.'

She meant yes to everything, even that she knew this was just the beginning, that they might think they loved each other completely now but it was nothing compared to what was to come. This could only grow stronger, they could only become closer. As if he followed her thoughts he kissed her then, tilting her chin to make her look at him.

'Don't leave me, that's all I ask. However bad it gets. . .and it will be very dangerous. We may lose everything.'

He meant Aquila Romana. She kissed him back. 'Never everything, Federigo, not while we are together, the four of us. While we have each other there is nothing that matters more than that.'

She knew it was time for him to open the letters now. While they were safe in this moment, belonging only to themselves, and whatever it was he might read could not really touch him. She almost thought she knew already. To make it easier she asked a few things that had been puzzling her.

'Why did you come back tonight? I saw you plainly before I came, and waited for you to leave.'

He laughed out loud then and she knew before he said it, 'We knew you would. Toro saw you take the key when Talia dropped it and we decided the only thing for it was to make you dance to our tune. I knew you'd be watching for a chance to leave the Bishop's Palace, so we staged an elaborate performance for your benefit. You don't seriously think I would go standing so conspicuously on walls in the middle of curfew for the devilment of it, do you?'

'You mean you wanted me to see you. . .then see you leave and think it was safe to get into the garden? You *utter*. . .!'

'If you say so! Then we followed you. We knew that Massimo had also been watching you closely. Vialli was set to follow him and warn us he was coming. Did you not hear the cat crying amorously in the lilac tree?'

'No, I didn't! Vialli did that?'

'Of course. He was very convincing.'

'He would be!' Cecilia was wondering then how she would ever face the others again after thinking she had been so clever, while all the time they had been laughing at her antics.

'Don't worry. We were all very impressed with you. Particularly when you nearly shot me.'

'I did not!'

'Well, you would never have hit Massimo the way you were waving it about!' The time had come. 'Now may I have those letters, please?'

The oilskin was cold against her fingers when she drew them from her pocket. There were only a dozen letters inside the wrapping, a little water-stained, but not enough to obscure the writing. Two different hands, two different authors. One his mother. The other—Cecilia saw the arrogant scrawl in the moonlight—Federigo. Federigo Mansini.

She watched her own Federigo as he read on, for almost half an hour, as he opened each new letter and she felt the chill of the deepest hours of night weaving into her cloak and began to shiver. But if she was cold it was as much at the look on his face, hard, hurt, but not perhaps really so very surprised.

At last he looked up and met her gaze.

'You guessed, of course.'

'That your mother had a lover called Federigo, yes. Nothing else would explain it.'

'He was her cousin. Killed in some war. I never knew him, but he was my father.'

The Mansini secret at last. And the most explosive of all. Federigo himself a bastard, and no more Duke of Aquila Romana than she was. Imagine if Massimo ever discovered this! Only what good would it have really done him, or anyone? Cecilia knew what was hurting Federigo the most.

'My God,' his voice was hoarse with pain as she reached out to take his hand, 'Massimo killed my father. . .the man I believed was my father. . .he must have done. Yes, I know he did. It explains Papa's look. It explains everything. Massimo killed him, and Giulio, and the two servant women. . .and all for this!' The irony of it was truly terrible. 'And all the time Federigo Mansini was my father!'

'Are you certain of it? Absolutely certain?'

He looked at her for a long time then and shook his head. 'Not completely—how can I ever be sure? My mother cannot even have been sure. But it is what she believed. . .'

'Because she wanted to.'

'My father. . .Papa. . .he loved her so much. I thought she loved him. How could she ever have. . .?'

'The way you do. It is possible to love two people at the same time.'

She felt him reach out for her other hand. 'How did I even live before you came? You make everything so simple! Yes, perhaps I can forgive my mother for what she did to Papa. . .he forgave her. And you're right, I may still be Prince d'Aquilano. But you have seen it yourself, how like Massimo I am, and yet I *do* know he isn't my son. We are both Mansini.'

'But was not your mother a Mansini too? It could be from her you inherited your features.'

'I want to believe it, even though she looked nothing like either Massimo or myself. Oh, not for the title, the right to call myself Duke. For Papa. I want *him* to have been my father!'

Cecilia twined her fingers into his and made him look at her. He had to listen to her now.

'He was your father, Federigo. You must believe it; for the sake of this city you must believe it! Without you what hope is there for Aquila Romana? You *are* the Duke; the people need *you*, not anyone else. Even if Federigo Mansini was your father, nobody but you and I must ever know it.'

'I know that, *angelo*. It is the only thing that makes this possible to bear. Even if it's a lie I have to keep what I have. Not for me, not for us. . .not even for our son, who will see Aquila Romana free, even if we don't. Just. . .'

'For Aquila Romana. And for Giulio, Federigo. He died for Aquila Romana, after all, and not only for you. He knew what was in those letters—maybe he had read them; maybe he guessed. He must have guessed to have looked for them at all. That is what he meant by "tell the Duke". . .he wanted you to know there was a dangerous secret at all. To find it—and destroy it.'

'Destroy these?'

'Yes, you must.'

She knew already that he would do so. He would take them to the fire the moment he reached home and watch them burn. Once the Mansini secret was gone Aquila Romana was safe. He was safe. They all were.

'So that is that?' He seemed to need to be sure of something she could not understand. But she knew so much better now; she knew to ask.

'What's wrong, Federigo? There is still something.'

And she saw him smile at last, the vivid, boyish smile

that so belied his age and all that he had been through. A smile she knew she had given back to him, and it was all for her.

'I was thinking what a vast number of bastards we have accumulated in this family. Indeed, I am hard put to it to think of anybody who isn't one!'

'And?'

'And I rather think we ought to get married at once—tonight, if I can haul the Bishop from his slumbers.'

'You will do no such thing; he's a very old man and——'

'And would prefer to see us wed than add to the family collection!'

Cecilia blushed hotly then—such a thing had never occurred to her.

'The most shocking little hoyden!' He was teasing at her with the old words again. 'You couldn't even care if we did, could you? Well, I care. I want my son—my first son—to be legitimate. Next time there must be no doubts about the heir to Aquila Romana.'

'Well, I wasn't proposing to leave the Bishop sleeping a full nine months, Federigo,' Cecilia smiled mischievously through her very real confusion, 'only until the morning.'

She felt his hand soft against her cheek then, and her heart quicken at the light in his eyes and his smile.

'So what do you propose we do with the next five hours, Cecilia *mia*?'

'I don't. . .know. . .'

He kissed her then and she knew that at last she had truly come home; this was home, this was safety. This was everything.

Then he whispered, 'I do.'

After all, they were alone here in the Mansini Garden now that the ghosts were gone. There was nothing here but the two of them, and love.

The other exciting

MASQUERADE
Historical

available this month is:

COUSIN HARRY
Paula Marshall

Through the bad temper of his grandfather, Alex,
7th Earl of Templestowe, found himself deprived of
part of his inheritance – Racquette, the home he
loved above others. And since he was led to
believe that Harriet Ashburn had cynically married
her dying husband for money, his reception of the
widowed Harry was brusque indeed!

Gentle and serene, Harry was startled by Alex's
resemblance to her husband, as Gilly might have
been but for his illness, and once she grasped
Alex's reasons, the devil took hold of Harry. If Alex
believed her an adventuress, who was she to
disabuse him?

Yours FREE an exciting

MILLS & BOON ROMANCE OR MASQUERADE

Spare a few moments to answer the questions overleaf and we will send you an exciting Mills & Boon Romance or Masquerade as our thank you.

Regular readers will know that from time to time Mills & Boon invite your opinions on our latest books, so that we can be sure of continuing to provide what you want - the very best in romantic fiction. Please can you spare the time to help us now, by filling in this questionnaire and posting it back to us TODAY, reply paid?

Don't forget to fill in your name and address - so we know where to send your **FREE BOOK**

 **See overleaf**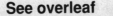

JUST ANSWER THESE 8 QUESTIONS FOR YOUR FREE BOOK

1 **Did you enjoy Dishonourable Proposal by Jacqueline Baird?**

Very much indeed ☐ Quite a lot ☐ Not particularly ☐ Not at all ☐

2 **What did you like best about it?**

The plot ☐ The hero ☐ The heroine ☐ The background ☐

3 **What did you like least about it?**

The plot ☐ The hero ☐ The heroine ☐ The background ☐

4 **Do you have any special comment to make about the story?**

_____

_____

5 **Age group:** under 25 ☐ 25-34 ☐ 35-44 ☐ 45-54 ☐ 55+ ☐

6 **Have you read more than six Mills & Boon Romances in the last two months?** Yes ☐ No ☐

7 **Would you like to read other books of this kind?** Yes ☐ No ☐

8 **What is your favourite type of book, apart from romantic fiction?**

_____

Thank you for filling in this questionnaire. We hope that you enjoy your FREE book. Fill in your name and address below, put this page in an envelope and post it today to:

Mills & Boon Survey, FREEPOST, P.O. Box 236, Croydon CR9 9EL.

Mrs/Ms/Miss/Mr _____ EDMAN

Address_____

_____

_____

| NO STAMP NEEDED | 0292 |

Postcode_____

Tick box R if you wish to receive a free Romance or tick box M for a Masquerade.   R   M